Seeking the Future

Mattew C. Perez

Seeking the Future

SEEKING THE FUTURE
By Matthew C. Perez
oriental@aol.com
East Hanover, New Jersey
07/27/2023

D'Fana Editions

Cover: Carlos E. Morel

Printing in Rodes Printing
Miami
2023

ISBN: 979-888831590-3

Acknowledgement

This novel would not have been possible without the unwavering support and advice from two wonderful individuals.

First, my dear wife, friend, and life partner Irene who often set aside her own projects and responsibilities to review, edit, and cleanse the manuscript from grammatical oversights and from my tendency to overuse commas.

Second, Angel De Fana a person whom I like to call friend. Without his technical guidance and his personal time invested reviewing and making material recommendation, this book would likely not have been published.

(This story is a fiction, all characters and events are likewise. Any similarity to real names and characters is pure coincidental)

I

Dina was the oldest child of an accomplished couple; a professor and graduate from Princeton University, and a pianist whose music filled the air waves of the New York Metropolitan area, as her performance was broadcast weekly by a local radio station.

Vincent was light complexion with blond hair. His full head of hair reflected a red tint when touched by the sun rays. His facial features were slightly altered by a thin and exceptionally well trimmed mustache. His athletic physique complemented his youthful appearance and yet contrasted with his warm and tender affection which he always shared with Dina.

Dina, like Vincent, had similar light complexion. Her light and soft blond hair gently and smoothly fell to her shoulders supported by soft curls which sheltered the back of her neck and fully covered her ears. Her eyes, radiant baby blue, projected the gentleness of her soul and the love for Vincent, guarded by her heart.

Life had been good to Dina in spite of the family's economic misfortunes, having lost most of their material wealth during the difficult and economically painful depression years.

Jaime quickly adjusted to the city's hustle and bustle in spite of coming from a slower paced life style, to which he was accustomed to in his homeland. His sun tan complexion and onyx like hair made him distinguishable when together with members of his social circle, whose appearance tended to be more northern European. Nonetheless, his personality and moral values, defeated any potential barrier resulting from different national, language and cultural background.

Thru his culinary abilities Jaime was able to further reinforce friendships and demonstrate his giving spirit. He was well liked and readily accepted in spite of his cultural and language differences and accompanying "funny" accent". However, Jaime continuously struggled with self, as he perceived his achievements to always fall short of his self expectations.

The group of friends' weekly get together became the show place for Jaimes' culinary demonstrations and sometimes experimentation. He filled the table and his friends digestive cavities with Caribbean gastronomical delicacies. Preparation of the various Cuban dishes reminded him of his native land, and of his home cooking tutor, his lovely mother Maria. He yearned to kiss and hold her on his arms.

Some of his favorite dishes to make, always warmly welcomed and frequently joyfully devoured by his friends were; Chicken with Rice, White Rice, Carne Ripiada, Black Bean Potage and Fried Plantains.

*

Unfortunately life's path presents unexpected and unmanageable challenges which often cause a detour or a direction change relative to vision and desire. Unbeknownst to Dina, Vincent had just discovered, after various medical tests, that the joyfulness which he had shared with his lovely wife would be no more. It was a late spring morning, the sky was blue and cloudless, the flowers' fragrance enriched the city air, and the sun radiated light and warmth as if it was eternity. Vincent walked down the street pale face, head down and oblivious of nature's gifts.

The doctor had shared with Vincent the result of his last exam, news which he did not want to accept. Shortly he will not be able to be with Dina, the love of his life. The thought, unbearable to contemplate yet insignificant when compare to the pain which it will inflict on Dina.

Many thoughts were pondered while walking down the avenue; should he tell Dina? should he run away? How can he help her deal with the fact that he was dying? Vincent knew that he needed to share his burden with someone; he needed to find a way to diminish Dina's pain.

Vincent walked aimlessly and obliviously passed the laughing children and the street vendors, calling attention to their luscious peaches recently receive from Georgia's hillside.

Unaware of her presence, he collided with a frail elderly lady whose face reflected the heavy burden of the years gone by, her eyes mirroring the pain of her life's struggle, and her frail body slowly recovering from the unexpected jolt from Vincent's athletic young torso. The impact with the feeble and helpless lady returned Vincent consciousness, from his immersed search to shelter Dina from the inevitable pain which the sad news will place on her gentle heart.

He new that his destiny was already defined and that the remaining chapters of his life were very few, for the final episode was already written. His boundless love for Dina diminished the uncertainty and concerns for the "ever after", his focus and primary mission for the rest of his life was to shelter Dina, as much as possible from the pain to come.

Vincent gently held the old lady's arm until she managed to stabilize her body's balance. He spoke to her softly and apologetically, his voice overflowing with kindness and remorse.

The elderly lady, whose appearance showed the rigors of economic struggle was flush with love and kindness. With a soft, weak, and gentle voice she responded to Vincent's apology with forgiveness. She looked into his eyes and he felt as if something had penetrated his inner soul and had detected the pain which he carried. She said in response "young man there is nothing to forgive, it was an accident, please do not remorse, it was an accident".

Vincent thanked her and volunteered to help her carry the small bag of groceries, which appeared to be a burden for her to do. At first she refused but then she allowed Vincent to walk her to her small apartment half a block away.

As they walked quietly down the street, each submerge in their own challenging thoughts, the frail old lady looked at Vincent and said "young man you appear to be carrying a very heavy burden on your shoulders, please remember that no matter how cloudy the skies may appear today, the sun will always come out tomorrow." Vincent surprise and intrigued by her comment asked "what makes you think that?" The frail old lady responded "your eyes are the mirror of your soul and their tears the reflection of your pain" Vincent looked puzzled by her wisdom and slightly smile as if acknowledging her observation.

They reached the entrance to the cellar apartment were she lives, Vincent handed the grocery bag to the elderly lady, thanked her for her understanding and wished her a wonderful day. The elderly lady remove her black babushka, exposing her angel like white hair, kissed Vincent on the forehead and said "son may God bless you and may he help you carry your heavy burden just as you have help me carry mine".

She slowly turned away from Vincent and walked carefully down the three steps, covered with fallen spring flower's petals, to her cellar apartment.

Vincent walked away pensive, not only about the wisdom of the elderly lady's observations but more so, wondering about his lovely Dina's golden years which he would not be able to share with her. Momentarily he questioned, if someday Dina would also wear a Babushka.

Undecided about his destination, Vincent continued his aimless walk searching his mind and soul for answers. The sun rays slowly began to be replaced by the late afternoon shadows, and the bird's music welcoming the spring was replaced by the sound of the horns, by the ringing of the bicycle bells, by the closing of car doors, by the screeching truck brakes, and by the multitude of people rushing home from work.

Unexpectedly Vincent's pace accelerated as if he knew his destination. Indeed he did, and his brain cells likewise accelerated processing his thoughts with the same certainty, as his body's strong muscles rapidly moved him thru the busy city streets.

Vincent adventurous and fund loving nature contributed to his bonding and growing friendship with Jaime. Both men are young, easy going, lovers of good food, enjoyed each others company, and above all very trustworthy. This is the reason which motivated Vincent to reach out for his friend Jaime, to share his sorrow, and to seek his advice.

It was five thirty Friday afternoon and Vincent, knowing Jaime very well, expected that he was already home since his job at a local Pills factory was only three blocks away from Jaime's apartment. Vincent was certain that Jaime was polishing his shoes, and ironing his shirt, before joining the group at the local dance spot.

Jaime enjoyed listening to music and watching his friends dance the exotic dances of the times including, the "flying Charleston" which requires a high kick forward and low kick backward, a move more appropriate for Vincent with his athletic characteristic.

Jaime preferred the Danzon, better known as the official Cuban dance of his time, and occasionally he also enjoyed Mambo. His preference, particularly when dancing with a partner that he admired greatly and perhaps desires, was an intimate and slow dance.

As he walked towards Jaime's apartment, Vincent remembered teasing Dina about the possibility of their participating in an enduring dance marathon contest, a practice very popular at the time. He smiled slightly, remembering Dina's reaction. She rapidly expressed her objection to his suggestion, and pretended to be annoyed at him by quickly saying 'What kind of girl do you think I am!?"

Vincent reached Jaime's cellar apartment located two blocks west of Penn Station. Jaime greeted Vincent with his usual warm embrace, typical of the fraternal expression common between Cuban men who have high regards for each other. At first Vincent, a Slovaks descendant, found this friendship expression somewhat uncomfortable. Often he remembers that, when he first met Jaime, he considered the hug to be an unmanly behavior. On occasions he has shared that reaction with Jaime, at which time they both laughed lightheartedly at the cultural idiosyncrasies.

Jaime's apartment was small but comfortable for a single man. The windowless bedroom was approximately eight by eight feet, and was furnished with a single bed, a small two doors dresser, and a night table supporting a simple lamp and a picture of Jaime's mother. On the wall hung a print of a Cuban land escape, including a Guajiro mounted on his horse crossing a shallow river bed which was bordered by three beautiful palm tress bearing flowers. Those flowers latter develop into a bean like fruits, also known as Palmiche, which is often used to feed the peasants pigs. On the back drop of the print was a flowering Flanboyan tree in full blossom, filling the landscape with brilliant red/orange flowers.

Next to the print hung the Cuban code of arms and above it two crossed flags. The U.S. and the Cuban flags, the flags of the two nations which he admired and loved dearly. Next to the bedroom was a kitchenette with a Formica table surround by four taburetes, a sturdy wood frame chair with cow hide seats and backing, a typical furniture style used by the Cuban peasants.

To the right of the bedroom and on back of the kitchenette was a small bathroom with a shower, a small sink, a yellowing white toilet, and the only window available in the modest apartment.

Jaime, knowing Vincent caffeine vice, offered to make Cuban coffee, a very strong espresso like brew. Vincent quickly refused the offer and, fully controlling his emotions, told Jaime that today he needs his friendship and advice more than coffee, and more than ever. They both sat by the kitchen table and Vincent related verbatim the doctor's evaluation and conclusion, resulting from the extensive battery of medical tests which he had to endure.

Vincent related that the doctor had told him that the tests had uncovered an advanced, terminal, and untreatable bone cancer condition. Vincent could not hold back his emotion any longer, and tears began to uncontrollably drop from his eye lids. To his own surprise, Vincent was seeking the comfort and confirmation of friendship and loyalty which is clearly communicated between two good friends, indeed two brothers, with a fraternal embrace.

Jaime was aware that Vincent had been seeing the doctor and was having some tests performed. He always thought that it was not a serious matter, but rather a minor ailment which will be readily cured with time and prescriptions.

Jaime understood why Vincent had carried this painful burden on his shoulders alone, he knew Vincent well. He knew that Vincent is a very private, proud, unselfish, and industrious man. He knew that Vincent will rather endure the pain or pay the price himself, if that action would shelter those that he loves from having to endure the pain or pay the price.

Vincent always closely safeguarded his personal issues; his health condition was not an exception. Those were some of the personal qualities which Jaime admired so very much about his friend. Although he often wondered what motivated Vincent to be as reserved as he was.

Upon hearing Vincent's slow and methodical explanation, as if Vincent had to pry every verb and every adjective from the inner most part of his soul, Jaime's felt his blood rush thru his veins, not unlike the melting snow rushing down the mountains in a balmy spring morning.

Jaime could feel the pressure building on the lateral part of his cranium, his brain cells appeared to be sending contradictory commands to the leg muscles, and momentarily Jaime thought that he was going to drop. Seconds later Jaime gained his inner composure, including the disappearance of the butterfly like feeling on his upper abdomen.

Vincent stood up as if wanting to escape, as if wanting to run away. He was struggling, not only with the consequences of his terminal health condition, but also he was dealing with having violated part of who he is. He who has always being independent, self reliable, and an extremely reserved individual had to seek refuge, in his friendship with Jaime, to lighten the heavy and unbearable burden which his destiny had revealed.

Jaime also stood up; he walked slowly towards Vincent, and stopped half of an arm length away from him. Jaime's light brown eyes were overflowing with but not releasing those moisture droplets with the brilliance of a most precious diamond and the purity of true brotherly love. He had to be strong for his friend and not shed those tears.

Jaime looked into Vincent's moist and resigned light blue eyes. He raised both of his arms and placed each hand on each of Vincent's shoulders. Jaime's fingers slowly moved and gently pressured both subscapularis muscle hoping to ease Vincent's pain.

Words were not necessary for the most profound and sincere understanding of what was happening and what was to happen, was being communicated without the sometimes distracting consequences of the spoken word.

Momentarily, it appeared as if the world had been placed on hold as both men visually acknowledge their understanding of life's consequences and their appreciation of each other's true friendship.

Vincent raised his arms and embraced Jaime, who likewise responded with a long and affectionate embrace as if it would be the last time. They move away from each other and the only words that Jaime could put together were "Please! Please don't go, let's talk" Vincent abruptly moved his upper torso towards the door as if wanting to run. It was not that he wanted to run from his dear friend, but rather because he wanted to hide his shedding tears.

They both sat quietly in the small kitchen, it was soundless except for the muffled sound of air entering and exiting the nasal cavities. There was no obvious physical movement in the room. If it had been possible to amplify the sound of the heart beats, the echo of the rushing blood, and the rhythm of the brain cells, the resulting symphony would have been a torturous and unbearable experience.

Jaime's search his brain cells for a gentle and supportive sounds which he could express to his dear friend. Instead, his mind wandered, many years past when he, for the first time in his life, experienced a loss which was almost as severe as losing his own life.

*

Uncontrollably Jaime's mind focus on his father's unexpected accidental death at a sugar mill called Santa Fe, in Cuba.

Jaime had just turned sixteen and was working at the sugar mill as an apprentice in the mill's parts warehouse. He clearly remembers wanting to continue his education and to someday perhaps becoming the mill's general manager. Unfortunately, his father's income was insufficient to sustain the family's needs. As the oldest male member in the family, Jaime was required to leave school at the age of fifteen to seek employment and supplement the family's income.

With his father's help, who played dominoes with the parts warehouse manager, Jaime was able to get hired as an apprentice warehouse clerk. Because of his lack of experience, and the apprentice classification, Jaime was paid half of the normal compensation of 300 pesos a month.

Jaime was bringing home one third of his father's earnings, nonetheless it helped fill the budgetary gap for the family, at that time.

There was one month left before the beginning of the "Dead season", the time when the seasonal sugar production was completed since all of the sugar fields had been cut, and all the sugar cane had been transported to the sugar mills via ox carts from the local farms or via truck and rail from the further distanced growers.

Jaime remembers that day as if it was yesterday. It was a Friday afternoon on the 28th of May when Mr. Fernandez, the Warehouse manager excitedly called him at the back of the warehouse, and told him to rush to the front office.

Jaime was taking inventory and had carefully climbed the top shelf, twenty five feet above ground, and did not welcomed Daniel's, his trainer, insistence that he stop immediately and go to the front office as instructed by Mr. Fernandez. This only meant that he had to once again carefully climb up the ladder, again, in order to complete the unfinished section of the inventory. This was always an onerous process for Jaime, since he was very fearful of heights.

Jaime reported to the front office's secretary. She instructed him to knock on Mr. Fernandez office's door and to wait for a response. Mr. Fernandez asked "Quien es" and Jaime meekly responded Jaimecito, as he is usually called by Mr. Fernandez.

The deep voice from inside the office quickly and forcefully responded "entra".

Jaime entered the office and immediately, sensing that something was a foul. His first thought was that he had done something wrong and that Mr. Fernandez was going to terminate his employment. He immediately thought that his response will be to ask for forgiveness for whatever he did wrong, in order to make sure to not loose the job. His family could not afford to be without his income.

Sitting on a chair next to Mr. Fernandez was Dr. Roblejo, who was in charge of the sugar mill's first aid clinic. Jaime somewhat nervous, but making his best effort to self control, walked slowly towards Mr. Fernandez's executive desk, stopped two feet away from the beautifully hand carved edge of the desk directly in front of Mr. Fernandez, and with weakening knees and a low and nervous voice said " Señor Fernandez en que le puedo servir?".

Jaime had not been in Mr. Fernandez's office before today, and was very impressed by the eight by four feet hand carved dark mahogany desk which sheltered him from Mr. Fernandez.

There was a moment of silence in the office, and Jaime could feel his heart pounding. His thoughts, looking for a shelter used that "dead moment" to visually explore Mr. Fernandez office and escape from what was coming.

The office approximately fifteen square feet accommodated the beautiful desk which served as a buffer separating Jaime from Mr. Fernandez. A tall executive chair, made of the same mahogany wood as the desk, grown not very far from the sugar mill along El Cauto River, comfortably tolerated the excessively overweight old man. Luxurious dark leather; decorated with fancy brass tacks, was used to attached the cushioned leather to the bottom, back and arm rest of the executive chair, as well as the that of the two arm chairs, placed immediately in front near each desk corner.

There were two end tables occupied by crystal lamps, covered with dark, gold fringe, decorated cream colored shades. The wall immediately behind Mr. Fernandez had large glass window exposing a beautiful tropical atrium were palm, malanga, plantain and a variety of other tropical plants and flowers thrived.

The wall to the left of Mr. Fernandez had a blackboard partially covered on either side by a red velvet curtain, hanging from a long ceiling rod, and touching the ash white Spanish tile floor. The blackboard revealed columns of figures and notations in English.

Facing Mr. Fernandez's desk was the door to the office, immediately above the door was a framed Cuban flag and centered on each side of the door, hung a four by three feet painting of Jose Marti and Antonio Maceo, two of Cuba's independence heroes.

The wall to the right of Mr. Fernandez was used to display various diplomas and certificates of recognition, which were hung on the first row. Below the diplomas were three pictures of Mr. Fernandez shaking hands, and standing together with executives of the parent company in the United States. The third row displayed a three feet by two feet aerial photograph of the sugar mill. The picture highlights the size of the complex which consists of four attached structures with three black colored smoke stacks exhausting white cotton candy like puff of steam, rising towards the clear baby blue tropical sky.

The roof, constructed of three by eight zinc coated metal sheets commonly use in the tropics, was supported by steel beams covered by brick red colored aluminum siding. The first structure, the Pit, was adjacent to the main street, the second structure was the processing facility followed by the third which was the packaging, product and parts warehouse.

The very large rail yard immediately in front of the Pit consisted of ten rows of rail lines gradually merging to a single rail line that disappears into the Pit structure. Next to the rail line, a dirt road, likewise ending at the pit structure, was fully covered with sugar cane loaded Ford and Chevy trucks, waiting to unload the neatly loaded sugar cane.

At the other end of the train tracks yard, approximately two miles from the Pit's entrance, a crane busily unloaded large bundles of cut sugar cane from the two ox team pulled carts, and deposited the load to the adjacent rail cars.

The rail cars, thirty five feet in length, were steel fabricated. The solid front and rear walls support the sidewalls of the rail cart which are attached to it by heavy duty hinges on the upper level. The bottom of the side walls is secured with a moving horizontal bar attached to it and inserted into apertures on the front and back walls.

The sidewalls of the sugar cane carts are constructed with vertical metal rods which are welded to an upper an lower flat steel beam, approximately one inch by three inch thick, hinged to the front and rear walls. These hinges allows the opening of the sides, prior to tilting the rail car sideways towards the Pit, thus facilitating the dumping of the sugar cane into the Pit.

Mr. Fernandez cleared his throat and it served to focus Jaime's attention back to the issue of the moment. Jaime awaiting a response to his early query asked again somewhat more confident and with a mildly impatient tone "Señor Fernandez en que le puedo servir?" Obviously something was very wrong, thought Jaime, having noticed Mr. Fernandez face turn red and Dr. Roblejo's eyes focusing on the floor.

Finally, Mr. Fernandez began to speak with a nervous voice, he said "my son I have very bad news for you". Immediately Jaime interrupted Mr. Fernandez, and rapidly and without hesitation said "Mr. Fernandez, I am very sorry for whatever I have done, I swear on the Virgencita de la Caridad that I will not do it again, I swear.! If I lose this job my father is going to kill me".

Once again silence permeated the room. Dr. Roblejo, an elderly gentleman whose white hair matched his garment and his white mustache contrasted with his yellowing teeth, permanently tinted by tobacco juices from the Cuban cigars which are not often absent from his lips, slowly and sadly raised his head and looked at Jaime. He search for the right words to lessen Jaime's shock from the terrible news that he was about to share, but could not find them.

Finally he said, "Jaime your father died in an accident half of an hour ago". Once again, sound was non existent. Jaime face turned as white as the doctor's white hair and the tears rushed out of his tear ducts as if with the speed of an eagle excitedly breaking thru the gently breeze at high speed, in pursuit of his prey. Mr. Fernandez rushed to Jaime's side, hugged him and tried to comfort him. Likewise, Dr. Roblejo went to Jaime side and placed his arm on Jaime's shoulders. They both expressed their heart felt sorrow.

Jaime, having exhausted his tears, asked about the details of how his father met his maker, where was his father, and if his mother and siblings had been told. Dr. Roblejo immediately proceeded to narrate the unfortunate and sad event.

Jaime's father worked at the front end of the sugar production process. He controlled the conveyor systems that moves and fees the sugar cane to the grinding equipment. The grinding equipment cuts the canes into small sections and squeezes all available juices from the cane. The juice is then condensed and converted into molasses, and subsequently to sugar granules, once all of the moisture is separated from the molasses.

Trucks and rail cars unload the sugar cane into a built in underground Pit. An open dumpster type of structure, with built in conveyor belts on the bottom used to continuously move the sugar cane to conveyor channels with gradually narrowed side to side dimension from four to one and one half feet. Thus, forcing the sugar cane to line up neatly and parallel to each other before being introduced to the grinding equipment.

Rotating metal arms are installed every five feet, throughout the length of the conveyor system beyond the pit, to cause the alignment of the canes as they travel through the length of the narrowing channel, and to assure an efficient intake by the grinding equipment.

Jaime was told that a metal rod from the rail car fell into the pit and traveled thru the conveyor channel until it became lodged between the conveyor gears and the rotating arms, thus jamming and stopping the conveyor system.

The maintenance supervisor responsible for handling this type of repair was ill and Jaime's father having overall responsibility for the front end operation and been the only person with sufficient experience to solve the problem, began the troubleshooting of the conveyor system.

The jamming triggered a safety mechanism that automatically turned off the power to the conveyor system. Thus, when Jaime's father arrived at the location where the metal rod was lodged, there was no need to turn off the power.

Jaime's father immediately proceeded to climb down to the problem area using a fifteen foot ladder.

Once Jaime's father reached his destination, he quickly identified the source of the problem and proceeded to remove the metal rod. It was not an easy task, thus he requested his assistant, Peter, to locate a metal cutting torch and to get it down to him.

Peter located the wheeled torch and quickly moved it to the problem location. Peter also located two more co-workers and with the use of a heavy rope he and his helpers carefully lowered the wheeled metal torch to Jaime's father.

Jaime's father immediately lit the torch, identified the best location to cut the metal rod and slowly and carefully moved the torch to the selected spot to cut the rod in half, to free the revolving metal arms and the conveyor system's gear.

Jaime's father unexpectedly turned off the torch, looked up towards Peter and requested that he Peter provide him with a face and eye protector mask. A protective device made of metal and a glass window to provide visual access while protecting the face.

Peter located the protective mask and lowered it to Jaime's father with a long twine which he had found nearby. Jaime's father action demonstrated, once again, his concern for safety at the work place.

Jaime's father repeated the earlier process; he lit the torch, located the target, and slowly moved the torch's flame to its predetermined destination. As the torch light began to make contact with the metal rod, sparks began to fly in all directions. The closer the flame source to the metal rod, the greater the discharge of brilliant sparks, many of which appeared to attack Jaime's father as if in revenge. As the torch light penetrated the center of the rod, the spark display was reminiscent of the Fourth of July fire work display at the U.S. Consulate in the city of Santiago.

In order to complete the cutting task Jaime's father had to lie down on the sugar cane bed underneath the revolving arms, facing upwards. This he did carefully and once again applied the flame to the rod. It was a matter of seconds for the flame's high temperature to cut thru the remaining metal.

Finally the task was completed and Jaime's dad began to pull the cut rod and free the revolving arms. As Jaime's father removed the rod from its resting place the conveyor belt unexpectedly began to move simultaneously carrying his body together with the sugar cane underneath the moving arms. In a matter of split seconds one of the rotating arms penetrated the left side of Jaime's father's upper torso, and a second arm entered his forehead, and unimpeded invaded and destroyed his cranial shell and upper frontal cerebral section.

His body was no longer moving! Blood rushed out of his chest cavity as if trying to match the flying sparks from the metal rod. Above, Peter and his helpers were running and yelling with every ounce of energy which they could muster "Cojone! Turn off the main switch! Turn off the main switch! Cojone! Don Jose has been hurt!"

Sixty seconds later, although it felt as an eternity at the time, a jolt was heard and silence filed the area, the main power had been turned off. Peter quickly climbed down the ladder, stationed at the edge of the conveyor system, to the conveyor belt where Don Jose's still, and bloodied body sections rested in a painful contrast to the yellow/ green sugar canes.

Peter knew that there was no hope. He knew that his maestro and friend was gone forever. Peter felt to his knees, made a sign of the cross, and began to pray "Our father…but deliver us from evil, Amen".

A mocking bird's melody from a nearby tree accompanied Peter's prayer as if the bird was singing a final ballad to Don Jose. Peter made a sign of the cross again and began to quietly and privately weep. The sirens and the emergency vehicles filled the vacuum from the momentary silence that had overtaking the site. Crowds gathered along the conveyor system and witnessed the removal of Don Jose's remains and honored him with unbridled crying and uncontrolled tears.

Jaime, having heard the details of his dear father's accidental death, felt numb with an emptiness never experienced before, as if part of his soul had been cut away. He felt the burden of his great loss, his father and best friend. He felt the burden of the great responsibility, which destiny had bestowed upon his shoulders.

*

Vincent began to speak to Jaime, not realizing that he had awaken him from a trance which had transported him to one of the most, if not the most sorrowful day of his life, his father's accidental death at the Santa Fe sugar mill in the province of Oriente, Cuba. Vincent told Jaime "my friend, now you are the only person other than my doctor and I, who is aware of my terminal bone cancer conditions, or as the medical experts called it Osteosarcoma."

Jaime not able to find compassionate words that could express the unexpected and heart breaking development, asked "what about Dina, when are you going to tell Dina?"

Vincent looked directly into Jaime's eyes and with a firm and decisive tone, confirming that he had gained his composure said, "My dear friend, that is precisely what I want to discuss with you, and why I need your advice and help".

Jaime's thought process was once again activated and he continued asking questions. Vincent, have you gone for a second opinion? How long has this been going on? What prompted you to go for the test? What? Vincent interrupted Jaime's barrage of questions and said, "slow down, slow down, I will answer all your questions in due time, but first help me help Dina.

Vincent explained to Jaime that Osteosarcoma, a form of bone cancer that attacks primarily young men ranging in ages ten to thirty years old, is a type of cancer that normally targets the long bones including; the pelvis, the legs; and the arms.

Vincent told Jaime that Osteosarcoma usually begins at the end of the bones where malignant cells grow out of control, "crowding out" the normal cells, propagating to the rest of the bone and promoting tumor growth. The malignant cells also migrate to other critical organs eventually destroying their functions and destroying life itself.

According to Vincent's doctor, his Osteosarcoma condition began on the upper arm by his left shoulder and has migrated and began to reproduce in the lower brain lobe.

As he proceeded to explain the diagnosis to Jaime, Vincent,

contrary to what he told the doctor, began to realize that he indeed has had signs or symptoms of the developing disease, as he remembers last summer country outing with the "gang".

*

It was the weekend after the fourth of July when the seven friends spend a weekend at a farm located in a farming area called Hanover Neck, approximately one and one half hour from the city of Newark. He remembers taking a ferry to the Hoboken terminal and then boarding a train to Penn station in Newark. Upon disembarking from the train at Penn Station the group gathered their luggage, unfortunately the ladies, Dina in particular, packed enough clothing to stay for two to three weeks.

The group followed Market Street West, passed Mc Arthur Highway and proceeded to the Mulberry Street Market Place struggling with the luggage load. They arrive at Jimmy's produce store, the first building on this extremely active market area, and located the White's Farm truck were Mr. White was stretched out on the truck's flat bed apparently taking a short nap.

Mr. White, Mary's parent's neighbor, a farmer, was delivering a truck load of eggplant and cucumber from his farm to the city's market. He was asked by his neighbors, the Richards and Mary's parents, to give the group a ride to the farm when he returns from his produce delivery. Mary was Dina's closes friend, confidant, and the Maid of Honor at Vincent's and Dina's wedding.

Mary awakened Mr. White with a sweet and gentle greeting, and began to introduced all her friends to him. Mr. White got up, briskly dusted his overalls, and told the "gang" to quickly place their luggage in the wooden crate attached underneath the flat bed, immediately behind the rear wheels.

He told the "gang" to climb on the truck bed, and make sure to hold on to the ropes attached to the wood post inserted to the sides of the truck's flat bed.

Before boarding the old Ford truck cab, Mr. White told the group that it was getting late and that he had to get back to gather and feed the cows.

Mr. White climbed into the truck's dusty cab, found his comfortable spot on the worn leather covered seat with protruding springs sticking out of the edge, and turned on the ignition switch. "Old Betsy", as he affectionately called his truck, refused to start. He tried again, and again without success.

Mr. White banged his fist right hand on the dash board, as if trying to beat and force Old Betsy's engine to start. He opened the door and jumped out of the cab yelling "Gosh Darn it"!

Mr. White opened the truck's tool box welded to the outside of the Ford's cab, extracted a crank bar and walked to the front of the truck. He inserted the crank bar into the hand crank inlet and turned it clockwise, once, twice, three times and nothing happened. Mr. White's face began to turn as red as the tomatoes that he brought to the market. He took a deep breath, gently padded the truck's hood and said "come on Old Betsy, my love". "Please don't let me down now!"

He grabbed the crank bar firmly and turned it. The six cylinders Ford straight engine responded shaking as if insecure. The combustion apparently had ignited for only two or three of the six engine's cylinders. Mr. White then said again "come on Old Betsy my love. Don't let me down!" The old truck's engine stopped shaking and the melody of the six cylinders working in partnership could be heard. Mr. White smiled, reflecting his satisfaction and gratitude to Old Betsy.

Mr. White looked at the "gang" who were sitting on truck's bed and told them "we are ready to go!"

The truck proceeded north on Mulberry Street and turned left on to Market Street. Mr. White has chosen to take South Orange Avenue, climb the South Orange Mountain via the South Mountain Reservation, continued on South Orange Avenue to Mt. Pleasant Road, and then pick up U.S. #10 which cuts thru Hanover Neck. The trip took approximately an hour and one half due to road conditions and the need to stop during the trip to let the truck's engine cool down, and provide and opportunity for the ladies to relieve themselves.

As Mr. White's truck approached the Richards's home, Old Betsy's horn began to honk scaring away the chickens and turkeys from the middle of the dirt road.

Anxious to see their daughter, the Peterson couple rushed to the farm house's porch to welcome Mary and her friends. The city folks jumped from the truck's flat bed and briskly walked towards the porch where a loving and warmth greeting awaited their arrival.

Vincent and Jaime volunteered to gather and unload the luggage from the wooden crate. Once their mission was accomplished, the two fellows thanked Mr. White for the ride and began walking towards the porch. Soon there after, the truck carrying Mr. White accelerated away from the Richards' house and away from the Richards' farm property, leaving behind a cloud of dust and many excited chicken and turkeys.

It was 5:30 PM and the Richards' family together with the "Gang of Seven" sat down to eat. Their visitors were tired and hungry, having taken in excess of half a day to reach their destination.

The supper table was a picture of plenteousness. Bowls of Beef Stew, Mashed Potato, Fried Chicken, Corn on the Cob, Green Beans, and Baked Beans, were the fare of the night. Mr. Peterson, sitting at the head of the table, thanked the Lord for thy bounty and encouraged all to enjoy the meal.

Mary's mother was sitting next to Dina and complimented her looks and stated that marriage agrees with her. Dina blushed slightly and said that marrying Vincent was the best thing that has happened to her. They talked about the trip, about the city, and about the difficulty which most folks are having trying to make ends meet. Mrs. Richards added that the White's almost lost their house after the Depression began, but fortunately all the farmers in the area got together and were able to raise enough money to "chase the bank" away.

Home made strawberry rhubarb pie, and French vanilla ice cream accompanied by fresh brewed coffee complemented the wholesome dinner.

Conversation around the dinner table was as plentiful, as the country bounty which the group had devoured. Jaime turned his head towards Mr. and Mrs. Richards, raised his water glass and thanked them profusely for their hospitality and for such a fantastic meal, especially for the Baked Beans for which Mrs. Richards is renown in the Hanover Neck area.

Fully satisfied and with the digestive system completely overloaded, the visitors sat on rocking chairs and hanging swing on the farm house's porch, admiring the blinking stars and savoring the fresh country air. A while later, Dina and Vincent said good night to the folks and retired to their bedroom. Vincent wanted to retire hoping that lying down would help relieve the very uncomfortable pain emanating from his left shoulder.

Vincent shared the fact that he was experiencing the shoulder discomfort with Dina who in turn gave both of his shoulders a long and gentle rub with Vic's Vapor Rub. Vincent rationalized that the shoulder discomfort may have been a consequence, of perhaps pulling a muscle as result of carrying the heavy baggage. He also shared that he expected that a good night of rest would address the problem. The shoulder discomforts dissuaded Vincent from taking advantage of the gentle and loving back rub, which Dina was giving him, and encouraged the beginning of a physically romantic evening.

*

Vincent refocused on his conversation with his friend Jaime, and asked him if he recalled their summer outing to the Richards' farm last July. Jaime welcoming the opportunity to add some levity to the moment quickly responded, "Yes, I remember clearly! I remember that I tried to wake you up "with the rooster" to teach you how to milk a cow. It was almost impossible to awaken you, I knocked on your door until my fingers hurt". Finally Dina opened the door and I told her that you had asked to be awakened to try to learn to milk a cow.

Dina obviously has more leverage on you than you have on yourself, because a few minutes later your came out dragging your butt. In any event, "trying to teach you to milk a cow ranks as one of the funniest experience in my adult life".

With a mischievous smile, Jaime reminded Vincent how they walked to the barn and selected a black and white, Hershey breed cow as the target for milking. Jaime found a small stool and placed it by the cow's right side next to the udder. Jaime told Vincent to sit on the stool and wait. Jaime proceeded to search for two buckets, one for the milk and the second to fill with water. Once he found the buckets and filled one with the water, Jaime walked to where Vincent and the cow waited.

The cow was somewhat restless and Vincent looked equally nervous. When Jaime reached his student and subject, he placed both buckets next to Vincent's stool and began the cow milking lessons; he said "OK, Vincent, first your need to wash the udder, place the water bucket underneath it and wash it with the cloth that is in the water. Hopefully you will not get too excited doing that. Remember this is work, not play time!" Vincent concluded his thorough cleaning job without any objection from the cow.

Jaime continued the instructions, "replace the water bucket with the empty bucket and take one of the teats with the palm of your right hand. Bend your thumb and squeeze the teat as close as possible to the udder, with your thumb on one side and the other fingers on the other side of the teat." Vincent followed the precise instructions, but regardless of how hard he squeezes the teats, the cow was not cooperating and milk would not come out.

Jaime decided that the next step has to be "show and tell". He knelt down next to Vincent, near the cow's udder. He squeezed one of the teats and to Vincent's surprise the milk came out as if Jaime had opened a water faucet. Vincent somewhat frustrated by his failure tried again. He held the teats one on each hand as instructed, squeeze them, and milk came rushing out, not to the bucket, but directly to Vincent's face and his crotch.

Reacting to the unexpected milk shower, Vincent felt back onto the hay and his head landed in a freshly produced and recently deposited "cow dung pie". Vincent got up, looked at Jaime and started cursing at himself, at Jaime and the cow. Jaime could no longer hold back the effect of the humorous situation, and began laughing uncontrollably at the innocent comedy act which Vincent had unintentionally played.

"OK Jaime! I hope you enjoyed reminding me of that fiasco", replied Vincent. Then he proceeded to tell Jaime that he had experienced a shoulder discomfort at Peterson's farm, which may have been the first manifestation of the bone or metastatic cancer condition which is now gradually destroying his young life.

Jaime asked Vincent what prompted him to begin the testing process. Vincent hesitated and then explained that he had decided to join the Air Force and that when the Pre-Induction tests were performed evidence of potential health concerns were detected.

The Air Force doctor recommended that Vincent should go to a specialist to confirm the preliminary findings from the Pre-Induction physical examination. The doctor also notified Vincent that a hold was being placed on his induction processing until there was viable evidence that his health condition were of no concern, and physical status met the Air Force standards.

Jaime asked Vincent what was his motivation for trying to join the Air Force and why did he keep it a secret. Vincent told Jaime that he had decided to join the Air Force not only because of the professional opportunities and the potential of possibly providing Dina a more adventurous and secured life, but also because he loves his country, the United States, and felt that every citizen who enjoys the fruits of the sacrifices of the many, has a civic and moral responsibility to fulfill his duty and to assure that future generations will be able to cherish and enjoy the same privileges which the current generation has enjoyed.

Vincent related that his family emigrated from Eastern Europe to the United States in 1915, when he was only five years old. He did not remember anything about the "old country" but he does remember the trip on the ship. It was dark and smelly and he remembers always being very hungry.

His family was welcome into the country. Vincent's mother had related, on various occasion, the difficulties which the family faced during the first few years after arriving in North America. She told Vincent that learning the language, finding permanent shelter and getting a job required a lot of perseverance and hard work. She further said, "However, this great nation has always provided opportunity for those that are willing to work hard and take care of themselves. Our family was no exception".

Vincent, showing that pensive expression which he generally musters before expressing an important point, told Jaime that he would be forever grateful for the freedom and opportunity which his family and he found in this great nation. He further stated "he felt indebted to our nation".

As to why he keep the volunteering into the Armed Forces a secret, Vincent explained that being accepted into the Air Force was not a sure thing and he did not want to be embarrassed should he had been rejected. Particularly since Dina's brother had been inducted and was currently in training.

Dina's older brother Victor, who joined the Air Force six months ago, had graduated from basic training last month. Vincent and Dina, nor her parents, could afford to witness her brother's basic training graduation, due to logistics and economic consideration. However, they did receive two photographs last week. The first photo, the official military picture, showed Victor in his full dress uniform. On the second photo, Vincent was receiving a certificate of recognition and saluting his commanding officer. Dina's brother looked very sharp and very proud.

Vincent got along very well with Victor. Vincent respected him and admired his character and personality. Indeed, Vincent considered Dina's brother to be his role model. Her brother was a very industrious individual, and his intellect was above average. His patriotism was second to none. Those are some of the personal traits which both Vincent and Jaime like to emulate. Vincent thought that perhaps his wanting to join the Armed Forces was an unconscious desire to fallow his role model's path.

Vincent changed sitting position on the chair looking for some additional comfort. He fixated his sight on Jaime's light brown pupils and said, "Jaime I have sheltered Dina from what we both know and I do not know how to gently tell her about the Osteosarcoma diagnosis".

Jaime took a deep breath, disengaged his sight from Vincent's eyes, momentarily lowered his head and looked down at the discolored wooden floor. Approximately thirty seconds later, he slowly raised his head and forced his eye's sight, once again, to find and make contact with Vincent's excessively moist light blue eyes. Jaime then asked Vincent with a tone, as if gently scolding him, "how could you possibly have kept Dina unaware of your tests, she is your wife!, she loves you very much, and promised to love you for better, or for worse" Vincent found himself needing to disengage eye contact with Jaime and redirected his sight to a framed photograph sitting on top of the small Frigidaire refrigerator standing next to the double burner GE gas stove, of Dina and him at their wedding.

Vincent remorsefully expressed regrets for having avoided sharing the on-going tests with his lovely wife Dina. He explained to Jaime that, contrary to her friend's perception that Dina is a very strong person, she really is very fragile and insecure. He suspects that her insecurity is a consequence of the difficult economic struggle that she and her family experienced as a result of her father loosing his employment, and, subsequently, his investment when the market crashed preceding the Depression of 1929. Jaime acknowledged his understanding of Vincent's justification for withholding such critical information from his lovely wife. He then said, "Vincent you must tell Dina as soon as possible, it is not fair nor, is it right to keep her unaware of what is happening, it is not right!"

Vincent looked at Jaime once again, and asked him if he had any thought as to how to best break the news to Dina causing the least amount of pain. He repeated to Jaime about his concern for Dina, her reaction and her ability to deal with his decease and its eventual consequence.

Silence prevailed as Jaime used every once of concentration, searching for a helpful response to his dear friend's request. Unexpectedly he thought and shared with Vincent a scenario for his consideration.

Jaime looked at Vincent and suggested that, he and Dina go to Coney Island beach this weekend by themselves. Vincent looked at Jaime somewhat bewildered and reminded Jaime that it was only the end of May and that the water was definitely too cold to go swimming. Jaime responded that he was aware of the time of the year and about the fact that the water was too cold. However, he reminded Vincent that Dina's birthday was next week and that the beach will be a desolate setting which will make it possible for them to spend quality time together and by themselves. Jaime was sure that the setting will provide appropriate opportunity for Vincent to explain his medical condition to Dina.

Jaime hesitated momentarily then raised his hands to Vincent's shoulder and rested both of them next on each side of Vincent's neck as if keeping him from getting away. Jaime than said, "Please allow me to be a bit philosophical". Jaime continued, "You and Dina will be sitting by the water on an isolated beach being caressed by the warm and soft spring breeze. Words may be few in between for they will be really unnecessary. Being together, gently holding hands, and feeling each other's warmth will be all that you both desire at the moment, to communicate each other's love and to open your soul to each other. The waves' ebb and flow will not only echo the melody of love, but they symbolically will represent the reality of life, as they have a beginning and an end, an origin and a destination, joy and sadness, and its cause and effect continuously creates and removes its carvings on the sandy beach"

Jaime dropped his hands from Vincent's shoulder and told him once again that the mood and beach setting should enable him to muster the strength necessary to finally disclose his health condition to his lovely wife.

Vincent silent, in deep thought, and with his eyes fixated, as if searching the vast emptiness of outer space, pondered his friend's suggestion. Yes he thought, going away and spending the weekend alone at the beach with my love is certainly an appealing proposition. I should then be able to find a way to gently tell her about the diagnosis. He looked at Jaime, gave him an approvingly smile and told him that he agreed with his suggestion and that he will talk to Dina about the week end escape to Coney Island.

*

The trip to the beach was much more challenging that Vincent had anticipated since the beach season had not started. The winter bus schedule to Coney Island from Mid Manhattan was quite limited. Service was only available for the weekend due to the limited demand since cold water bathing was not what the public wanted, except for the few brave souls, members of the Polar Bear Club who enjoyed challenging nature's frigid waters challenge. Precisely the setting that Jaime had suggested, and that Vincent and Dina needed to deal with such a heartbreaking conversation.

On Saturday morning after staying overnight with Dina's family in Irving Town, Vincent and Dina boarded the #1 bus at the town's center. Being a non working day, the trip was faster than usual to Newark's center. They got off at the South West corner of Broad and Market Street and entered a local general store to purchase snacks and drinks for their trip. They the walked East on Market Street towards Penn Station to board a train to Manhattan where they could change to another train which will take them to their beach destination - Coney Island.

It was one thirty, Saturday afternoon, May 27, three days before Dina's birthday. The young couple had registered at a small motel named Esperanza, bearing the owner's wife's name after a two and a half hour trip from their home town. It was a small twelve cabin motel, which reflected the effect of the harsh winter that had recently gone by. Vincent picked up Dina and carried her into the small room as if they were on their honey moon. Vincent kissed her tenderly and lovingly, and then lowered her body until her feet contacted the rustic wooden floor. They embraced and kissed once again with the same passion as their first kiss and with the same intensity as if were to be their last.

They both sat on the side of the bed, quietly looking at each other. Suddenly, Vincent felt a painful shock run from his shoulder and down his left arm, as if he had been hit by lightning, or perhaps a reminder of the equally painful conversation which he had to have with the love of his life. Vincent's face showed the unexpected pain long enough for Dina to detect his physical reaction mirrored by his facial expression. This unusual physical reaction behavior cause Dina's to be became alarmed and excitedly asked Vincent "Are you OK, My Love? What happened?" Vincent simultaneously struggling with the pain, and with his desire to conceal the truth for the moment, forced his face to yield a small smile and told Dina that he must have pulled a muscle when carrying her. They both looked at the bed and shared a sweet and meaningful smile.

Dina got up and began removing their clothes from the Duffle bag into the makeshift closet provided by the motel. She picked up her one piece burgundy colored bathing suit and handed Vincent his black trunk. Dina entered the very small bathroom to change and Vincent remained in the bedroom to put on his trunk.

The bathroom was very clean but unable to hide the wear and tear of the use frequency. There was a small sink sitting on a home made, sherry wood, cabinet with two doors each with an an antique silver knob on. Above the sink hung an oval mirror without frame, appearing to support with its upper end an antique, vertically positioned single 60 Watts light bulb fixture. A half inch bronze pipe protruded thru the wall, on back of the light fixture, providing mirror support and as well as being the conduit for the electrical power. This was the only light source for the small bathroom. The toilet, appearing to have been recently installed, was to the right of the sink opposite the bathroom door.

The room included a shower, a disappointment to Dina who on occasion enjoys leisurely submerging her youthful and envious looking body into a full tub of warm water, spiced with fragrances and opaqued from the popping bubbles. The shower wall was covered with yellow tiles that extended to the corner immediately opposite the toilet. A thick, white cloth curtain hung in front of the shower, from ceiling to floor, to keep the splashing water from invading the small mosaic tile floor supporting all the fixtures.

Once finished dressing, combing her hair, applying her deep red lipstick, and lightly spraying her favorite cologne immediately below her ears, below the neck and above her young and firm bosom, Dina came out of the bathroom with a smile, confirming her feeling of expectation and joy. Vincent looked up at his wife, smiled broadly, and as if reading Dina's thoughts, told her, "Sweetheart, you look radiant, I am indeed a fortunate fellow and I love you very, very much". Dina heard exactly what she was hoping to hear. Her ability and effort to supplement her natural beauty with color and essence, in the small bathroom, produced the result and provided the reward that she was anticipating.

Vincent held Dina closed to him, kissed her on the neck, below the ears, and lovingly asked her if she was ready for a walk on the beach. She look at him and with a smile, which projected a sweetness only matched by the most delicious and pure honey from Pennsylvania's flower fields. She then responded to Vincent suggestion, "it was getting late and that she was starving". Consequently, they decided to walk to Mickey's Fish Emporium, a hot spot they have frequented with their friends, and which was located only half a mile away.

Vincent and Dina put on their spring sweeter. Each grabbed a towel and Vincent also picked up the blanket before proceeding the walk to Mickey's and enjoy a bowl of delicious Manhattan clam chowder, followed by their famous deep fried cat fish preceding a thirst quenching "Cuba Libre", which their dear friend Jaime had introduced to them.

As they approached Mickey's Fish Emporium, a mile away

from the rustic motel, the dim lighting projecting from the lonely building tamed their enthusiasm and caused a momentary frustration as they thought that their favorite restaurant may not be open. As they approached the restaurant they could hear the soft melody of a favorite song by Jimmy Grier & His Orchestra title "Stay as Sweet as You Are". The frustration which they entertained on their way to the restaurant was no longer there. It abandoned their thoughts as quickly as the ocean waves erased the footprints on the sandy beach.

It was four thirty in the afternoon, Vincent and Dina walked passed over the white sand dunes, protected by the sea shore's thin bladed green grass that partially sheltered the beach sand from the ocean waves and from their discharge of fury against the land, as if in punishment.

They had a fantastic meal at Mickey's. The clam chowder had been sold out, but the fish chowder was just as exquisite. The deep fried Cat Fish was as superb as always. It was so good that he requested a second serving of Cat fish that he shared with his lovely wife. As Dina watched Vincent eat with such gusto and with an inner smile, perhaps even a childish one, she thought that the fresh air had awaken Vincent's appetite and wondered if subconsciously Vincent was preparing self for a romantic adventure, which she hoped would follow as the evening approached.

The dessert deserved similar accolades. Eating the creamy and chocolaty Boston cream pie was heavenly, and the grand finale, the Italian Espresso Coffee with a touch of Anisette was the golden seal for an unforgettable dinning experience shared by this loving couple.

Having left the restaurant, Dina and Vincent took their shoes off and walked across the solidly packed lukewarm white sand towards the approaching waves. The sea was calm this late afternoon. The waves turned white, foamy, and bubbly when the gentle spring breeze guided them to meet the awaiting shore line.

The waves and the beach embraced and dissipated the foamy and bubbly water. The dry sand was not longer dry, as if the two forces had became one.

The ocean color, emerald green near the shore line and deep blue as it approached the horizon, contrasted beautifully against the clear and cloudless of the darkening baby blue sky. The gentle breeze was blowing back Dina's beautiful, soft, blond hair. The Seagulls were dancing on the air as if welcoming the couple to their sanctuary. The small birds were rapidly walking, if not running, on the sand trying to capture insects disturber by the ocean waves, before they could dig holds and seek protection under the sand.

Unlike all of their previous outings to Coney Island beach, today Vincent and Dina had no problem locating a desirable spot to open their blanket and enjoy the dying sun, the sand, and the ocean breeze. Indeed, they felt as if they were in a dessert Island. The nearest sun worshipper was about half a mile away trying to entice the elusive prey to bite the helpless worm hiding the threatening hook.

Vincent and Dina lay down on the blanket avoiding carrying sand on their feet, they faced the gorgeous early spring, clear late afternoon sky. As they restfully lay on the blanket and their body warmth tamed the cooling air, they admired and were entertained by the flexibility and beauty of the Seagull's as they gracefully danced on the air.

They were lying on an isolated beach being caressed by the warm and soft spring breeze as Jaime had wisely described. They were together, gently holding hands, feeling each other's warmth, and truly enjoying the richness of the moment which demanded nothing more than silence and joyfulness.

The richness and calmness of the moment was too great to be resisted and both Vincent's and Dina's consciousness was overcome by the body's natural need and desire to slow down and recess into a dormant mode. Their consciousness faded and they both entered a stage of mental and physical rest.

As the red sun started to slowly and quietly recede into the awaiting Horizon, a seagull rapidly flying down towards Vincent, as if having been trained by a fighter pilot, dropped a discharge which landed on Vincent's bare chest. The unexpected impact and the warmth and moisture of the fecal matter awakened Vincent who had been startled by the experienced. He looked at his chest and could not help but exclaim "Oh Shit!" He carefully moved away from Dina to avoid awakening her, ran to the water, knelt down and washed all the evidence of the target practice from his chest.

Vincent returned to the blanket, laid down next to Dina and began to strategize how to best approach "the subject" with Dina.

The sun continued its journey to the horizon, being admired by Vincent while while mentally exploring the possible options to handle the escapade mission. The beauty of the reddish sun rays, the darkening clear blue skies and the scattered cumulus clouds breaking the diminishing sun rays, was too overwhelming for Vincent to selfishly enjoy by himself. He turned towards Dina and whispered "I Love You" into her ears. Dina apparently, on a deep sleep, was not responsive to his message. Thus Vincent followed by gently kissed her moist lips, which had been covered with the cherry flavored deep red lipstick at the motel's bathroom and later refreshed after their wonderful meal at Mickey's. Dina responded immediately by jumping to a sitting position and romantically embracing and kissing Vincent. The mischievous look on Dina's face exposed her pretending to be asleep after he whispered into her ears. They both remained lying down and admiring the late spring sunset.

They silently watched the sun disappear into the Horizon, with only a ring like section of it remained projecting weakening red and golden rays, barely visible. The symbolism of a dying sunset motivated Vincent to share storm which their lives, their love, will have to deal with in the near future.

Dina was aware that Vincent had registered for a Pre-Induction physical to joint the Armed Forces. She had mix feelings about his decision. On the one hand, she did not want anything or any one to separate her from Vincent. On the other hand, her very strong patriotism and unbridled love for her country help her understand and accept the justification for Vincent's actions.

Dina's acceptance was perhaps one of her most difficult life decision for she had to deal with internal conflict within herself resulting in a "checkmate" and her consequent acceptance of his action.

Vincent looked at Dina restraining his inner emotions and began to talk about the military physical, and the administrative process he had to deal with. He mentioned to her that he wanted to share, in detail, what happened during the Pre-Induction process. She interrupted him, not wanting to talk about his going away at this time for she wanted to remain submerged in the natural beauty and enjoy their precious get away from life's challenges.

Dina told Vincent that there is something that she too wants to share with him but that she rather they relish the beautiful late afternoon. She added that there was plenty of time for them to talk about the military, but that right know she rather just enjoy each other's company.

Unbeknownst to Vincent Dina had gone to the gynecologist on Monday, and received confirmation of what she had suspected, the exciting news that she was going to be a mother. She has been dying to share the wonderful news with Vincent, but she did not want the baby to become an impediment for Vincent to fulfill his dream and perceived obligation to join the Air Force.

Dina's request provided Vincent the justification to avoid the difficult subject, thus he acceded to Dina's suggestion, and decided to postpone the conversation to the following day.

The clear skies and the shinning sun were replaced by a blanket of darkness decorated with the brilliance of diamond like lights in a half hazard display, provided by the brilliant stars. As with all things in life, exceptions are also found in that infinite space. Nature provides some of those brilliant lights known as stars in very organized groups and shapes, commonly known as the "Big Dipper" and the "Little Dipper"

Exhaustion from the day's activities and exposure to the fresh air has taken its told on the loving couple. They decided to return to their cabin, freshen up and have a snack at the local diner. After cleaning and changing from the beach clothing, Vincent and Dina walked to the diner. Each enjoyed a plate of pea soup, a vanilla milk shake and shared an apple pie a la mode.

After dinner, the couple walked on the deserted local boardwalk. Afterwards, they retired to their cabin where they physically and unrestrainedly celebrated and enriched the love which they have for each other.

"The Sun's rays" invaded the small cabin room and touched the side of Dina's winter white face, as if wanting to share its power and a late summer tan gift with her. The slowly increasing warmth from the sun's rays serve as the wake up call for Dina, who slowly opened her eyes and gently rubbing them. She looked at the old alarm clock sitting on the three drawer white painted dresser, and was surprised to see that it was 8:30 in the morning. They both are early risers and it was already late morning based on their usual wake up practice.

Recalling the wonderful late lunch, the enjoyable beach setting, and the romantic and passionate evening at the cabin, Dina concluded that there could be no better justification to have violated the customary "early rise" practice.

Sunday was an unforgettable continuation of the wonderful time experienced the day before. It was a care free day occupied by the young couple consuming delicious foods, lounging on the sandy beach, and thoroughly enjoying each other's company. They wanted to make the most out of this day because they had to return to their hometown late Sunday afternoon. Vincent and Dina had promised his parents, the Wagner's, they would join them for an early Sunday evening dinner.

Dina and Vincent's mother became very good friends, and always had a rewarding time together. Particularly, when they spent time in the kitchen and Vincent's mom shares her favorite recipes with Dina.

The young couple arrived at his parent's elegant home, and greeted each other with affection and warmth. Dina told Vincent's mom that she was looking forward to the visit and to the delicious dinner.

Sunday's dinner at the Wagner's usually tends to be somewhat formal. The table was elegantly set with glistening glass ware, and with Mrs. Wagner's cherished China, which she purchased in the United Kingdom during one of her many trips accompanying her husband, while on business travels. Colorful cloth napkins, polished silver ware, and a beautiful spring flowers display on the center of the twelve chair dinning table complemented the very attractive table setting presentation.

This afternoon the dinner was to be enjoyed by only four people, the two Wagner couples. Mr. Wagner Sr. sat at the head of the table, Mrs. Wagner to his left, Dina to his immediate right, and Vincent next to Dina. The fare for the evening; a very appetizing looking pork roast, accompanied by mash potatoes, mixed vegetables and apple sauce, was waiting on the table having been efficiently and quietly moved from the kitchen by Lucrecia, the family's long time maid.

Lucrecia, a heavy set middle age lady, that many years ago the Wagner's met and became very fond of her during their vacation to the island of Guadalupe, an island located approximately one hundred fifty miles, west off Mexico's Baja California peninsula. The Wagner's were able to persuade Lucrecia to come to work for them, as their maid in the United States, taking care of little Vincent.

Lucrecia welcomed the opportunity to move to the states and to have a secured source of income which she could use to help her financially struggling family at her home.

Vincent cared for Lucrecia very much for she was like a second mother to him.. Upon seeing her come in to the dinning room; he got up, walked around the large dinning table, and affectionately hugged and kissed her on her forehead. She looked at him and instantaneously released a joyful smile which demonstrated her true affection and devotion to Vincent. She asked him "how are you my darling?" "I am fine Lucri", as he has always affectionately called Lucrecia.

Vincent gratified with having felt the same love and affection which had been shared with him by Lucrecia for so many years, returned to the table and sat down by Dina.

Once they were all sitting comfortably on the cushion padded, mahogany wood chairs, Mr. Wagner raised his glass and toasted to his wonderful family and to the future Wagner's that he hope will, in the not too far future, occupy some of the empty chairs around the dinner table.

Dina's heart beat increased unexpectedly, she felt an uncontrollable warmth bathing and adding a mild blush to her slightly wind burn and lightly red face. She discretely took a deep breath of air, managed to tap all her self control in order to keep the fact that she was carrying Vincent's child a secret, until she found the proper time to first share the news with her love.

The dinner table's conversation was extensive as it is always with Vincent's parents. The subject's menu which they shared was as varied and gratifying to the mind as the scrumptious meal was gratifying to the stomach. Vincent and Dina also shared with his parents the great time which they had at Coney Island's beach the last few days. Dina could not help relating the Seagull "target practice" incident which Vincent experienced, while she was sleeping on the sandy beach and which he shared with her after it occurred. Everyone at the table chuckled at Vincent's expense.

Mr. Wagner expressed his concern about events in Europe and about its possible consequences on their homeland. He related some of the recent news which preoccupied him: Hitler renouncing the Treaty of Versailles, introducing compulsory military service, and announcing plans to create 36 new military divisions. In addition Mr. Wagner mentioned that Ethiopia asked the League of Nations to take action regarding Italy's aggression, and that Japan demanded that China remove forces from Peking and Tientsin.

Mr. Wagner's facial expression clearly related his preoccupation and uncertainty about the increasing world tensions, and the effect which the potential consequence of these tensions may have on the nation and, in particular, on the lives of the people that he loves so much. He related that he was aware of the extensive discussions and negotiations which the legislative body, in the United States Congress, was holding in regards to the proposed bill known as the "The U.S. Neutrality Act"

The proposed "U.S. Neutrality Act" was intended to shelter the United States from getting involved in a potential war. This effort was motivated by the belief of many Americans that the involvement in WWI had been a mistake. The favored strategy was; to forbid shipment of war materials to belligerent nations at the discretion of the President, and to forbid U.S. citizens from traveling on belligerent vessels, except at their own risk.

Mr. Wagner, whose earlier cheerful mood had been mellowed by the world events discussion, lifted his wine glass once more, and with an energetic and joyful voice said, "To my family, happiness for always. To Dina, the most recent and wonderful addition to our family; we love you very much and may you have a wonderful birthday. And now let's enjoy the desert. Lucrecia, please bring the dessert".

Lucrecia walked carefully carrying a tray with a twenty four inch round cake, covered with freshly made whipped cream. The base was surrounded by recently picked strawberries, and the cake decorated with pink roses and ribbons made with colored whipped cream. The whipped cream ribbon extended to the top of the cake and the "Happy Birthday Dina" message was framed by it. A single candle inserted in the center of the cake above the letter "i" illuminated the surface of the cake.

As Lucrecia placed the cake immediately in front of Dina, she began to sing accompanied by all, "Happy Birth...dear Dina, Happy Birthday to you", applauses and congratulatory comments followed the conclusion of the song.

Dina's expression of gratitude and child like embarrassment, projected from her contented facial expression.

The cake was accompanied by a creamy, farm fresh made ice cream that the Wagner's had arranged to be delivered from Lancaster, Pennsylvania where the herds of milking cattle are naturally nourished by the fertile farm fields.

It had been a wonderful evening with the folks. However, it was time for Vincent and Dina to start thinking about returning home and getting ready to go to work the next morning. Dina discretely squeezed Vincent's hand under the table, an understood signal to her loving husband that it was time to "wind up" the visit.

Vincent looked at his mother and said "Mom we have had a marvelous time but unfortunately we have to get back home and get our things ready to go to work tomorrow" and to his dad he said "Dad I enjoyed our conversation immensely, I truly understand and share your concerns regarding current world events and its repercussion on our nation".

Dina also expressed her gratitude to Vincent's parents for the wonderful meal, including the delicious cake and home made ice cream in recognition of her birthday.

The two couples got up from the table. Dina turned to Mr. Wagner and hugged him as she would normally embrace her father. Then she turned to Mrs. Wagner, and momentarily waited for Vincent to receive and respond to the unbridled affection which only a mother could offer. Dina kissed her on the cheeks and warmly hugged and thanked her again for the superb meal and for remembering her birthday.

Vincent turned to his dad, looked directly into his eyes and told him "Dad, I love you", then he moved closer and strongly embraced him, as he had never before, while repeating "Thanks dad, I love you".

Mr. Wagner, befuddled for a split second by the intensity of the embrace, responded accordingly both physically and verbally. Once they finished their expression of affection, Mr. Wagner experienced a cold wave flooding his entire body, accompanied by a feeling of finality which he immediately rejected, a very uncomfortable feeling that something very bad and unexpected was going to take place.

Dina and Vincent gathered their light cotton spring sweaters and her knitted black pocket book and proceeded to walk towards the front door. Vincent stood next to his mother left shoulder, extended his right arm over it, brought her close to his right shoulder with a gentle squeezed, and kissed her on her forehead. Then he turned towards the dining room and yelled "good by Lucri, I love you!" Vincent opened the front door and he and Dina walked out into the night as the door closed slowly behind them.

*

Mr. & Mrs. Wagner's home is located on a cliff on the New Jersey side of the Hudson River, across from a major construction project which was going to provide additional car and truck access to the city. The available vehicle and passenger ferry services and the Holland tunnel, located closer to the southern tip of Manhattan Island, have become insufficient conduits for the continuing vehicles and passengers traffic increase.

This new access to the city has been named "The Lincoln Tunnel" and according to the newspapers it will be approximately 1.5 miles long. The construction plan, designed by Ole Stinstad, provided for three tubes to be available once the entire project was completed. It was anticipated that when constructed, the new tunnel would provide significant traffic relief for travelers trying to reach the middle of the island of Manhattan from Weehawken, New Jersey.

The Wagner's not only enjoyed a magnificent view of the Hudson River's activity and that of the Island of Manhattan, but also they could clearly follow the construction progress on the New Jersey entrance of the Lincoln Tunnel.

Vincent's and Dina's return to the Island of Manhattan could have been a lot less complicated and faster had the tunnel been completed. Instead, they had to take a taxi to the Hudson River ferry station in Hoboken and then wait for the next available Ferry to New York City which ran significantly less frequent on Sunday evenings than the remaining days of the week.

The young couple waited patiently by the water's edge. The night breeze was cool and inviting for lovers to seek each other's warmth. Vincent and Dina willingly yielded to this natural need and gently embraced while admiring the star filled sky, the brightly lit buildings, and street lights, bathing the river's shore.

It was seven thirty in the evening and the Ferry Boat slowly approached the docks announcing its arrival with a distinctive and awakening Ferry boat horn. The boat's horn sounded twice immediately prior to beginning the final approach. The crew actively began manning their assigned positions with heavy ropes on their hands ready to throw them to the waiting "hands" on the dock, and secure the boat.

The onboard passengers began to anxiously move forward towards the boat's exit ramp, while the waiting passenger impatiently gathered at the entrance gate as if expecting that this behavior would accelerate the debarkation and departure.

Dina and Vincent remained by the water's edge as if not wanting to let the Ferry boat's arrival disrupt the enjoyment of such a magnificent view, complemented by the sharing of each other's warmth in a cool and unforgettable spring night.

The crew began boarding the Ferry boat and the captain sounded the first of three horn signals alerting the potential passengers to come on board. Dina and Vincent separated from their embrace. He held her right hand with his left one, and ran to the boarding plank laughing, as they would have done during their teenage years.

The couple boarded the ship and handed the welcoming crew member the return ticket stub, the other half of the round trip fare which they had purchased in the Manhattan. They raced up to the upper deck and sat closed together on the aft section of the boat trying to shelter each other from the Hudson River's crisp breeze and where they could clearly see the lower level and the dock area.

The Ferry boat's second horn signal, somewhat longer lasting than the first, sounded off and the remaining passengers rushed to the boarding plank. The crew members began to once again occupy their post to get the boat ready for departure. Moments later the third and longest lasting horn signal sounded off. The ground crew began to unfasten the ropes from the dock when suddenly a brand new Cadillac, black town sedan, series 10 V-8, rushed on to the Ferry's boarding gate and four, elegantly dressed men, got out of the car and immediately boarded it.

The car's design caught Vincent's attention. He had seen pictures of the newly released Cadillac model on the papers but had never seen the the actual vehicle until tonight. He thought that it had a very elegant and smart design, not to mention the power displayed by eight cylinder engine.

Vincent's curiosity about the late arriving passengers was awakened not only by the impressive vehicle but also by the boat's crew's behavior. Vincent observed that the boat's crew greeted the four passengers with a combination of intense hand shaking and surprising behavior as confirmed by their nervous expressions, and apprehensive behavior.

The Ferry boat navigated East on the Hudson River waters uneventfully and effortlessly, assisted by the low tide and the calm waters. Most of the passengers sought shelter from the cool breeze in the enclosed lower level while others, primarily young couples, enjoyed the night's panorama and resisted the fresh air coolness with the warmth generated by their mutual affection and tenderness.

The Ferry began its approach to Manhattan's side river line and proudly signaled its arrival at the dock with its first horn signal. As usual, most of the passengers on the lower deck quickly got up and began their slow movement to the exit plank. The four well dressed gentlemen remained on their seats as if without any intention to disembark, but rather to continue on a long journey.

On the upper deck, the couples, submerged in their mutual infatuation, also ignored the Ferry's arrival's warning and continued sharing each others affection as if desiring to avoid its ending.

The last horn warning, relaying a signal of finality and disrupting the hustle and bustle of the vibrant city's mid-town. Immediately preceding the warning, the passenger's felt a thump and a quick stop. This caused some of the anxious travelers to partially loose their balance and to quickly search for anything to hold on to, and thus avoiding falling on the wet and dirty deck.

Dina and Vincent got up walked fore and watched while the passengers hurriedly walked across the wooden ramp which was fenced with thick ropes on both sides to provide the exiting passengers with at least psychological support when exiting the vessel, in addition to safeguarding the anxious fear from falling into the chilled Hudson River waters.

After most of the travelers walked down the ramp ashore, one of the crew members walked onto the exit ramp and yelled with what appeared to be all the energy which his lungs could muster, "All ashore! last call". He then began visually exploring the surrounding Ferry's landing area, as if he was a member of an "advance unit" checking the fields for enemy entrapment. Then he returned to the inside of the lower level cabin.

Following the announcement, Vincent and Dina gathered their possessions and walked to the fore stairs leading to the exit ramp. They, Vincent ahead of Dina, began slowly and carefully taking one step at a time, as a precautionary measure as they descend to the exit level and proceeded to the exit ramp.

As Dina and Vincent reached the last step, the four gentlemen arriving in the fancy Cadillac, were also exiting out of the lower level cabin and walking towards the exit ramp. The young couple stopped their final descent, and made way for the four late arriving, executive looking individuals to pass by and exit the Ferry boat.

As the last presumed executive exited thru the cabin door, his jacket got caught by the door's handle, and as he pulled it back his belt and the right upper portion of his trouser was exposed. The individual did not realize that the gun which he was carrying, hanging from a shoulder strap and nested on his right side, was inadvertently exposed. Vincent's eyes captured that momentary image.

His face changed from a pale white complexion to a reddish

blush, giving away his reaction to the unexpected discovery and resulting rational concern. He quickly digested his discovery and choose to keep that knowledge to himself, and maintain a reasonable distance from the small group of assumed executives. He held Dina's arm and slowed down their pace as if trying to continue enjoying the scenery, the real intent being keep distance from any potential danger.

The crew member who had made the exit announcement approached the young couple from behind, and politely asked them to please move ahead. They advance forward, measuring their pace, and began walking down the ramp making their best effort to remain behind as much as possible from the four armed men.

As the young couples walked down the ramp, burst of machine guns fire was heard not too distant from the Ferry boat. The passengers walking down the ramp momentarily froze, and their face displayed the inner fear which they were experiencing. Suddenly, thereafter bullets was flying in the direction of the Ferry boat and ricocheting from the paved dock floor. Flashes from machine guns were seen coming from various buildings which are part of the Ferry Line complex. The four men drew their weapons, ran towards the dock's building seeking shelter while returning fire towards the attackers.

Vincent, extremely concerned for Dina's well being and with his adrenaline already primed from his early discovery, quickly review his options and concluded that jumping into the chilled Hudson river water was the safest option to protect himself and Dina from the imminent danger they faced.

Without sharing his thoughts, he looked down at the river's water next to the Ferry boat to confirm that the water was free of debris, then he picked up Dina's body as if carrying her through the wedding night threshold. Then he lifted her body above the safety rope, and gently let her body drop safely into the river. Bullets continued flying around Vincent as if he was the target. Immediately after, he pushed his body thru the open space between the parallel ropes and let his body fall into the river not far from his wife.

Dina struggled to keep afloat while simultaneously screaming for Vincent with a fear unequal to any other life experienced. She excitedly struggled to keep afloat, dealt with the frigid waters, and make certain that the love of her life had succeeded and escaped from the treacherous bullets.

When Dina saw Vincent fall into the water, she felt a wave of emotion and a natural warmth filled every artery and vein in her young body which momentarily relieved the discomfort from the chilled Hudson River water.

Dina rapidly swam to the spot were Vincent had fallen and was struggling to stay afloat. She reached him, helped him remain above water, and asked him, with all the tenderness and love that she could express under the circumstances, "My darling, are you OK?" With a nervous and unsecured voice, Vincent responded that he was fine.

Dina embraced Vincent while trying to assure that both stay afloat and searching for the warmth that they had treasured on the upper deck of the Ferry boat. As she held his upper shoulder above the water, Dina felt a warm and unexpected contrasting feeling on the part of her arm which was above the chilled river water. She raised her arm above his shoulder and with the aid of the reflection from a dim dock light; Dina noticed that her white sleeve was stained with blood like color.

Dina looked at Vincent, whose eyes were barely open, and told him with a very shaky and painful voice "Vincent have you been hit!" Vincent looked at her and with an energy less smile told her "Dina, I love you forever".

His body went limp and began to escape from Dina's embrace. She held him as secure as her strength allowed, and tried to swim to the dock wall, crying and emotionally pleading towards the Ferry boat crew to help her wounded husband.

The shooting ceased, and cars could be heard speeding away. Three bodies, two facing down and one as if staring at the celestial beauty, rested on the arriving plaza. Their blood was flooding nearby area, and their hand remained grasping their weapons as if they were the only thing that those shooting victims really trusted and priced.

Three members of the Ferry's crew jumped into the water. Two of the men grabbed Vincent's limp body from Dina and the third one helped her reached a boat launching ramp to egress from the river.

The two remaining Ferry's crew members were impatiently waiting at the water's edge with blankets for the young freezing couple, a most needed and welcomed shelter from the chilly water. Dina was wrapped with a blanket and guided towards the warm office building nearby, Vincent was laid on another blanket which had placed on the ground and then carefully covered with the other half of the blanket.

Dina knelt next to Vincent, caressed his forehead, and with a tone driven by profound love and echoing extreme level of tenderness and reassurance, told him "hold on my love! Soon we will go to the hospital. They will take good care of you. Everything will be fine!"

Dina was not only trying to comfort Vincent, she was also trying to convince herself that the love of her life was going to be fine.

Sirens began to break the eerie silence that engulfed the Ferry boat's docking place and soon, thereafter, the machine guns ceased spitting the fearful flashes that disrupted the evening quietness at the river's side. The light evening breeze gradually cleansed the immediate area from the threatening smell coming from the spent machine guns and pistols bullets.

Onlookers, curious about what had happened, rushed to the

Ferry boat's dock area and began to quickly gather near by. The speculations rumbling tempo gradually increased until the police cruisers began arriving at the site. The first police cruiser, with high beam, red and blue flashing lights, and blasting siren slowly broke thru the crowd and stopped suddenly about twenty feet away from the Ferry boat's launching pad.

The Police Cruiser's bright lights illuminated the Ferry boat's launching pad, providing Dina with a clearer view of her love, who was lying on the wet, greasy, and scummy cement pad not far from were the police cruiser stopped. His face, extremely pale and almost lifeless looking, his eyes barely open, and his forehead allowing his body moisture to escape as his body defense mustered all physical resources to protect himself from wound related causes. Dina struggled to reject the fatalistic thoughts crossing her mind and flooding her heart with unbearable pain. Her sweetheart was not going to make it she thought, rushing to his side.

Dina's concern for Vincent's condition overshadowed her own physical discomfort. Her body was not only struggling to regain acceptable temperature levels, having been in the river's chilled water, but she was also experiencing significant discomfort in her lower abdomen. Sporadic sharp pain on forced her arms to hold the lower part of her stomach and prompted her teeth to fiercely bite her lower lips to conceal it, as well as her concern for her fetus condition, from her wounded partner.

The five police cruisers and a black sedan caravan arrived shortly after the first police unit arrived. Two men in blue exited from each of the vehicles and began dispersing the crow and cordoning the crime scene area. Four detectives, smartly dressed with tailored like, dark gabardine coats got out of their car and proceeded towards Vincent, Dina, and the three rescuing crew members, who were waiting for the ambulance to arrive, and rushed the wounded victim to the nearest Hospital facility.

The detectives approached quietly, introduced themselves while simultaneously displaying their NYC detective badges to the folks watching and trying to provide comfort to the wounded and to Vincent's and his wife. They began questioning the crew members who had helped rescue the couple from the frigid Hudson River water, hoping to prompt them to share any information that could provide leads about the committed crime. They also questioned Dina, not expecting much relevant information, but hoping to give her some comfort and assurance about her husband's wounds. While Dina had very little information to share with the detectives, having been dropped into the water by her husband as soon as the shooting began. The only thing that she was able to witness and share was that the four late arriving passengers boarding the Ferry on the Jersey side, ran away from the Ferry's dock once the shooting began, while simultaneously returning fire towards the source of the flash of lights from the machine guns barrels that were rapidly spitting bullets, apparently aimed at the them.

The Ferry crew, apparently being conditioned to the police line of questions; "Saw Nothing, Heard Nothing and Knew Nothing".

The detectives asked for details about Vincent's condition. They requested all the passengers and crew members to provide their name, address, and telephone numbers. Once they recorded the requested data, the detectives proceeded to look at the crime scene and to search the body of each of the tree victims, still lying on the bloody and dirty plaza looking for personal identification.

Another siren could be heard approaching and its flashing lights were detected once they were about half a block away from the crime scene. Dina looked up and identified the emergency vehicle. The vehicle's arrival provide her with a sense of optimism, thinking that with prompt hospital care her husband's wound would be dealt with and bring a quick recovery. Her previous pessimistic thoughts were consequently replaced with hope and positive expectations.

The ambulance stopped next to the detective's Black Sedan. The two man crew exited the ambulance's cab and proceeded towards the rear of the vehicle. They opened the rear double door, climbed on to the van, and began to place the first aid tools on top of the wheeled cot. Once they gathered their equipment, they both stepped down from the ambulance's cab and pulled the wheeled cot off the ambulance and rolled it to were Vincent was laying.

Dina impatiently watched the ambulance crew's methodically follow their routine, as they probably have done hundreds if not thousands of time before. She successfully managed to control her desire to urge the First Aid Squad to please pick up the pace, for the life of the man she loves was at stake.

The First Aid Squad approached the scene where Vincent laid, helplessly and almost lifeless, apparently unaware or perhaps resigned to his imminent destiny. Unable to receive a response when they asked Vincent how he felt, the taller ambulance crew member named Vito, according to his worn looking Columbus Hospital tag, directed his questions to Dina. The second first aid person, Damian, checked Vincent's vital signs and inspected the severity of the wound.

Vito began to satisfy the necessary requirements administrative questions by asking Dina her husband's name, address, age, allergies if any, and his health conditions. He immediately recorded her response on the printed form provided by the hospital.

As Vito was finishing the interview with Dina, he detected, on her face an apparently uncontrolled facial expression change from a gentle and nervous look to one of excruciating pain. This raised his concern. Immediately afterwards, she experienced a recurrence of pain which she previously felt on the lower part of abdomen again causing her arms automatic response of holding the area were she previously experienced similar episode. Vito, surprised but professionally calm, asked Dina where was she hurting while simultaneously prompting her to sit down. He then asked his partner to check her vitals as soon as he finished with Vincent.

Damien, having finished checking Vincent's viral sign, proceeded to check Dina's heart beat, blood pressure, and body temperature. He found that in all cases the readings exceeded normal levels. Upon learning of the results, Vito prepared another form for Dina, following the same line of questioning as he had done processing Vincent's case.

Once the required first aid protocol had been satisfied, Vito and Damien lowered the wheeled cot to almost ground level. They placed another blanket next to Vincent and delicately moved his body on to the new blanket. Each of them grabbed one of the blanket sides opposite Vincent and firmly and deliberately lifted his once healthy torso onto the wheeled cot. Vincent was secured to the cot with the leather belts with metal buckles.

Damien reached the rear of the ambulance, and without further delay, he, with Vito's help, suspended the securely tied cot into the ambulance . Damien began to push the cot towards the rear section of the ambulance and locked the cot in place. Vito asked Dina how she was feeling and she responded that the dagger's puncture like pain had subsided for the moment. She told Vito "Please don't worry about me. Please take care of Vincent". Vito assisted Dina up into the ambulance, on to a bench that had been installed parallel to the side of the ambulance, an area closed to Vincent's head,

Vito stepped outside the ambulance, closed the double doors, and walked to the driver's side of the cab. He entered the cab, started the engines, turned on the emergency lights and sirens, and slowly moved the ambulance through the Ferry Boat Docking Plaza on to the street. Once on the street, Vito accelerated the tired, old ambulance's engine and proceeded to Columbus Hospital. This medical facility, located at 214-218 East 34th Street, near 5th Avenue, opening in 1896 to service the City's growing Italian community.

The trip to the hospital was rapid and uneventful. The blasting sirens disrupted the evening quietness and encouraged the reduced number of vehicles and horse drawn carriages to make way for the rushing ambulance.

Upon arrival at the emergency room gate, the Vincent was taken out of the ambulance and briskly moved to the emergency room. Dina was placed on a wheel chair and was taken to a First Aid cubicle, adjacent to the operating wing. Once she was settled in the First Aid cubicle, Dina asked to use the telephone to call her and Vincent's family and share what had occurred. Unfortunately, much to her despair, she was unable to reach Vincent's family.

The doctors on duty were assiduously trying to contain Vincent's blood loss without much success. The bullet which had ricocheted from Ferry boat's fore plate, had penetrated Vincent's upper back and severed part of the pulmonary artery, very close to the heart. He had excessive internal bleeding requiring significant blood transfusions.

The emergency room doctors requested support from Dr. Wilson, the Vascular Department's Head, world renowned and an eminence in his field. Mr. Wilson was having a quiet dinner at home with his family on the upper East Side of the City. Upon receiving the emergency call, he contacted the local police precinct and requested the assistance of a police cruiser to rush him to Columbus Hospital.

Mr. Wilson, together with a team of six other surgeons, tirelessly struggled to stop the bleeding and to stabilize Vincent's vital signs without success. The doctors were convinced that they had lost Vincent on two occasions during the four hour battle between life and death. Miraculously, on two occasions, they managed to recover his pulse and regain weak heart palpitations.

The battle proved to be too great for the team of doctors and for the patient. At the end of the courageous struggle, four hours later, the vibrant life that used to be Vincent, was no longer there.

Unaware of her devastating loss, Dina slept comfortably on the emergency room bed after being given a light sedative.

The doctors had examined her and had diagnosed the source of the unbearable recurring pain. Dina's body had aborted the fetus, consequence of the emotional and physical shock from her horrible experience; witnessing the shootings, her concern for Vincent's well being, and her body's impact on the chilled Hudson river water. Sadly, Dina was not longer carrying Vincent's child.

It was approximately 3AM the next morning when Vincent's parents arrived together with the Peterson's, Dina's parents. Dina had called her parents that night and shared the terrible events that occurred during their journey back to the city. She asked her father to please call Mr. & Mrs. Wagner right away, and relate what had occurred.

Mr. Peterson called Mr. Wagner immediately after ending the telephone conversation with his daughter. He was able to reach the Wagner family and related the limited information which he had gained from Dina during her telephone call, including the heart breaking news that Vincent had been badly wounded and was in the operating room.

Mr. Wagner, knowing that the Petersons did not have a vehicle, having lost most of their material possessions during the height of the Depression and, recognizing that transportation to New York City at that time of the night would be extremely onerous, told Mr. Peterson that he and his wife will pick them up at their home.

Mr. Peterson, a scholar and an intellectually wealthy individual, without hesitation told Mr. Wagner that his offer was very generous and he thanked him very much for his thoughtfulness, but that imposing on him at that time of the night was not necessary. He also expressed his desire to not delay their arrival to the hospital.

Mr. Wagner persisted, insisting that he and the misses wanted and needed to pick them up and to travel together to the hospital. Mr. Peterson, recognizing that he was dealing with a genealogically stubborn trait, and with the reality of the difficulty to expeditiously reach Columbus Hospital in the City, gratefully acceded to Mr. Wagner's offer.

Mr. Wagner awoke Mrs. Wagner and gave her consciousness an opportunity to understand to the reality of the moment. He then told her about his conversation with Mr. Peterson and about the heart breaking news that their only son had been seriously wounded, as he and Dina returned to the city on the ferry boat.

Mrs. Wagner, not yet overtaken by the shock and the emotion of what had occurred, asked "how about Dina?" Mr. Wagner responded that she was fine to the best of his knowledge.

She immediately began to cry in an unbridled fashion. Her heart felt a pain that will not dissipate until she could confirm that the pearl of her eyes and the image of her soul is out of danger.

The Wagner's effortlessly dressed and rushed to their awaiting 1933 Cadillac Sedan. Mr. Wagner opened the rear left side door for his wife and then sat behind the steering wheel. He started the engine, which responded without hesitation, and began the journey to the center of Newark where the Petersons lived, a trip that Mr. Wagner had made only a few weeks ago when he was invited to participate in a recognition to Amelia Earlhart by the City of Newark, New Jersey in honor of her non-stop flight from Mexico City to the Newark Airport.

After approximately an hour on the road, the shiney and quietly running vehicle pulled up to the curb in front of the Peterson's home. Mr. Peterson was standing on the porch projecting an impression of a person enjoying the beauty of the night. The truth was his concern for the "children" in the hospital and his anxiety to comfort and care for them could only be partially tamed by passing time on the porch while waiting for The Wagner's to arrive.

Mr. Peterson called his wife, told her "the Wagner's are here", and asked her to get ready to go. The two couples' greeting was very brief as the Petersons proceeded to board the vehicle. Mr. Peterson sat on the passenger side of the vehicle and Mrs. Peterson sat on the back, next to Mrs. Wagner.

Mr. Peterson shook hands with Mr. Wagner and once again thanked him for his generosity. Mrs. Peterson kissed and hugged Mrs. Wagner. They then both began to cry in unison as if they had practiced for a part in a Broadway play. Indeed, this was not a play. Actors can only dream of being able to replicate half of the pain's intensity and heart-felt sorrow expressed by the two mothers' tears.

The two couples, anxious for updated news about their "children" and with tears ready to overflow should the unthinkable be found, walked into the emergency room and identified themselves as the parents of Mr. & Mrs. Vincent Wagner.

The emergency room receptionist, upon hearing the couple's identity, asked them to sit down for a few minutes in the waiting area and told them that Doctor Wilson will be with them momentarily.

Approximately thirty minutes earlier, after loosing his patient, Dr. Wilson had instructed the emergency room reception staff to call him at the Internist's Resting Lounge, where he will be holding a post operative review with the team involved in the failed effort to save Vincent's life.

Dr. Wilson interrupted the review of the followed operating procedures including the rationale and available options in the effort to save Vincent's life. He hurriedly, after being called, walked to the emergency room reception area to meet the his parents, perhaps the biggest burden which Doctors must deal with.

The receptionist directed Dr. Wilson to the Wagner and Petersons. He walked to where they were waiting for him, introduced himself to the them, and requested that they follow him to his office.

Dr. Wilson, followed by the four exhausted and fearful parents of the deceased entered his office. The doctor sat behind his desk as if seeking a safety net to shelter himself from the pain that he knew will be inflicted on the innocent recipients of his team's inability to save a perceived promising life, an innocent life that was extinguished, consequence of a rebellious and uncontrolled societal behavior.

Mrs. Wagner and Mrs. Peterson sat on the two chairs located in front of the doctor's traditional office desk, covered on one side with numerous piles of documents and on the other side with an equal stacks of books, most likely medical texts. Mr. Wagner and Mr. Peterson moved two folding chairs, leaning against the wall, next to the two anxious mothers. They both sat down and focused their attention on every word shared by Dr. Wilson's words.

Dr. Wilson, a very experienced and accomplished professional in his field, has always found the task of communicating his failure to protect a life from the claws of death to his patient's relatives to be a torturous process. In every case, he struggles up to the last instant, questioning the best approach to ease the pain which he has to cause by sharing the sad outcome with the recipients of his information. He questions himself as to whether it is better to "get to the bottom line" right away, as his accountant friend generally practices with his financial clients, or to gradually build up the dialogue so that implications prepare the recipient parties to the final "dagger" which will likely deeply wound their happiness.

Mr. Wagner, demonstrating his assertiveness and strength of character, interrupted Dr. Wilson's internal negotiation and bluntly asked him, "Doctor, how is my son? Is he going to make it?" The direct question overrode Dr. Wilson's dilemma and left him with no choice but to follow his accounting friend's approach.

Dr. Wilson, unable to look at Mrs. Wagner and allow his unusually watery eyes to betray him, locked his sight on Mr. Wagner's eyes, and with a very professional voice, devoid of any normal human feelings, informed the two couples, directing his focus and voice to Mr. & Mrs. Wagner, that "he did everything humanly possible to save their son, but sadly he was not successful. Your son died forty five minutes ago. I am very, very sorry!"

Mr. Wagner disengaged his eyes from Dr. Wilson sight as if to wanting to punish him for his failure, but truly seeking the neutral floor as the target to hide the pain, and to conceal his emotions from everyone present. Mrs. Wagner and Mrs. Peterson filled the quiet and somber room with the echoes of broken hearts and overflowing reservoirs of tears. Mr. Peterson dropped his head and uncontrolled pearls of moisture gently and slowly traveled down his aging face.

Mrs. Peterson, after gaining her composure and with reddish and tearful eyes, asked Dr. Wilson about her daughter, Dina. He responded that Mrs. Wagner was not his patient, but that he had spoken with the internist in charge in the emergency room and was told that Mrs. Wagner was going to be fine. Dr. Wilson began to say "except" and was quickly interrupted by Mrs. Peterson who said, "Except what Doctor? Is she alright!?". Dr. Wilson took a deep breath of air and responded, "Except that she lost her child".

The two ladies looked at each other with an expression of extreme surprise, and began once again to cry tearlessly, for all the tears had already been exhausted while seeking an outlet for their profound pain.

Mr. Peterson looked down once more, held his head with both hands and lightly sobbed for the lost of his Grand Child. Mr. Wagner, who had up to now demonstrated the admirable strength to maintain his composure under all circumstances, wept without shame. Not only did he loose his son this unforgettable day, but he also lost his dream – a grandchild. A reality that he was not aware existed. He lost his dream to have a grandchild who would carry his name, spread his ancestry's seeds, and enjoy his fortune.

Mrs. Peterson gently dried her eyes as part of her effort to compose herself once again and slowly raised her head to allow eye contact with Dr. Wilson. She saw an expression of sorrow and painfulness in his demeanor. Then she asked the doctor if she could see her daughter and if he knew how Dina has handled the news of her husband's death and of the lost of her fetus.

Dr. Wilson informed the family that Dina has been under medication and has been asleep since prior to Vincent's demise. Thus, Dina has not been made aware of the great loss and drastic change that her life has taken.

Dr. Wilson expressed his concern about the impact that the news will have on Dina. Therefore he solicited the family's co-operation to minimize the shock and potential psychological consequences.

After confirming that Dina had not disclosed her pregnancy to the family, as he had inferred from her mother's and mother in-law's early reaction, Dr. Wilson suggested that perhaps it would be best to have Dina's gynecologist break that sad news to her first thing in the morning. He felt that this strategy will relieve Dina from dealing, at this time, with having to explain not having previously disclosed the pregnancy to her family.

Dina's gynecologist, Doctor Alvarez, a very attractive brunette whose brilliant emerald green eyes projected self assurance and a caring attitude, walked confidently into Dina's hospital room a few minutes before seven a.m. Although recently graduated from the Bellevue Hospital Medical College, which this year became the New York University College of Medicine, the young doctor has gained Dina's full confidence and friendship.

Doctor Alvarez is a Spanish citizen, whose father is a high ranking military officer, affiliated with the Spanish Nationalist movement, headed by General Franco. Fearful of the political climate and of a potential civil war in Spain, he encouraged his only daughter to come to the United States to pursue her professional dream and become a medical doctor. Doctor Alvarez's mother accompanied her. Both mother and daughter established a home in a residential section of lower Manhattan.

As the doctor approached the bed, Dina opened her eyes and directed her hands to rub her eyes lightly. Once she removed her hands away from her sleepy and drained eyes, She greeted the doctor with a semi-dazed appearance having just awakened and still recuperating from the sedative given to her last night, very late in the evening, to promote rest from the horrible experience, which she had been exposed to the day before.

Doctor Alvarez was prepared, as she could be, to deal with the reaction of the information, which she was going to disclose to Dina. She was trained to maintain a professional emotional distance from her patients and, thus, responded to Dina's greeting with a short answer "Good morning, Dina, how do you feel?". Before her words were forever deleted from Dina's brain receptors, the doctor told her that there was a problem with the baby. Dina immediately suspended both arm and carefully rested both of them on her lower belly, a mother's natural instinct, as if trying to comfort and shelter the flourishing life which she has been carrying and protecting from danger. Witnessing Dina's physical response, Doctor Alvarez told her that she was very sorry but that the body had aborted the fetus. Most likely, as a consequence of the emotional and physical shock which she had lived through the night before.

Doctor Alvarez remained silent and allowed Dina to fully absorb what she had been told. A few seconds later, Dina began to cry intensively while holding her belly and continuously repeating in a gradually lowering tone, "My baby! My baby! My baby!"

She briefly stopped crying, as if refocusing her thoughts, and then began to cry again with the same desperation and hurtfulness, repeating "Vincent never knew, Vincent never knew!"

Doctor Alvarez compassionately allowed Dina to cry and unburden her aching heart without interruption, for she knew that the worse was still to come.

Once Dina exhausted her expression of sorrow, but continued quietly sobbing, Doctor Alvarez sat down next to her bed and held Dina's hand. She looked at Dina, and with all the gentleness and compassion that her young inexperience heart could possibly marshal under these circumstances, began to say "Dina". At that precise moment Dina's parent's entered the room. Noticing that the doctor was talking to Dina, who was not aware of their presence as of yet, Mr. & Mrs. Peterson momentarily froze in place.

Dr. Alvarez, also oblivious to Dina's parent's presence continued. "Vincent did not make it, I am very sorry!" Dina's expression of sadness changed instantaneously to one of disbelief and rejection of what she had just been told. Every word that she had just heard was loaded with poisonous venom which was gradually destroying her inner being.

The doctor's message carried the same dagger that invaded her womb and destroyed her fetus, except that this time it broke her heart and threatened previously unreachable regions of her soul.

Dina pulled her hands from Doctor Alvarez hold, turned her body upside down, began hitting the bed uncontrollably with both arms and cried intensively loud repeating "No, No, No!" Followed by "That can not be! You are lying to me!" Dina's parents rushed to her side, desperately wanting to comfort their daughter.

As they approached her bedside, an intense scream escaped from Dina's vocal cords that filled the quiet hospital corridors, after sharing it with all in the room "Vincent, I Love You", expressing the compounded suffering that she had experienced during the last twenty four hours, The echoes rapidly returning to the source ten fold, competed equally with the intense recurring screams "Vincent, I Love You", "I am sorry, you never knew!"

Dr. Alvarez, recognizing Dina's acute emotional condition and the potential risk of long term consequences, quietly got up from the chair next to the bed and proceeded immediately to the nurse's station.

Julia, the head nurse was sitting by the nurse's station handling administrative tasks as Dr. Alvarez approached her.

The intensity and magnitude of the pain conveyed by Dina's scream was such that even Julia, a professional nurse trained and accustomed to deal with the patient's emotional and physical pain, could not control the flow of a compassionate tear from her own eyes.

Dr. Alvarez instructed Julia to sedate Mrs. Wagner, the patient in room #113 right away, and also told her to keep the patient sedated for the rest of the morning.

Dr. Alvarez moved away from the nurse's station, and with decisive steps, walked towards her office down the hall. She unlocked the door, entered her office, and locked the door behind her. In the privacy and secrecy of her empty office, Dr. Alvarez released the emotion which she could not longer hold she began to cry quietly.

Dina continues discharging her pain, less intensively than before, a reflection of her exhaustion and depletion of energy. Nonetheless, she continued weeping and agonizingly and intermittently repeating "He did not know!", "He did not know!", "Life no longer has any meaning for me!", "I want to die!"

Mrs.& Mrs. Peterson have been by Dina's side since Dr. Alvarez departed from her room trying to console and reassure their loving daughter that she is not alone. Mrs. Peterson poured all the motherly love that she possesses into Dina, to help her find a path to mend her broken heart, without avail.

Julia walked into the room with a loaded syringe and approached Dina's bed side, opposite Mrs. Wagner. She looked at Dina and with a firm and reassuring voice told Dina "Darling, you are going to be alright."

Julia explained to both the patient and her mother that the doctor prescribed an injection to help Dina get some much needed rest. Julia injected Dina's upper left arm and slowly pushed the syringe's plunger until all the fluid, which will deliver temporary tranquility to her wrecked soul, was delivered.

The sedative prescribed by the doctor rapidly fulfilled its mission. Dina's crying and devastating pleads slowly subsided until silent permeated the antiseptic hospital room. Dina slept quietly, her mind no longer punished with the realities of what had occurred. Her parents remained by her bedside while she slept.

*

It was approximately a quarter to seven, on Monday morning, when Jaime returned to his apartment, having gone to a local bakery to purchase freshly made Italian Rolls, and to the corner delicatessen to purchased a quart of whole milk and a New York Sun newspaper. The only bread that somewhat resembles the light flavored and soft, Cuban bread that he was accustomed to eat in his homeland, and that he loves to butter and dunk in his warm and sweetened Café con Leche, always remembering his mother during the early morning, boiling the lightly salted whole milk and, once boiled, pouring it three quarters of the way into a white custom printed coffee cup, then topping the cup with a rich, flavorful, freshly roasted and brewed coffee from local beans.

As planned, Jaime returned home having fulfilled his mission. He took off his coat, hung it in the small clothes closet, and began breakfast preparation. Jaime proceeded to prepare his breakfast which today consisted of a ripe plantain omelet, toasted and buttered Italian bread, accompanied by his Café con Leche.

Jaime had already sliced and fried the ripened plantains and had prepared the two eggs before going out to the local deli. Milk had not been added to the mixed eggs since he drank the the remaining milk last night before going to bed. Upon returning home from the store, he added a bit of milk, salt and pepper to the already mixed eggs, poured the mixture into the already heated pan with the bottom lightly covered with melted butter. Once the eggs mixture began to fry and change from a liquid mixture to a solid texture, he carefully placed the thinly sliced and fried ripened plantains on half of the then frying round-shaped omelet. Before completely frying, he used his spatula to cover the plantains with the other half of the omelet. Simultaneously, he boiled the milk and heated the water to brew the anticipated Cuban Espresso coffee.

Jaime prepared his Cuban coffee following the traditional Cuban peasant's technique. The dark and flavorful roasted and, finely grounded coffee beans powder is deposited into a sock like cotton pocket, which has an attached wire ring and extended handle and hangs from inside the four inches circular aperture on the "colador", as it's called, inserted into upper plate hole, leaving enough space on its bottom to place the container that will capture the rewarding brew. Once the water boils, it is poured in the opening of the cotton sock. The hot water bathes the fragrant coffee bean's powder. It extracts its hidden treasures, and drains it to the bottom of the sock where it discharges its cargo of palate pleasure into the waiting container, directly below the sock. The container, already holding naturally brown sugar, welcomes the black liquid gold and its sugar cane sweetness made perfectly ready to satisfy the urges and to awaken the senses of its recipients.

The table is ready for Jaime to enjoy his morning feast. The plantain omelet, the cup of hot milk, the lightly toasted and buttered Italian bread ready to be dunked in the cup of Café con Leche. The Cuban coffee container is on the table waiting to provide Jaime it's usual pleasure and nutrition.

The Monday morning edition of the New York Sun, which Jaime hurriedly picked up, lay folded next to the breakfast setting, also waiting to yield its intellectual nutrition.

Jaime sat down. He poured the Cuban coffee into the hot cup of milk, stirred the mixture and confirmed its strength. Not satisfied, Jaime added more black gold into his cup. He then added a spoon of the rich natural brown sugar and stirred the mixture again. Jaime took a quarter of the toasted and buttered Italian roll, dunked it into the Café con Leche and, gratified savored the delicious brew. As Jaime began to pick up his fork to enjoy the plantain omelet, he hesitated and instead, picked up the newspaper and began to read the morning's news headline: NEW YORK CITY FERRY LANDING SHOOTING LAST NIGHT, THREE DEAD AND ONE MORTALLY WOUNDED.

He then reads the sub heading: GANGSTERS SHOOT IT OUT AT THE 45TH STREET FERRY LANDING.

The eye catching headline was too intriguing for Jaime not to continue reading. He cut a small piece of omelet, began to eat it, and refocused his attention to the article, which he continued to read:

"Monday 6:00 AM
Reporter: John Neil

According to police sources, there was an intensive shootout at the West 45th Street, Ferry Landing. Three members of the Terranova gang were gunned down by suspected members of the Luciano crime family. Unidentified sources indicated that Ciro

Terranova, better known as the "King of Artichokes", a nickname given him because of his significant control of the produce distribution in the city, was the target of the shooting. However, it has been reported that Mr. Terranova managed to jump into the river and escape from his assailants.

Unconfirmed reports indicated that Luciano has been trying to muscle into Ciro Terranova's produce business ever since the City's Mayor declared and ordered the arrest of Ciro Terranova, if found in the city.

Other unconfirmed reports indicate that Ciro Terranova had arranged a gang meeting in Little Italy, as he has done in previous occasion. Also it is claimed, that Ciro took the late hour Ferry from New Jersey to avoid police and fellow gangster traps at the Holland Tunnel exit. It is also speculated that Ciro had "greased" the Ferry captain and crew to keep his medium of sneaking into the city, quiet.

The three gangster who died at the site were: Mickey the mouse, a capo and otherwise known as a made-man in recognition of his organization status; Jimmy the stick, a longtime and trusted soldier; and Lou the enforcer, a soldier known to pleasure "smoking out" his targets. Mickey was nicknamed "the mouse" because of his canny ability to effortlessly brake into any place at any time. "The stick" name was giving to Jimmy because of his appearance. Lou earned his nickname by his enthusiasm and success executing instructions from his crime-boss.

The mortally wounded Ferry passenger, a city resident named Vincent Wagner, was taken by ambulance to the nearby Columbus Hospital where he succumbed early this morning while the surgical team performed a delicate and valiant effort to save his life.

Jaime's right hand involuntarily released the hot Café con Leche cup that he was holding. The cup dropped precipitously onto the tiled floor. It shattered into half a dozen fragments, bathing the floor and Jaime's trousers with the once anxiously desired morning drink. Jaime placed the newspaper on the table and covered his face with both hands trying to overcome the shock, and seeking reinforcement for an instant thought, that the fourth victim although named Vincent Wagner, may not really be his best friend. Jaime picked up the paper again and continued reading the article hoping to gain additional information regarding the fourth victim. The remaining paragraph:

"The police chief has assigned their gang crack team to continue investigation of this homicide.
End."

The article did not provide the confirmation which he was seeking.

He quickly got up from the table, and realizing that he needed to change his wet trousers, he rushed to his bed, got a clean pair of trousers from the small closet,   changed and the graved his spring jacket from the small closet where he had placed it once he returned from his trip to the bakery and deli. He rushed out of the house to make a telephone call from the nearby public telephone at the corner deli.

Jaime arrived at his destination with very little time left before having to report to his job. In another five minutes he had to begin walking to his job, in order to arrive on time.

The company that employs him, Nutritional Reserve International, Inc., (NRI) is an excellent place to work. It has been very good to Jaime. However, they are very strict and structured. Their attendance and punctuality enforcement is   mandatory and its violation consequential. Employees are allowed no more than three tardiness occurrences per year, before being disciplined and possibly terminated, if compounded with other violations of productivity or behavioral requirements.

In addition to providing a fair, and for the most part secure income, particularly in view of the post depression's economic crisis, NRI is a very structured and disciplined organization. Jaime considers this practice an admirable business behavior and consistent with what he has witnessed regarding the comportment of the North American society in general. He has already concluded that when he returns to his homeland, he will certainly implement and nurture this behavioral management standard.

Jaime walked into the oak wood and clear glass telephone booth, located at an inside corner of the Deli, picked up the ear handle of the Western Electric model 301 pay telephone with his left hand and pressed it against his left ear. With his right hand, he turned the hand crank that sends a ring signal to the operator center. He got no response. Impatiently, Jaime rapidly rotated the hand crank again. A professional sounding and helpfully sounding female voice responded, "Please, deposit ten cents!" Jaime extracted a dime from his trouser's right pocket, the lonely available coin awaiting his reach, and deposited it in the coin box on back of the street telephone's voice piece, as instructed by the operator. A "cling" sound, generated by the coin being deposited in the slot, a confirmation of the deposit coin for both the user and the operator, filled the sound vacuum of the telephone line. Immediately after, the same pleasant voice that had asked for the ten cents to be deposited said "Operator. How may I help you?"

Jaime responded with his distinctive native Cuban accent that influenced his second language, "Operator, I need talk to Sr. Wagener." The operator responded "With whom do you need to talk to Sir?" Jaime responded again "Mr. Wagener". The operator asked Jaime for Mr. Wagner's telephone number. Unfortunately, Jaime left the Wagner's telephone number at the apartment in his haste to leave and make the telephone call before having to rush to his job.

Upon learning that Jaime did not have the needed telephone number, the operator asked him if he new Mr. Wagner's address. Jaime provided the address to the operator and she responded, "Hold on a minute please". Approximately sixty seconds later, Jaime heard the first ringing tone. A sense of relief and hope filled his being, thinking that he will be able to confirm that Vincent was not the "mortally wounded" person which had been reported in the morning paper.

The telephone rang again, and again, and again. At the tenth ring, the operator cut onto the line and told Jaime that she was very sorry but there was no answer and to please try again later. Jaime heard another "click" and the line went silent.

Jaime, with his hope deteriorating and not able to reach his friend, exited the telephone both, waived to the person behind the counter, exited the deli, and began his daily morning walk to his work place.

As he purposely and briskly walked to his job's facility, located in industrial sector of Manhattan's West Side, he had to cope with its very busy streets and crowded sidewalks. He reviewed his pressing objectives for the day, trying not to think about his friend. At the job in NRI, he is one of eight line supervisors. He is being considered for the floor's Senior Supervisor's position to replace Alfred who worked for the company during the last 10 years. The Senior Supervisor in charge is responsible for the production activities managed by the eight lines supervisors. This job will become available next week when Alfred, the current floor Senior Supervisor who joined the Marines, leaves for processing and basic training at For Dix in South Jersey. Jaime, knowing that he is being considered for that job slot, has been anxiously anticipating the potential promotion and looking forward to the additional income which he will bank and save to, perhaps, accelerate his achieving his plan to return to Cuba and fulfill his dream to purchase a farm and raise a family there. This promotion would increase his take home pay. It would be a welcomed twenty percent weekly pay check increase, which he would likely bank.

Jaime knows that he must focus his attention on his job responsibilities and on the interview scheduled with the Plant Manager, Mr. Smith, for this morning. However, he has to also confirm that his friend Vincent is not the deceased person reported by the newspaper. Knowing that telephone calls are not permitted during work time, Jaime decided to skip going to the factory's cafeteria at lunch time, skip lunch altogether and try calling Vincent and Dina again.

Jaime arrived at the factory with one minute to spare. He intermingled with other arriving co-workers and entered the factory through the employee's side entrance. He found his time card and inserted it into the mechanical time keeper, which responded with a metal sound feedback worthy of a musical instrument.

When he arrived at his station, seconds before the Starting Bell rang, the girls already sitting at their station greeted Jaime with a "buffet" of "Hellos" and "How was your weekend?" comments. Mary, the very attractive and "well distributed" blond young lady, who sits two stations away from his production line, locked eyes with Jaime and rewarded him with a smile, overflowing with "honey".

Mary has been pursuing Jaime since shortly after joining his production line. Her lively personality and good looks has been both enticing and punishing to him. It has been enticing because he has perceived that getting together with Mary could bring lots of enjoyment to his disciplined life. It has been punishing because he has had to restrain his Latin characteristic in obedience to the teachings of one of his mentors, who was Mr. Fernandez, the sugar mill's Part Warehouse Manager.

Mr. Fernandez had taken Jaime under his "wings" after Jaime's father's death, and imparted much of his business behavioral knowledge to the attentive and receptive pupil.

Having been a young man himself, and knowing the physical drives and temptations which men must deal with at that early age, Mr. Fernandez in numerous occasions, alerted Jaime against "pissing where you eat". A somewhat vulgar expression, but one that by its vulgarity, etches a valuable and wisdom loaded message into the mind of its recipient.

Jaime has, since gaining that street wisdom, always resisted temptations and has abstained from the like behavior at the work place by avoiding relationships that would interfere with the company's expected level of professionalism.

The bell rang and the employees previously engaged in personal conversations regarding their weekend happenings, stopped talking and began their daily chores and work asignments.

Jaime's production line consisted of eight stations, including his. The line length is thirty two feet long by three feet wide, consisting of eight four feet modular tables. It is bordered on the far end by a continuous belt that moves the vitamin's bulk containers to the station operators, and also carries the loaded retail bottles to the packing operation.

The Line Supervisor is responsible for controlling his operators' productivity by assuring adequate supply of retail bottles, lids, products and labels. He is also required to maintain the employees focus on the production task in order to assure meeting at least the customary production quantity and quality standards. In addition to his supervisory role, Jaime was responsible for the line's OQC (Outgoing Quality control).

At 9:00 a.m, the sound of the machinery and the operators' quiet whisper, sharing their thoughts with those to the their left and right as they try to overcome the mental boredom of the repetitious task, which they perform, was interrupted by a loud speaker instructing Mr. Jaime Gonzalez to report to the personnel office.

Jaime was not surprised by the paging, since he was expecting to be called for the interview. He instructed Julia, the operator sitting to his right, to take over his station until he returns from the office. Julia has been trained by Jaime to cover for him when he is on vacation and when he has to leave his station to participate in production and training meetings, or other reasons.

Jaime reported to the personnel office, as instructed. Mr. William, the head of personnel was waiting for him in his office with good news. Unknown to Jaime, the interview formality had been waived in view of his excellent record with the company.

Jaime entered Mr. William's office and was asked to sit down. Mr. Williams pretending to review the records waited long enough to awaken Jaime's expectation. He leveled his eyes sight to Jaime's eyes, and told him "Mr. Gonzalez, the company recognizes and appreciate your service. Management has decided to waive the customary interview. The decision has been made to promote you to the position of Floor Supervisor, effective next Monday. Congratulations!"

Jaime was very pleased that the company had trusted and recognized him with the additional responsibility. However, momentarily he was much more pleased not having to face the interview process. He always felt somewhat insecure handling interviews. He thought that, perhaps, language insecurity may have contributed to this feeling.

Mr. Williams shook Jaime's hand and told him that the company will announce his promotion this Friday at a planned general meeting, followed by a memo to be posted on the Bulletin Board after the meeting. Jaime thanked Mr. Williams, who acknowledge the thanks, and instructed Jaime to return to his station.

Shortly after the visit to the personnel department, Jaime was sitting at his station feeling gratified about his promotion, but carefully withholding any reaction that may give it away to his co-workers before the announced his promotion to Floor Supervisor has been made, as he had been instructed to safeguard it.

The rest of the morning continued uneventfully, but with growing anxiety, as he impatiently waited for lunch break and the opportunity to try to reach his friends Vincent or Dina.

The twelve-noon bell rang, and the industrious sounding production floor immediately became a beehive of activity caused by employees exiting the working area. A choir of mixed sounds, generated by the excited, hungry and anxious employees, anticipated their work brake and meal intake.

Jaime swiftly departed the work area and walked to the exit door. He picked his time card and inserted it into the time clock slot as he had done early this morning. The clock responded with the usual clanking sound. He then proceeded to the telephone installed on the outside back corner of the building.

The corner booth was occupied when Jaime got there. He stood near by the telephone booth waiting for his turn to make his worrisome telephone call. His blood pressure began to rise in response to the telephone availability delay, and because of his concern of not having sufficient time to call and finally confirm that his dear friend, Vincent, is alright.

Jaime walked back and forth in front of the telephone booth as a means of releasing his anxiety and projecting his impatient state to the person in the booth. The young lady talking in the telephone was oblivious to his presence.

*

At noon time Julia, the head nurse, walked into the Dina's room with a lunch tray. Mrs. Peterson was sitting quietly next to Dina's bed, knitting a light weight, white cardigan for her daughter. Mr. Peterson sat behind his wife, with his head back and supported by the light green wall, sleeping. Dina appeared to be awakening from the sedative that Doctor Alvarez had prescribed.

Julia placed the food tray on the rolling work table sitting next to the bed and asked Dina if she was hungry. The negative response did not surprise Julia. Nonetheless, she firmly told Dina that she had to eat and provide her body with the needed nutrition to have the strength to deal with the challenges ahead.

Julia also told Mrs. Peterson that there were two extra sandwiches for her and her husband. Mrs. Peterson expressed her gratitude and assured Julia that she will make sure that Dina consumed at least the soup, if not all of the food provided.

Dina looked at her mother, who could not wait to ask her how she was feeling. Dina with still tearful eyes responded "Mom I feel empty, as if part of me has been yanked away". Her mother forcing a reassuring expression told Dina that she understood her feelings, but that time will help heal her pain, and that she was there for her. She further told Dina that she was a young person and life challenges, opportunities and relationships will certainly cross her path again. Mrs. Peterson also told her daughter that Vincent will always occupy a special place in her life, and that she is sure that his wish would be for her to move on with her life and pursue happiness.

Dina's father opened his eyes and noticed that Dina was awake. He walked to the side of the bed opposite his wife, kissed his daughter on the forehead in a loving fatherly way. He told Dina, "My darling I am so sorry that life has burdened you with so much suffering. Please remember that you do not have to carry this burden on your shoulders alone. You have us and we have you. We shall together lighten your burden and help your journey through this most difficult time. We love you very much and we are here for you!"

Dina looked at her dad, extended her arms as a signal that she wanted to hug him. He moved closer to her and they embraced in a comforting and reassuring way. As he receded from the embrace, Mr. Peterson urged Dina to please have something to eat. He reminded her "there is much to be done, and you need all the strength that you can muster".

After much persuasion from both parents, Dina picked up the soup spoon and slowly began to consume some of the chicken broth. Her mouth was dry and the broth was a welcomed refreshment, as the warm moisture awakened her palate as it bathed her mouth and upper throat. Her stomach, on the other hand, was not as welcoming to the broth. The acid reservoir, which her stomach had become, was trying to reject the needed nutrition and threatening to reverse its flow.

Dina consumed half of the soup and followed it with a cool cherry Jell-O, hoping to neutralize the uncomfortable and unwanted stomach discomfort.

Doctor Alvarez entered the room and with a cheerful voice, greeted Dina and asked her if she was able to rest last night. Her response was short and to the point and told, I am very tired, Doctor. He then introduced himself and greeted her parents as well. After the greeting and introduction, the doctor informed Dina's parents that all the vital signs were normal and that there was no medical reason for Dina to remain in the hospital. He further stated that he will sign the patient release form at the nurses station right away so that she can go home whenever they wish.

The Petersons smiled at the good news and thanked Doctor Alvarez for taking care of Dina and for his concern for her welfare. Dina, apparently accepting that "life must go on", but more important, wanting to leave the antiseptic environment of the hospital's setting, she sat up to begin getting ready to leave the hospital. She, too, thanked the doctor for his caring and support.

The young lady in the booth finally, after a twenty minutes long telephone conversation, exited the booth and made it available for Jaime to make his telephone call. Jaime searched his pocket and located the only coin which he had, a dime. He cranked the telephone and soon after, a voice which sounded somewhat older than this morning's telephone operator responded "Please, deposit ten cents"

Jaime deposited the moist dime which he had been holding as he impatiently walk back and fort trying to send a visual message to young lady in the telephone booth, into the coin box on back of the pay telephone's voice piece. After the usual "clicking' sound, he heard the operator's standard greeting "Operator, How may I help you?" Jaime told the operator that he needed to speak to Mr. Wagner and, before he was asked, he provided the street address to the operator. After a quick thank you from the operator, the telephone's ringing sound provided Jaime a momentary comfort. He thought that finally he will be able to put his mind at ease.

The telephone rang continuously as it did during the morning call. Finally the operator came back and told Jaime that she was sorry, but that there was no answer. A second cling sounded and the telephone communication was terminated.

Jaime felt very disappointed and frustrated. He resigned himself not having gotten the answer, which he was seeking, and returned to work having no choice other than waiting for the end of the work day to try to reach his friend Vincent again. He returned to the work place just in time to punch back in before the bell rang, without having had the opportunity to eat or drink anything.

At Columbus Hospital, Dina was changing from the dreary looking hospital gown to the clothes which she wore the day before. Her father had located a local dry cleaner and, after sharing the circumstances for needing the garments cleaned right away, the attendant agreed to cooperate cleaning the clothes promptly. Unfortunately, the attendant was unable to get rid of Vincent's blood stain from the white blouse sleeve, requiring Mr. Peterson to take a detour to Macy's on 34th Street and purchase a new long sleeve blouse for his daughter. He was concerned that the blood stained blouse would, further trigger last night's event's memories and, perhaps, be detrimental for Dina's emotional recuperation.

Mr. Peterson called the Wagners, who had returned home, and shared Dina's condition with them. He mentioned that shortly they will be leaving the hospital and going to Dina's and Vincent's apartment, where they planned to remain for the night providing her some company. They also told the Wagners their plan for the morning was to help her with funeral arrangements and try to convince her to return to Newark with them.

Mr. Wagner took advantage of the funeral discussion to share that his family has a crypt with four available chambers at the Evergreen Cemetery, located in Hillside, a small suburb town adjacent to the South West boundary of Newark. He added that this cemetery is where Stephen Crane, the famous author of the well known book titled "The Red Badge of Courage", was buried in the year 1900. Mr. Peterson confirmed that the author's famous book was one of the literary works which he regularly discussed with his students when he was a teacher. He then shared one book quote which he regularly used to entice his students to read the classic text -"Directly he was working at his weapon like an automatic affair. He suddenly lost concern for himself and forgot to look at a menacing fate. He became not a man but a member. He was welded into a common personality, which was dominated by a single desire."

Mr. Wagner emphasized that he and his wife would very much like to have Vincent's remains put to rest with the other members of the family. Furthermore, he shared that he will call Dina and ask her permission for them to handle all the funeral's financial arrangements, and to let her know that one of the remaining burial chambers at the Evergreen Cemetery will be saved for her, should she wish upon her death, to have her remains lay next to him.

Mr. Peterson considered the Wagner's suggestion to be timely, practical, and a financial lifesaver for his daughter. He knew that the young couple did not have much time to build a "nest egg" to finance this unexpected and unfortunate tragedy. Additionally, he and his wife, having been significantly economically affected by the depression, did not have sufficient financial resources to cover all the costs incurred for Vincent's funeral. Mr. Wagner's news regarding the availability of the crypt, and his decision to assume financial responsibility for the funeral's expenditures, was a great relief for Mr. Peterson.

It was mid-morning when the Peterson family walked out of the hospital. It was a beautiful spring afternoon. The temperature was close to sixty five degrees and the trees were all dressed with pink and white blossoms. The fragrance filled the afternoon air allowed Dina to fill her lung with its freshness, flooded with perfume, and cleansing it from the institutional hospital air, unfortunately, without the usual joy and satisfaction that she has been accustomed to experiencing while walking the street of New York City with her departed love.

The late morning street prettiness or the perfumed air did not matter to Dina. She had lost her best friend and lover and, with that, she lost her appreciation for any form of beauty. At that moment, she felt as an abandon vessel, navigating adrift in the middle of the Ocean without any origin and without any destination.

As they approached the sidewalk in front of the hospital, Mr. Peterson signaled a yellow taxi going East across the street. The driver quickly turned left, crossing the solid line, and pulling up to the curb nearby his new fare, the waiting three passengers.

Mr. Peterson opened the rear right door of the taxi for the ladies to enter. Once they were inside, he closed their door and proceeded to open the front passenger side door, to enter the cab.

The driver, unshaven and with a half chewed, probably a one day old cigar held by his cavity filled, yellow teeth, asked Mr. Peterson, "where to", with what appeared to be a heavy Italian accent. Mr. Peterson gave the driver Dina's address who then accelerated his smelly and noisy cab as if he was in a hurry to go to the bathroom.

The driver expertly navigated through the busy streets of Manhattan and reached Dina's apartment in less than fifteen minutes. Mr. Peterson could not wait to reach their destination in order to escape from the driver's unsavory cigar smell. The ladies exited the cab in front of Dina's place and Mr. Peterson remained inside the taxi long enough to pay the fare and tip the driver.

Dina's apartment was located in quiet, tree covered, Manhattan Street, not very far from the Island center. The building, a brick front, four apartments structure was built fifty years earlier. The quality structure's construction can now be better appreciated by the excellent condition of the building five decades later.

The Peterson family walked up five steps to the front entrance platform and Mr. Peterson opened the unlocked door for the ladies. The family walked into the foyer and Dina handed the apartment's keys to her father, who opened the door of the first floor apartment.

Dina walked into the apartment's living room, followed by her parents. The room was elegantly finished with mahogany-framed windows and red brocade front window curtains, sheltering the room from the street, and providing additional privacy for the newly weds. The living room was sparsely, but tastefully furnished. Apparently, Dina was either very selective with her furniture choices or economically conscientious, choosing not to incur excessive expenditures until the funds become available. It is likely that the later criteria may be most probable, in view of her parent's experience.

The apartment consisted of a living room, a dining room with an adjacent kitchen, a bathroom with an elegant and inviting ceramic tub, and two bedrooms. Vincent and Dina selected this apartment primarily because of the two bedrooms, in anticipation of the family which they planned for early in their marriage.

Dina's guided her parents to the second bedroom for them to use for the night. The second bedroom where her parents were sleeping tonight was adjacent to the bathroom and on the opposite side of the main bedroom, both located on the apartment's back section, away from the street.

The Petersons, in their haste to reach the Hospital, did not bring additional clothing for an overnight stay. Dina provided Mr. Peterson with one of Vincent's bathrobes. She outfitted her mother with a brand new bathrobe, which she had received as a wedding gift and had never used.

Dina parents went to their bedroom to get ready to bathe and put on the bathrobes lent to them. Once they finished bathing, both parents returned to the living room and joined their daughter. She was sitting still and pensive looking on the living room's wooden sofa, as if in a trance. When her parents approached her, she forced a smile for them, and requested they sit down next to her.

They sat together, and avoided the current events. Their conversed about the family and, at times, reminiscing about their daughter's childhood experiences. Time passed with conversation and, on occasions with silence as each of them submerged into self thoughts about the life changing events which engulfed and changed their lives for ever. Their conversations aided the passing of time, and at approximately four thirty in the afternoon, Mrs. Peterson told Dina that it was getting close to dinner time. She suggested that, if Dina had no objections, she would gladly prepare some food for them to eat. Dina, not particularly caring about eating, but concerned that her parents not be deprived of their nutrition, acceded to her mother's offer.

Dina suggested that her mother warm up a pot of beef stew, which she had prepared yesterday, before departing to Vincent's parents in New Jersey. Dina's mother went to the kitchen to set the table and prepare the evening's meal.

Mr. Peterson took advantage of that opportunity, being alone with Dina, to address the sensitive burial subject with her. He expected that it would be a difficult matter to address without causing his daughter to fall back into a depressive mode. Unfortunately the matter needed addressing. Thus there was no choice, the matter had to be discussed and addressed.

Before Mr. Peterson was able to sort out the strategy on how to approach the subject, Dina looked at him and surprisingly calm said, "Dad, I need your help making the funeral arrangements". Mr. Peterson, somewhat taken aback, responded without hesitation. "My darling, of course I will always be here for you!". His daughter's request provided the impetus to initiate the needed conversation to decide on the the required funeral arrangement.

Mr. Peterson then related the conversation that he had with Mr. Wagner regarding their family's wishes, that Vincent be entombed in their Evergreen Cemetery family mausoleum, which currently has four remaining crypts. Mr. Wagner reminded his daughter that the cemetery is located in the suburban and sparsely populated town of Hillside. The small town that borders the South West side of Newark and is sandwiched between the two cities of Newark and Elizabeth.

He also shared Mr. Wagner's gracious offer to reserve the crypt for her, next to Vincent's resting place, should Dina desire to have her remains, when the time comes to rest next to her deceased husband. Upon hearing the thoughtful offer, Dina experienced a sense of relief, for she did posses the needed financial resources and was well aware that her family may perhaps, in a more dire financial situation than she is. She then considered, in silence, the gracious offer to preserve a "slot" for her in their family's mausoleum. She thought to herself that death was not in her agenda, at least not until she reached a long and ripped old age, as most young people have the tendency to think consequence of ignoring the human fragility.

Mr. Peterson suggested to his daughter that she has to decide where to hold the funeral services tonight if possible. He shared in his opinion, that she should select a funeral home in the City of Newark rather than in Manhattan because: First of all, both families live on the other side of the river; Secondly, the cemetery is located in Hillside, a town adjacent to the City of Newark; and Thirdly, the cost of funeral services in Newark will be significantly lower than that in New York City. He reminded Dina that the economic factor should be an important consideration even though Vincent's family were very gracious to volunteer handling all the expenses.

While Dina digested her father's recommendation, he continued the mental process of reviewing all available options, and he tried to anticipate the logistics associated with Vincent's funeral service and burial. His desire being, of course, to minimize the burden of his lovely daughter's shoulders, for she has a sufficient weight to carry with the loss of her partner in marriage, and the integral missing part of her life's dream.

While thinking about what needed to be done, Mr. Peterson remembered that one of his students, Nuncio Spatola, in his English evening class at the West Side High School, located on High Street, in Newark and not far from the Court House, guarded on the front of the building by an impressive and very visible statue of the 16th president of the United States, Abraham Lincoln. An individual which history has credited as being the Republican President who preserved the United States of America's Union, and who also is credited with bringing about the emancipation of slaved people. Nuncio was part owner of the Spatola Family

Funeral Home and also was the brother of the business manager, Angelo Spatola.

Mr. Peterson remembered that Nuncio was very grateful and proud, having significantly improved his English language comprehension and communication. And Nuncio credited him, a number of times, for those accomplishment. Mr. Peterson remembers always responding to Nuncio, that he only provided the "direction and road map" and that the credit really belonged to who dedicated the time and effort, fulfilling the mission to reach the desired destination. He further remembered that one night after class, Nuncio approached him and told him "Mr. P, I am indebted to you for all your help. You may not want to hear this, but if you ever need our family's service, with funeral arrangements, please make sure that you talk to me first". Mr. Peterson remember smiling at Nuncio and telling him, "your offer was very thoughtful, but I hope not to have to take advantage of your gracious offer for a long time".

Mr. Peterson decided to share that bit of information and dialogue, with Dina. She smiled briefly, acknowledging her father's extensive circle of acquaintances. She asked him where the Funeral Home was located, and if it was a nice place where Vincent's services could be handled with the decorum that he deserves and his parents expected.

Mr. Peterson explained to his daughter, the Spatola family had purchased an old mansion on High Street, Newark, renovated it, and modernized it into an elegant Funeral Home facility. He added that he had recently attended services for a colleague who had fallen from a horse at a nearby farm, and the service was handled with the upmost level of professionalism and correctness.

Dina concluded that her father's suggestions were very practical and, above all, provided resolutions for issues that she'd rather not dwell on for very much longer. She looked at her Dad, hugged him, and thanked him for his help. She then said 'Dad, I do not know what I would do without your help".

As Dina was rewarding her father with a kiss on his cheek, her mother walked into the living room and told her husband and daughter that dinner was ready.

Father and daughter got up from the sofa, as if a sergeant had given the order, and, together with her mother, walked into the dining room where the steaming beef goulash, improvised by Dina's mother, was hiding the freshly boiled Linguine steaming underneath, which had been served on each of the three plates. The family sat down to eat their last meal for the day.

*

It was approximately twenty after five in the afternoon and Jaime had managed to find an empty telephone booth halfway home. He entered the booth and reached into his pocket for a coin to initiate his call to Vincent. Unfortunately, he had used his last and only coin during the unsuccessful lunch time call effort. Jaime, demonstrating an unusual behavior, angrily expressed out loud a few selective profanities in his native language and sheltering self in the telephone booth, from being embarrassed by his indiscretion heard by passers by. Jaime exited the telephone booth and began walking in an accelerated pace to his apartment two blocks away.

As he approached his block, neighbors' greetings were ignored as he was unmindful of his surroundings, hoping to confirm the inevitable. He entered his apartment, after a brief struggle with the keys and lock. He walked directly into his bedroom where he had a cigar box as an improvised piggy bank and took five ten cents coins. He exited his house with the same haste as he entered it, and directed his steps to the corner deli where he could try again to reach his friend, Vincent.

Jaime entered the deli and walked directly to the telephone

booth, it was empty. With a sigh of relief, he entered the booth and cranked the telephone mechanism. A voice responded immediately, "Please deposit ten cents". Jaime quickly deposited one of the dimes that he taken from the old cigar box into the coin slot in back of the pay telephone's voice piece.

He heard the click from payment confirmation, followed by an operator's voice saying, "Operator, How may I help you!?" Jaime told the operator that he needed to speak with Mr. Wa-ge-ner, and gave the operator Vincent's telephone number before being asked.

The telephone rang once, twice, and on the third ring, Vincent heard a connection feedback.

Mr. Peterson told Dina that he will answer the call for her. He got up from the dining table, walked to the living room where the telephone sat on a corner dark mahogany table, picked up the ear piece, and responded to the call.

To Jaime's bewilderment, an unrecognized voice on the other end responded, "Hello, can I help you" Jaime, unsure if the operator had dialed the right party said, "I want to talk to Vincent Wa-ge-ner". Mr. Peterson, not recognizing the inquiring voice, asked who was speaking. Jaime responded without hesitation, "It is Jaime." Mr. Peterson told Jaime to please hold on a minute. He covered the telephone's mouth piece with his left hand palm and asked Dina if she new a Jaime, with a heavy Spanish accent.

Dina always has considered Jaime a good and reliable family friend, and a person she could always lean on when the dark clouds shadowed happiness and expectations. She also knew that Jaime was one of Vincent's closest friends, if not the closest one. She always attributed their political alignment, economic perspective, and philosophical compatibility to be the catalyst, which promoted the growth and maintenance of their friendship.

Dina did not have the courage or stamina to pick up the telephone and tell Jaime that Vincent was gone. She asked her father to tell Jaime to please call later this evening, when Dina will be available to talk to him.

Mr. Peterson uncovered the mouth piece and told Jaime that it is impossible for him to speak with Vincent and or Dina at this time, to please call later this evening when Dina will be available. Jaime, not quite understanding or wanting to understand the message, asked, "May I know who I am speaking with?" When he heard the response "Mr. Peterson", Jaime realized that he was talking to Dina's dad. He felt slightly relieved, comfortable, and responded, "Mr. P", as he usually addresses her Dad, "this James", the name used by the Petersons when speaking to him.

Jaime anxiously shared with Mr. P his day long preoccupation regarding Vincent's well being, caused by the article which he read in the New York Sun's morning's edition.

Mr. Peterson, recognizing Vincent's and Jaime's close friendship, felt remorse and empathetic knowing that his response will also fill Jaime's heart with sorrow. Indeed, it was necessary to share the sad news with Jaime without further delay. Allowing the uncertainty of Vincent's demise to continue will certainly be an unjust action. Therefore, Mr. Peterson decided to follow the path of full disclosure, without consulting Dina. He took a deep breast of the late afternoon's fresh air, lovingly spiced with the smell of the Hungarian Goulash that his sweetheart had prepared, and told Jaime, "James, the victim reported in the New York Sun's article was our Vincent".

A brief silence ensued, Mr. Peterson inspire once again, and recharged his lungs with a new supply of energy laden oxygen. Jaime gradually coiled his upper torso towards the telephone booth's wooden wall until the thump, caused by his head contacting the clear varnished wood, brought him back to the awareness of the moment.

Both Jaime and Mr. P struggled with the consequences that the expression a few words, "the victim was Vincent", represented and emphasize as a reality; the sadness, sense of loss, suffering, and life changing outcome that said words had, and will have, in the lives of so many people, and in particular on Dina's life, a loving daughter, and on a dear and perhaps best friend of the deceased.

Mr. Peterson broke the uncomfortable silence and said, "I am very sorry, James", a short and disengaged "me, too" reply from Jaime followed. Mr. Peterson heard a "click", confirming that the other party had terminated the conversation.

Jaime sat quietly in the telephone booth, head slumped forward, and with manly tears spilling from the corner of his eyes, something which he had not experienced in recent years. His upper body coiled again and slowly moved forward until his head lightly banged against the telephone booth wall again, afterwards receding to his normal sitting position. This movement continued for half a dozen times until his body rested in the forward position, with his head pressed against the smooth wood surface of the telephone booth's wall.

Jaime's current painfulness and sadness were familiar. They transported his thoughts many years back, to when he lost his best friend, at an early stage of his life, his father. As he revisited those deep feelings that had been buried in his sub consciousness, caused by time and the power of acceptance, he recognized the similarities and binding relationships between Fatherhood and Brotherhood.

Fatherhood is a lifetime bond originated with a seed deposited in the welcoming mother's womb that provides much needed shelter, nutrition, comfort, and security. A seed, whose miraculous development influenced by forces greater than mankind's capacity to comprehend; blossoms in a finite time, abandons the safety and comfort of the mother's shelter and a new stage in life's journey begins, learning and sharing until eternal peace is realized.

Brotherhood is a bond that is beyond having originated from the same paternal seed, or from having traveled the identical birth canal. Brotherhood is a bond that overcomes obstacles, ignores greed, flourishes in complete trust, is congruent in perspectives and philosophies, admires each other's strength absent of envy, and provides support for each other's weaknesses.

Jaime recognizes that the sadness and anguish which he is experiencing is because the loss of Vincent is more than just loosing a friend, he has lost a brother.

A young lady looking at Jaime sitting, and apparently in deep thought, in the telephone booth, politely tapped the small rectangular glass window on the booth's door. Jaime, awakened from his stupor, exited the telephone booth somewhat embarrassed for having held back the young lady from making her telephone call, just as he had experienced during earlier in the day, during his lunch break.

Jaime had dealt all day with the preoccupation and concern that Vincent may have been the victim of the shooting, a preoccupation that he rejected with hope and false justification. The words, "the victim was Vincent", although painful and penetrating, as if a knife had been driven into his guts, provided a needed closure to the torturous thoughts that pervaded his thinking throughout the day.

There was not much to do, or much that Jaime wanted to do, this evening. His thought began to focus on Dina, his dear friend. He felt that it was incumbent upon him to provide her with moral support during this most difficult time. Without hesitation, he signaled a taxi, boarded it, and gave the driver destination instructions. Jaime had decided to go to Dina's and Vincent's apartment.

Dina and her parents had finished their meal. Her parents, having traveled through life a lot longer, and having experienced many losses of love ones, were able to accept the inevitable afflictions, eventually confronted by all humans in life's path, were able to consume the delicious Hungarian Goulash prepared by Dina's Mom. Dina, on the other hand, barely ate any food, notwithstanding her parent's insistence. A German style, Black Forest cake, Vincent's favorite, together with a pot of freshly brewed Colombian coffee, waited invitingly, to be served.

A knock on the front door delayed the family's dessert. Father, mother and daughter looked each other with puzzled expression, not expecting any company. Mr. Peterson got up from his chair and walked to the front door to find out who was seeking their attention. He opened the door and saw Jaime patiently standing by, his youthful presence partially blocking the reflection of the night light above the porch.

It was a clear night. The sky was beautifully decorated by bright starts, reminiscent of Christmas trees fully loaded with brilliant white miniature lights, and partially illuminated by a beautifully clear, full moon.

The magnificent night was shamefully wasted by the absence of one young loving couple, expressing their passion, while walking down the blossomed embellished promenade.

Mr. Peterson greeted James, and told him "I am surprised to see you, Please come in". Jaime thanked Mr. P and walked into the building's foyer. Mr. Peterson closed the door and both men entered the apartment and walked towards the dining room, Jaime following.

Mr. Peterson announced James's arrival, while crossing the living room and walking towards the kitchen. Dina got up and quickly walked towards the living room to greet Jaime, to seek solace and to mutually comfort each other for the tragic loss that they both have experienced.

Their loss was of a different nature, with different consequences, but in a way, with the same magnitude of human torment.

Dina and Jaime looked at each other wordless, both of their bodies united into a fraternal embrace expressing and sharing the sense of loss that they both were experiencing. She began to sob softly, and her tears began to bathe his upper left shoulder. His face rested next to her silky blond hair and his lung began to be filled by the soothing fragrance broadcast by her young and beautiful body. Jaime exerted all his masculine strength retaining the tears from spilling over, to assure that his voice did not betray his feelings, and his difficulty fulfilling the expected manly behavior. Neither one of the two dear friends wanted to cease their comforting embrace. They held each other tighter, and tighter, as if wanting to fuse both bodies into a single mass, better able to cope with the suffering and sorrow they both shared.

Mr. Peterson was surprised by the unexpected intensity of the embrace and by the degree that the two young people were able to understand their mutual pain, and were able to comfort and communicate with each other without expressing a single syllable.

Mr. Peterson, having studied human behavior and having taught hundreds , if not thousands of young people, and not to mention many years of experience recognized that unbeknownst to the couple, a forbidden natural attraction has been clandestinely self cultivating. An observation that he will keep to his inner most self, certainly during this most critical time.

A few moments later, Jaime realized that it was prudent to disengage from their embrace, even though it provided much comfort for their souls as they dealt with the unbearable life's torment, not wanting to imply cause for her parents to infer that the warm and appearing to never end embrace was more than just an expression of true and lasting friendship, particularly in the presence of Mr. Peterson.

Jaime considered Dina's dad's values to have been molded in a different era, and thought that her father may not understand the feeling of brotherhood that existed between the three close friends, and which he hoped would continue to thrive for the remaining two.

Jaime moved slowly away from Dina while tenderly holding her left hand.

The tips of his right hand's fingers continued holding her left hand. This was the only remaining bodily contact between the two of them. They both would have preferred to continued sheltering each other's anguish with the warmth and the peaceful feeling, which their embrace provided but should not be. Certainly not in her parents' presence, for their inference may be misguided.

The three of them, Mr. Peterson, Dina and Jaime walked together, back to the dining room and where Mrs. Peterson was focused on cleaning the pots and dishes soiled from their dinner.

Jaime greeted Mrs. Peterson with a warm and sincere smile, followed by a polite kiss on her left cheek. Mrs. "P" reciprocated with a kiss on his right cheek and a warm and welcoming hug and smile.

Dina pointed to the chair next to her father and suggested that Jaime sit there.

They all sat down and the Peterson family was about to begin to enjoy the awaiting appetizing threat when Mrs. Peterson, realizing that Jaime may not have had his supper yet, asked him if he had already eaten. Jaime politely responded that he did have something to eat earlier and was not really hungry at this time.

Jaime had eaten a sweet and juicy peach from Georgia during his lunch time, which he had purchased at the fruit stand, on his way to the deli to call his friend Vincent. Dina, knowing Jaime and his routine, and knowing that he prepares his own meals after work, was sure that he was being polite and was attempting to not inconvenience them with concerns about his not having had supper.

Dina told Jaime "It is not possible for you to have eaten. First of all, it is too early and secondly there is no way for you to have been able to prepare your meal in such a short period of time". Jaime's attempt to "bluff" his way out of what he considered to be an inconvenience to Mrs. Peterson, was neutralized. Dina insisted that he have something "solid" to eat before enjoying dessert. Mrs. Peterson reinforced Dina's insistence and added "not to worry, we have enough Hungarian Goulash left to feet an army". Without asking, Mrs. Peterson got up from the table and went to the stove to serve a soup bowl full of Goulash. She placed it in front of young man, her daughter's friend. Although his reputation has been, his having an unusually aggressive appetite, Jaime thanked Mrs. Peterson and shared with her not being very hungry at this time. Further mentioning that his usual appetite had banished. Mrs. Peterson insisted that he eat something, and he said "thank you, but I am not hungry". She then removed Jaime's plate and returned half of the goulash, that she had previously served, back into the pot, and placed the half filled plate on the table and back in front of Jaime. Feeling obliged he forced himself to consume the delicious looking fare.

They all engaged in light general conversation, making sure to avoid any subject related to Vincent's death, while Jaime enjoyed the healthy and fulfilling Hungarian Goulash.

After Jaime finished eating and recognizing that his dormant hunger had been partially awaken, he looked forward to savoring the delicious looking cake sitting on the kitchen's counter top. Mrs. Peterson immediately began serving generous portion of the German Black Forest Cake to the welcoming recipients.

They all began ingesting the gratifying sweet treat that they had been anxiously anticipating, followed by an excellent cup of American style coffee to close the meal. Jaime politely forced himself to drink what he considered to be a "watered down" brew when compared with "el cafecito cubano", which is a strong and dark espresso coffee served in a demitasse and brewed with

Seeking the Future

fine grind French style roasted coffee beans. Afterwards, they all, except Mrs. Peterson who stayed in the kitchen to clean up, retired to the living room where they experienced post dinner symptoms of feeling slightly bloated, but fully satisfied.

The living room conversations inevitably lead to the taboo subject which was avoided during dinner. Jaime asked if the arrangements for Vincent's funeral had been made and, if so, when and where. He further stated that he was at their service to help in any way that they may consider useful.

Mr. Peterson explained to Jaime that the arrangements will be made tomorrow morning. He also informed Jaime that the funeral services will most likely be held at Spatola's Funeral Home in Newark, followed by internment at the Wagner's family's plot in The Evergreen Cemetery located in Hillside, New Jersey.

Mr. Peterson also told Jaime that Dina will be going to New Jersey tomorrow morning and will, most likely, remain with them in Newark for a few days after the burial services. He suggested that Jaime call their home tomorrow at noon to find out the final funeral arrangements schedule

The telephone rang just as Mr. Peterson had finished sharing the available funeral arrangements information with Jaime. Dina picked up the shiny, white and gold trimmed, porcelain coated, telephone handle, which had been horizontally cradled on the Western Electric newest telephone fixture, greeting the caller with a mellow "hello".

The cheerful voice on the other end was that of Mary Richards, Dina's best friend and confidant.

Mary's cheerful replied, "hello darling, how are you this beautiful evening" and without providing an opportunity for Dina to respond, Mary released a sequential salvo of questions and statements without stopping to catch a breast of fresh air "How have you been my dear?. Did you have a such great romance at Coney Island that kept you from returning home as scheduled?. I called you a number of times last night and could not get you! How did Vincent react when you surprised him about the great news that he was becoming a daddy? Was the weekend as romantic as you expected? I can wait for you to tell me all about it." Dina could not now deal with her dear friend's usual inquiry litany. She interrupted Mary, with a somewhat curt and petulant command "Mary, please, shut up for a minute".

The tone and pitch that Dina used to deliver her telephone command to Mary was very surprising even to herself, if not shocking to her family and friend present in the living room. Her tone and words were considered very much out of character for Dina who has always been very patient and polite on the telephone.

Mary felt devastated and completely deflated by the way her best friend and confidant injured her pride and attacked her caring and enthusiasm. She then thought that something had to be wrong.

Mary, reflecting her injured pride, fired back with a comparable tone, "What is wrong with you?" Dina could no longer control herself. She lost her love and now she has possibly alienated her best friend. Dina's delicate self control has now been fractured. She began to cry helplessly on the telephone. Mary, with a loving and caring tone asked "Dina, Darling, what is wrong?" Dina could only harness the strength to express three words "Vincent is dead". Mary, with a very decisive voice, told Dina "I am going over right now".

Jaime got up and walked over to the sofa where Dina remained crying and wordless. He gently removed the telephone from her grasp, placed the ear piece on his ear to confirm if Mary was still on the line. Jaime say "hello". Silence followed. The conversation had been terminated. He replaced the ear piece on the cradle, after hearing an open line tone.

Jaime sat next to Dina. He placed his right arm over her

shoulder and brought her upper torso close to him. He provided a comfortable nest for her proving head to rest and feel the comfort that can only be realized with a very close friend, or a lover.

Dina's head remained immobile for a few minutes, her exhaustion overwhelming any concern for the time, the setting, or the inferences. Emotional fatigue overcame her ability to remain awake and her eyelids slowly dropped, shutting down her consciousness window and allowing her to enter a momentary state of relaxation and disengagement from life's complexities.

The door bell rang shortly after Dina fell to sleep and momentarily startled her. She synchronized her bearings and realized that Mary had arrived. She jumped from her sofa and intercepted her father, who was moving towards the door to open it. She asked her father to please let her get the door.

Dina opened the door and Mary was standing there waiting, with her tears freely running down her face, winning the battle against the makeup which she had so methodically and effectively put on.

Words were not necessary at the moment. The two friends firmly hugged each other and continued to hold each other with all the strength that they could muster, while unabashedly letting their reservoir of tears empty downward, towards their cheeks, washing away the limited remains of the mascara which they had previously carefully applied.

Dina's first words to Mary were apologetic, for having wrongfully treated her earlier during their telephone conversation. Mary acknowledged it and told Dina that under the circumstances she understood, and there was no need for her to be concerned for she clearly understood under the circumstances.

Dina and Mary Richards walked into the living room with locked arms comforting each other and simultaneously wiping their moist eyes with the tissues they had grabbed, in the living room, as they passed by the table with a tissue box sitting on it.

Both Jaime and Mr. Peterson stood up and greeted Mary. Mr. Peterson politely kissed her on the left cheek and returned to his seat. Jaime briefly embraced Mary, kissed her on both cheeks and also returned to the sofa where he had been seated. Mary and Dina both sat down next to Jaime.

Mary was anxious to understand how Vincent died. She looked at Dina and began to inquire, following her customary onslaught style of questioning, about how Vincent's death occurred. She said "Dina, Oh My God, how is it possible that Vincent is dead? How did it happen? Was it a car accident? Was he mugged? What happened?" Jaime, knowing that Mary will continue the bombardment of questions without providing a break and allowing the answers to the barrage of question to be answered , holding his arms ,interrupted her with three words, "I will explain"

Jaime pulled the New York Sun's article where he had read the details of the shooting from his trousers' right side pocket, and handed it to Mary. He then asked her to read the article. He further stated that most of her questions will be answered by the article. Mary took the newspaper article and began to read it while the Peterson's, Dina and Jaime remained silent:

Monday 6:00 AM
Reporter: Jim O'Neil
According to police sources
The police chief has assigned their gang crack team to continue investigation of this homicide.
End.

Mary looked up to Dina with teary eyes, hugged her, and began to cry again. They both continued crying in unison. After the crying was no more, Mary made eye contact with Dina, and with a blended expression of sisterly love and empathy, told Dina that she was staying with her tonight.

Dina was already uneasy about being alone in her bedroom tonight, lying in bed without Vincent at her bedside. Her parents will be staying with her this evening, but they would be in their bedroom and she, lonely and heart broken, on her bed by herself.

Mary explained that she will be glad to sleep over so that they can keep each other company, She further shared her feelings that their being together will be helpful for both of them to deal with what has happened, by sharing details and mutually learning to cope with the resulting emotional burden caused by the horrendous experience and and unmeasurable loss, which they both felt.

Dina has always enjoyed Mary's company. Her liveliness and optimistic perspective was always a very welcome quality and at times very much needed. Dina smiled lightly and told Mary that she would love to have her company tonight and hopefully tomorrow, when they go to Newark to make funeral arrangements. Mary response was a single word "Great", followed by, " I am always here for you"!

The five friends and relatives shared each other's company for a brief period before Jaime, recognizing that it was getting late, excused himself and told The Petersons, Mary and Dina that he had to go home to get his things ready for tomorrow's work routine. Jaime kissed the ladies, shook Mr. Peterson's hands, and departed from the familiar apartment. He began his familiar long walk through the city's streets towards his own apartment.

It had been a long and painful day for Dina and for her parents. They all decided to retire early and try to regain a reasonable level of energy to cope with the challenges that tomorrow would bring, as they make the necessary arrangements for Vincent's funeral.

The Petersons proceeded to their room. Dina and Mary went to the kitchen, hoping to find some coffee left over from dinner. Unfortunately, Dina's mother lived up to her reputation and the kitchen appeared as if it was Macy's store window's kitchen display. Everything had been "sterilized" and placed in the corresponding storage spot. The cleanliness and orderly condition of the kitchen discouraged the young women from pursuing, getting the craving satisfaction provided by drinking the caffeine brew.

The two friends went outside and sat on the building's front steps to try to enjoy the fresh and soft evening spring breeze and to share their secrets, absent of unwanted ears.

Dina shared with Mary her inability to tell Vincent, over the weekend, that he was going to be a father. She confided that Vincent's dying without knowing about her pregnancy made acceptance of his departure that much more difficult to deal with.

Mary interrupted Dina and asked her if the baby was okay. Dina began to cry and between sobs, told Mary that she lost her baby also. She told her that she lost the two most important things in her life; her love and the mirror of her love, her child.

Dina shared, "I feel that I have nothing left to live for." They both cried quietly again, shadowed by the remnants of the full moon, partially covered by puffy white and slow moving clouds, and caressed by the spring blossom fragrance of the early spring night.

The morning was young, approximately six thirty, and Dina's parents had already bathed and were getting breakfast ready. The smell of the freshly brewed coffee saturated the apartment's morning air. Dina, no longer accustomed to her senses being invaded by the rich coffee aroma while still sleep, was awakened by the inviting brew extracted from the rich Colombian coffee beans.

Dina and Mary got up, beautified themselves with the magic that only a woman understands and truly appreciate. They joined

Dina's parents, who were already eating their scrambled eggs with toast covered with freshly made blueberry jam, supplied by the nearby local store, and savoring the delicious coffee. They all greeted each other with a refreshing good morning! The girls occupied the empty chairs with the two plate settings and began to help themselves to the morning meal. Mr. Peterson served the coffee and Mrs. Peterson handed the milk to Mary.

While the two friends were eating their breakfast, Mr. Peterson informed them that he will like to catch the 8:15 am Ferry to the Terminal of Central Railroad of New Jersey (CRRNJ), at the Jersey City side of the Hudson River. He said should give them enough time to catch the Blue Comet train to Newark's Penn station. A taxi will then provide the final trek to their home on High Street.

Mr. Peterson shared his knowledge of state history by mentioning that the CRRNJ was located in a Jersey City area known as Communipaw Cove. A marsh and grassy area well known for its oyster beds, and the being the site of the Dutch Settlement's first ferry from the West side of the Hudson River to Manhattan.

The trip to the Peterson's home was uneventful, as the group successfully arrived at the CRRNJ station in time to catch the Blue Comet as it departed to Atlantic City, with a stop in Newark.

The Petersons and the girls arrived at their home, at ten minutes past ten, in the morning. Mr. & Mrs. Peterson went to their room to change their clothes, while Dina called the local cab company to schedule a pick up and take them to Spatola's Funeral Home. A quarter of an hour later, a yellow cab was waiting at the door for its passengers.

Dina entered the cab's rear door, followed by Mary. She then asked the driver to please wait for her parents, who will be coming out of the house momentarily. Mr. Peterson and his wife approached the cab. Mrs. Peterson opened the rear right door and, after asking Dina to shift to the center of the seat, she sat down next to the door, joining the two younger passengers already waiting. Mr. Peterson sat on the front passenger side. He instructed the driver to take them to Spatola's Funeral Home, located at 240 Mount Prospect Avenue. The driver gave a look and shook his head and responded, "I know, I know".

When the family and Mary arrived at the funeral home, they exited the cab and Mr. Peterson asked the driver to wait until they finished their business to take them back home. The driver responded, "OK, OK".

Mr. Peterson rang the door bell. A well dressed and closely shaven young man, dressed in a traditional funeral home black suit and black shoes, opened the door and welcomed his potential new clients with a customary professional greeting. Before Mr. Peterson was able to introduce himself, the young men said "Hello Mr. Peterson, How are you? Remember me, I am Nuncio". Mr. Peterson responded, "Off course I remember you. That is the reason I am here"

Nuncio invited the Peterson's party to come into the office and sit down. He quickly gathered additional chairs to accommodate the four visitors and potential customers. As Nuncio sat on the wheeled, high back office chair his potential clients settled on their seats. As they did, Angelo, Nuncio's brother, walked into the office and introduced himself to Mr. Peterson and to the rest of the family.

Angelo asked Mr. Peterson, "How may we help you?" Mr. Peterson response entailed a brief explanation regarding how his deceased son-in-law, Mr. Vincent Wagner, was caught, two night ago, in the middle of a gangster shoot out at the ferry boat landing in midtown Manhattan and was seriously wounded. He pointed to his daughter Dina, and told Angelo and Nuncio that her husband, Vincent, did not survive the shooting in spite of the doctor's heroic efforts to save his life. He then shared the sad news that

Seeking the Future

Vincent passed away yesterday, early morning, at approximately two o'clock, and that they needed assistance with the funeral arrangement.

Angelo, having significant experience in the funeral business, had already adjusted his facial expression, body language and demeanor to the accustomed projection of an empathetic and caring professional.

His words were soft, deliberate and purposeful. His objective was to sell his services in a manner that will provide comfort, help relieve the family's anxieties and trepidation, while balancing the grief and financial obligations associated with the loss of a loved one.

Angelo, with his expertise, is cognizant that the funeral arrangement's complexity and challenge is not inversely related to the family's financial strength. Thus, he tries, as discreetly as possible, early in the negotiations, to ascertain the family's financial flexibility and objectives.

Angelo reviewed the menu of available services with the family and provided a range of costs for their consideration. Mr. Peterson, recognizing that the entire process could be expedited by sharing the family's objectives, restrained by frugality as circumstances may permit. Thus, he told Angelo that the family desire is to have a service that maintains the necessary decorum, while avoiding unnecessary and unwarranted expenditures.

The message provided by Mr. Peterson could not be clearer. Consequently, Angelo suggested that they walk down to the casket sample display room to select the appropriate coffin.

They agreed, and went down to the cellar, a twenty four feet by twenty feet cavity, built during the conversion of the residence into a funeral home. As they reached the last step and turned left to the display section, they spotted four open caskets placed in a slight angle to maximize space and to avoid interference with the customers walking area.

Angelo explained to the family that they offer four styles of caskets; basic, good, better, and best. The caskets are displayed in reverse order. The first one, style "Best", was made of polished Mahogany. Its luster made it possible to see your faces silhouette on the wooden surface. It had six guilded metal handles, three on each side for the "pallbearers" to carry it. A crucifix, optional, was attached to the inside of the lid. A white sating material decorated the interior walls of the casket. The same quality material, shaped into a cushion and pillows, stuffed with goose down, covered the bottom and sides of the casket, sheltering the cadaver from the raw mahogany. A very discrete card, on top of the pillow, indicated that the cost of this unit was $1,250.00, a very significant sum.

The "Better" style was in the same price class as the "best" style. The interior decoration was of a slightly lesser quality, soft pink color, apparently decorated for the "gentler" sex. The side handles were black coated, plain cast iron. The price card on the pillow indicated a $1,000.00 cost for the casket.

The "Good" style was made out of polished oak wood with cotton material liner, cushions, and pillows. The casket exterior had been crafted to a lesser extend than the higher price styles. Built in slots were incorporated into the outside wooden panel for the pallbearers to carry it. The price for this model was $450.00

The last style, the "Basic", was very plain. It was a traditional gray painted pine box. The interior lining was made of inexpensive and loosely woven beige cotton material. The bottom cushion was stuffed with dried hay, as was the material covering the rawpine. This casket did not provide handles for the pallbearers, it needed to be held up from the bottom of the unit. The cost for this style was $150.00.

Dina was very confused and unsure as to what style to select. Her emotions and grief encourage her to want to select the best coffin for her love. The "Better" style cost a fortune that she could not afford, and she felt that the "Plain" style was beneath her husband's economic status. She continued asking herself what is the right thing to do?

Mary was next to Dina as they reviewed the available casket inventory and as Dina struggled with the decision she had to make. Dina looked at her friend with an inquiring look that prompted Mary to suggest that she consult her father. Dina squeezed her father's hand to get his attention. He looked at her, and she, with watery eyes and with the helpless look reminiscent of her childhood behavior, asked for her father's help in making a selection.

Mr. Peterson looked at his daughter and told her, "Darling, I know this process is not easy for you, or for anyone else. Please consider my perspective and it may help you make a decision: I subscribe to the philosophy that one should do all that can be done, or is wanted to be done for the ones we love when they are alive. Whatever we do after they are gone is done not for the intended recipient but rather for ourselves. People sometimes make unaffordable decisions or long term financial sacrifices for their departed soul, responding to inner remorse, perhaps trying to make up for a lifetime of neglectfulness, trying to express love and caring which was not adequately communicated to the person while alive, or fulfilling other people's expectations."

As Dina digested her father's viewpoint, he interrupted her and added, "I know that you loved Vincent very much, and he knows that as well. There is nothing you could do after his death to convey that unbridled love, which you did not already do and shared with him while he was alive. Choose the casket that is reasonable and yet provides the decorum that will make you comfortable, and that will satisfy some of the family and friends' expectations."

Dina understood her father's perspective and agreed with his philosophy. She told Angelo that she had decided to select the "Good" style for her husband's funeral service.

The group walked up to the office, where they reviewed the service options, made their selection, including date and time, and signed a contract for $2,000.00, minus a ten percent discount provided by Nuncio, a discount which Nuncio had arranged with his brother when the Petersons were downstairs in the display room selecting the desired model. The amount quoted included the cost of the casket, the funeral services, including one and one half days of viewing, the cemetery arrangements, and transportation of the deceased to the Church and to the cemetery afterwards. Angelo requested a $50.00 deposit, which Mr. Peterson rapidly extracted from his pocket and handed it to him.

Mr. Peterson, his family and Mary thanked Angelo and Nuncio, who patiently and professionally assisted them with the planning and logistics for Vincent's funeral service. They exited the Funeral Home, and boarded the waiting taxi which returned them home.

*

The taxi's experienced driver used his knowledge of the city to direct the vehicle from the Northeast section of Newark, not far from the beautiful Branch Brook Park to High Street, located in the Southwest section of the city. Branch Brook park was a favorite summer picnic destination for the Petersons, as well as for many other city families. This park was not only the first county park, but also one of the largest city parks in the country. The construction began in 1895 and in 1898 the public approved a $1.5 million dollar expenditure to continue its construction.

The afternoon occupied The Petersons and Dina contacting friends and family to communicate what Vincent's funeral service will be held, Thursday evening and all day Friday starting at 2:00PM until 9:00PM. They also shared that the interment will be in Hillside, at the Evergreen Cemetery, Saturday, at nine o'clock in the morning. Before any call was made to family and friends about the funeral arrangement, Mr. Peterson, together with his daughter, who would not be unable to hear the called party's comments, placed a call to Vincent's parents. As they explained the funeral arrangements and related schedule to Mr. Wagner, he wasted no time reminding Dina's father and insisting that he will assume all the costs associated with his son's funeral and internment. Mr. Peterson responded expressing the most sincere gratitude on behalf of his family and his daughter in particular. Once the call mission was fulfilled, both parties hung their receivers and the conversation ceased as they sadly stared at each other.

After her father hung up the receiver ending the conversation, Mary, who was only able to hear her father's comment, inquired the motive which prompted his expressions of gratitude on her behalf. Mr. Peterson, who intended to share Mr. Wagner's intent and insistence before his daughter asked, shared that Vincent's father will assumed all the cost's associated with the funeral.

Dina, who had been dealing with the emotional challenge of not only the lost of her beloved husband, but also the lost of the once growing seed in her womb, product of the that profound love and joy, which they shared, felt financially unburdened and deeply appreciated the partial sense of releif of not, also, having to deal with the challenges associated with Vincent's funeral arrangement costs.

After this most critical telephone call was terminated and prior to any other calls being made, Mary volunteered to contact the remaining members of the "Gang of Six" in the evening, and update them regarding Vincent's death and service arrangements.

*

The funeral service was about to begin as the sun started its westerly escape, and the flocks of Canadian geese invaded the sky flying in their magnificent horizontal "V" formation, to their evening retreat.

The parking lot at Spatola's Funeral Home had been empty until the arrival of the late model Ford sedan, owned by Gabriel, Mary's fiancé, who had driven Jaime, Cathy, Cathy's boyfriend, George, from Manhattan, for the service.

The four entered the funeral home and were professionally and assertively welcomed by Nuncio, who directed them to the room were Vincent's body had been laid for viewing. They entered the rear section of the viewing room through a double door. The room was approximately fifteen feet wide by forty feet in length. Twenty rows of eight wooden chairs each were perfectly aligned, beginning approximately ten feet from the casket. The chairs waited to accommodate those paying their respect. Two adjacent cushioned couches were located against the right wall between the casket and the third row of chairs. The room was conservatively decorated with soft, dark pastel colored curtains and wall paper. Landscape antique style paintings hung between the sets of gilded light fixtures on both walls.

Vincent's body rested as if sleeping on the polished oak wood, cotton lined, cushioned casket. His mother and mother-in-law sat next to Dina on the couch closest to Vincent's body. Dina's apparently never ending tears continued moisturizing her fancy kerchief. The ladies were all dressed in the traditional black dresses and their husbands, in matching black suits.

Mary sat on the first row and first chair right across from Dina. Gabriel, Jaime, Cathy, and George walked up the right side isle to where the relatives had been seated. They embraced, kissed and expressed their deeply felt condolences to Vincent's and Dina's parents.

They all gathered around Dina and Mary, who stood up, and as a group, hugged each other. The young ladies began to sob a symphony of sorrow, while the young men bravely attempted, but without success, to restrain the natural expression of grief.

The evening was a long, with abundant continuous expressions of empathy, sorrow, and understanding of the untimely and unexpected departure of a wonderful young man. Tears were shed by many, regardless of age and gender. Embraces and kisses were plentiful and spontaneous, as if they were the elixir that would cure the wounded hearts. Perhaps the real sedative that lightened the burden of the moment was exhaustion and the concern and effort to acknowledge the many expressions of sympathy, caring, and sharing of the sense of loss.

Dina's and Vincent's friends, recognizing the family's stress, provided greetings and introduction support whenever possible to relieve some of the social pressure from the grieving family members.

The Pastor, who married Vincent and Dina, arrived and was warmly greeted and welcomed by Dina and the couple's parents. He briefly spoke to the family before beginning the planned religious service. The pastor conveyed a message of understanding and sharing the families' grief, the extreme sense of loss, and the need to accept and overcome the anguish, with hope and peace and conviction that Vincent will welcomed in God's Kingdom.

During the religious service, the Pastor guided the grievers with prayers and reinforcement of the Christian faith, including the belief that upon our death, our soul will be welcomed in Heaven and peace and happiness will prevail for ever after.

As the end of the service neared, Gabriel held Mary's left hand and walked toward the front of the casket. Cathy and George, also holding hands, followed behind them. Jaime, and Dina followed all her friends. They gathered in front of the seventh member of the gang. His body lying peacefully in the Oak coffin, they bowed their heads, and each said a prayer to their God on behalf of their dear departed friend.

Jaime whispered a request on Dina's ear. She looked at him, and with an approving but very controlled loving smile, nodded positively to his request. Jaime, knowing Vincent's love for his country and his desire to fulfill his civic responsibility by serving in the military forces, extracted a small American flag on a miniature pole and placed it on Vincent's right hand, lying next to his body. A tear escaped from Jaime's right eye socket, a tear this time not for Vincent's but rather for a great nation who lost a dedicated, loyal and loving servant.

Jaime and Dina stood standing by Vincent's remains, after the others returned to the front row chairs, mentally revisiting all the pleasures and lessons gained from their friendships, She, as his loving wife, and he, as his considered best friend. He touched Vincent's and hands bid farewell to his good friend and confidant. He promised to do his best to help Dina handle and deal with her painful loss. He returned to the front row and sat there for the rest of the service.

Dina approached the open casket, knelt down, and said a prayer for the love that is no longer. Droplets of crystal clear expressions of her true love for Vincent escaped through her eyes, as she held his impacting very cold hands with hers. She laid the right side of her face on the smooth wooden surface, as if wanting to share her warmth with him and his with her, as they have cherished so many times before. Dina slowly raised her body, kissed Vincent's forehead and quietly told him, "I love you my Darling, and I always will". Dina stood up, raised her left arm to a horizontal position, and looked at her wedding ring. She kissed her wedding ring, pulled it from her finger, and gently placed it on Vincent's hand. She then whispered, "Darling, this ring signified our promise, to love and be faithful to each other until death do us part. I want you to take this ring with you as a symbol of my everlasting love for you, for this ring will remain engraved in my heart and you will always posses a very special place in my soul".

Dina kissed Vincent's forehead once again and returned uncontrollably tearful back to the couch with her family.

*

Saturday morning's weather contrasted significantly with that of the day before. It was dreary, misty and a penetrating coolness washed away the anticipated spring morning freshness. It was as if nature was acknowledging Vincent's loss and expressing its natural sorrow.

The family and friends gathered at Spatola's Funeral Home at eight in the morning. The pastor held a brief service, followed by the transfer of Vincent's body to the hearse, to be transported to The Evergreen Cemetery after a brief Church ceremony.

After the service was completed and the vehicles were lined up for the trip to church and cemetery, Gabriel, George, Jaime, and Mr. Peterson, who volunteered to served as pallbearers, proceeded to where the casket was located and witnessed the closure of the casket by the funeral director.

They wheeled the casket cart to the door and carried it out of the building into the back of the hearse, accompanied by the muffled cry of the loving friends and family which followed the procession.

Two hours later, the family and friend gathered in front of the Wagner's Mausoleum, each holding a red rose which, when deposited on the casket symbolized a final farewell and closure to a life that they once very much loved and shared with. A life that no longer was, a life that has been replaced with memories of love and lessons shared and learned.

The pallbearers carried the casket from the hearse. They walked slowly and carefully to the Mausoleum were the funeral director instructed them to place the casket on the floor, prior to placing it in the assigned crypt and, subsequently, permanently sealed by the cemetery staff.

The immediate family stood close by the Mausoleum entrance's door, surrounded by the family and friends. The Pastor read the interment prayer, blessed the remains, and all there gathered repeated the "Our father...,." prayer.

The funeral director thanked all attendees for their presence on behalf of the family, instructed them to walk in a file in front of the Mausoleum entrance where the open crypt with the casket with the resting remains could be seen, and to deposit their flower which they were holding, on the container that had been placed at the entrance to be deposited in the crypt prior to sealing it. The funeral director further instructed that upon depositing the flowers, all should return to their vehicle, as the interment service has been concluded.

The attendees kissed, expressed their condolences to the family again, and departed with tears in their eyes. Dina, her parents, Vincent's parents, and the five members of the gang of six stayed behind at the mausoleum, waiting to witness the sealing of the casket inside the crypt.

II

Already a week has gone by since Vincent's burial took place last Saturday. Dina had stayed home with her parents after the funeral in response to their strong insistence. The Petersons believed that their company and tender loving care was the needed prescription to help her deal with the loss of her husband and baby. Dina had not shared her body's rejection of the fetus with her parents. Mr. & Mrs. Peterson had decided not to broach the subject with Dina. Their belief was that Dina will share that great loss with them, at some future time, when she is emotionally ready to move on with her life.

Since returning home from the burial service, Dina's behavior has fluctuated between deep depression and appearance of some normalcy. Her food consumption has been negligible; the little that she has eaten had been primarily in response to her parent's encouragement and persistance.

Dina has spent most of time at her parent's house sitting by the window, and attempting to read a 1932 Pulitzer Prize winning novel by Pearl S. Buck titled "The Good Earth". Her father suggested that it would be a good read for her, he thought especially in her state of mind. She has been unable to distract her thoughts and allay her pain with the author's narration of human suffering and the character's resiliency to overcome life's sometimes harsh challenges. Instead Dina continued to look at the sky.

Sometimes brilliant, sometimes threatening, sometimes peaceful and serene, the sky provided Dina with a changing and soothing back drop as she revisits her previous life's adventures and fulfillment with the lover that she no longer has.

Mr. Peterson walked into the living room and sat next to Dina, bringing her back from her journey of the past. He kissed her on the forehead and, with an encouraging smile, asked her, "How are you feeling, darling?" Dina responded with a kiss on his right cheek. With a soft and wounded like voice told her father that she longed for Vincent very much. She added, only to put his mind at ease, "I will be fine, Dad!" A declaration that she wishes would be the case, but at this time she perceived it to be unreachable.

Mr. Peterson reminded her that for all practical purposes, her life just began. He told her the best strategy for her would be to return some sense of normalcy to her life. He reminded her that she has economic and employment responsibilities that need to be fulfilled, in particular, during the very difficult economic environment which the country is experiencing.

Dina's father suggested that, if at all possible, she should try to return to work on Monday. He reminded her that she has a good job as executive secretary, working for Mr. Brown at the Brown, Brown and Bookbinder legal office. He emphasized that her services are probably sorely needed in the office to handle all the depression related bankruptcy cases.

Mr. Peterson did not share with his daughter that his real motivation for encouraging her to return to work was his conviction that burying herself in her work will provide Dina the opportunity to heal her deep and painful emotional wounds and, hopefully, the emptiness she experiences, no longer having her partner. Mr. Peterson kissed Dina on the forehead, as he did before, and quietly exited the living room area. He left her, hopefully to digest his recommendation and, perhaps, begin the return to normalcy, where life's path may be flooded with honey and fragrances rather than rocks and thorns, as it now must feels for her.

Dina recognized her limited options and concluded that, as always before, her father's recommendation provides the most realistic and practical course of action for her to follow. She told her father she decided to return to Manhattan tomorrow morning and make the necessary preparations for her return to work.

Mary Richards called Dina before supper time as she has done every night since returning to Manhattan. She asked her how she was feeling and if she had decided which day she will be returning to the city. Mary Richards expressed her desire to get together with her as soon as possible. Dina shared with her friend the recent decision to return to Manhattan tomorrow.

Mary Richards was delighted to hear the news about Dina's return home. She felt that it was an indicator of a return to some sense of normality for her friend. Additionally, it will allow her, and the other members of the "gang" to have a quiet get together to remember Dina's birthday.

Latter that evening, after getting together with Gabriel and sharing the news about Dina's return, Mary Richards called Cathy and told her about Dina's plan. She also asked Cathy to share the good news with George as well.

Mary Richards waited for Jaime to call her from the public telephone to let him know about Dina. She had informed Jaime that she calls Dina every night before dinner and, since then, he has called her every evening to find out how she was handling her grief.

Dina finished talking with Mary Richards just as her mother called everyone to the dining room, with the anticipated announcement, "dinner is served"

The family gathered at the dinner table. The parents and siblings occupied all but one of the six chairs. The sixth chair belongs to Peter, the Peterson's oldest son, who is currently serving in the Air Force.

Dina's mother had made pot roast, mashed potatoes with brown gravy and sauteed spring squash, one of Dina's favorite meals.

Lucy, the youngest daughter, was very talkative during the meal as she normally is. She had just graduated from Central High School and was excitingly looking forward to begin her trainee job in the purchasing department of one of the most prestigious department stores in Newark, Bambergers.

Lucy had just received a letter from the Bamberger's Personnel Manager this afternoon, notifying her about having been selected for the trainee position. She proudly shared with her family that she was one of three candidates selected out of twenty five applicants remaining in the last round of interviews.

The trainee position excited Lucy, not only because the income stream will be very helpful to the family during this most difficult period, but, more so, because it will give her the opportunity to visit clothing and cosmetics show rooms in Manhattan, where she will be exposed to the latest fashions and fragrances. Lucy's secret ambition is to be a fashion designer. This job opportunity at the Bamberger's purchasing department will place her in a professional path related to the goals that she has set for herself.

The conversation at the dinner table was monopolized by Lucy's enthusiasm and job anticipation. Robert, a year younger than Lucy and a senior in high school interrupted Lucy's discourse and told the family that he was thinking about joining the Marines when he turns eighteen. Mr. Peterson, upon hearing this, emphatically told his son that he was very proud of his desire to serve in the armed forces. However, he insisted that Robert finish his senior year and graduate from High School before joining the military. Robert was not surprised at his father's reaction and dictate. It was indeed a reaffirmation of a previous response to his proving about his desire to join the "service".

Momentarily, the conversation ceased and the only prevailing sound was that of the silverware making contact with the colorful flower decorated flatware.

Dina did not eat one of her favorite meals with the same zest as she has in the past, nor did she participate in the family conversations. She was physically present but her thoughts were emigrating to the past while her siblings were dealing with the realities of the present and exploring the possibilities in the future.

The sound of a vacuum brought Dina back to the reality of the moment from her cerebral trip. She told her family that she has decided to go back to her apartment tomorrow morning and prepare herself to return to work on Monday.

Dina's mother yielded a gentle smile, projecting a satisfaction that perhaps the natural adjustment to life's challenging trial was beginning to take a hold for Dina.

Mr. Peterson looked at Dina's eyes, nodded his head, and told his daughter that she has made the right decision.

At eight in the evening, "on the dot", Jaime called Mary Richards and asked her the identical questions that he asks every night, "How is Dina doing? When is she coming home?"

Mary Richards told Jaime that Dina was coming home tomorrow morning, and that she is planning to return to work on Monday. She reminded Jaime that the "Gang" had not had the customary birthday get together for Dina and that it would be great if they could have it this coming Saturday night.

Jaime hesitated to reply to Mary Richard's suggestion. He did not want to disclose that he already made plans for that evening. Jaime had already made a commitment to go to the movies with Silvia, a young lady that he met at the evening school where he is taking English classes.

Silvia, a very friendly and vivacious young lady, sat next to Jaime in their class room.

Jaime has not developed any emotional attraction to Silvia, but he liked her fun loving personality. They decided to get together this Saturday evening to go see a new movie titled "Captain Blood", a swashbuckling adventure, starring Errol Flynn and Olivia de Havilland.

Jaime suggested to Mary Richards to change the get together to Sunday afternoon at his place. He will then have had the time to make chicken with rice and fried bananas, Dina's favorite dishes. Mary Richards told Jaime that she liked his suggestion as well as the Chicken with Rice fare. She promised to check with Dina and the others and let him know tomorrow after work.

Mary Richards called Gabriel to discuss Jaime's proposal to hold the get together for Dina Sunday afternoon at his place. Gabriel reminded her, with a mildly annoyed voice, that they had planned to go to the movies that afternoon to see the new "hot' film, Captain Blood. She told Gabriel, "you are right sweetheart, but we can always go another day!" Gabriel, unable to control his feelings, reminded Mary what he has told her a number of times, "you always want to change our plans when it comes to Jaime". He then followed with a cutting remark "I do not care. Do whatever you want!" Mary Richards' reception of her boyfriend's remarks was akin to cleaning a recent wound with alcohol. His comment penetrated her soul and added further bitterness to the exclusivity of sweetness, which months before engulfed their relationship.

*

This Friday Jaime arrived at the factory earlier than usual. Today was his last day as Line Supervisor and it was Alfred's last day before leaving to join the Marines.

Jaime wanted to provide Julia, the Assistant Line Supervisor, with additional instructions before turning over his responsibilities to her. He also needed to go over some of the record keeping requirements with Alfred to assure that continuity was maintained.

After talking to Julia, Jaime personally and individually thanked all the line operators for their past support. He also told them of his hope that they will continue to support him in his new roll. A kiss on both cheeks for each female operator sealed the gratitude that he was expressing.

When Jaime stopped by Mary's station, he was somewhat apprehensive, knowing her forwardness and persistent prompting for his response to her advances.

Today Mary's outfit was more provocative than usual. Her self packaging certainly emphasizes nature's generous and efficiently distributed gifts. It required Jaime's to muster self control, beyond what should be expected from a healthy young man.

Jaime thanked Mary, took a deep breath of air, and kissed her on both cheeks, assuring that his body language or his facial expression did not divulged his thoughts to her, thus possibly encouraging her expectations.

Once he finished talking to the line operators, Jaime gathered his personal things from desk and carried them to his new station, where Alfred was waiting for him. He and Alfred worked together for the rest of day.

It was early Friday evening and Jaime had already finished eating leftover white rice and a chick peas stew that he had prepared this past Wednesday. He was exhausted and very hungry, having to deal with the pressures of assuming his new responsibility.

As he was eating, Jaime concluded that he will be going to bed early tonight. Tomorrow, he thought, will be a hectic day shopping for Dina's get together and getting ready to go to the movies with Silvia. He found himself looking forward to getting together with Silvia and, perhaps, finding an opportunity to getting to know each other better.

Just as Jaime finished cleaning his dishes and putting them away, a habit inculcated into his behavior by his dear mother, the door bell rang. Jaime's curiosity was arising since he was not expecting any company. He walked to the door, opened it, and greeted the smiling visitor who, before he could say anything, asked if she could come in.

Jaime pleasantly surprised by Mary Richards' unexpected visit, prompted her to come in, and told her, "Mary", as he normally addresses her, "it is always a pleasure to see you! My doors are always open for you". She entered the apartment and sat on the taburete immediately across from the bedroom door.

Mary has always felt very comfortable around Jaime and at ease discussing subjects, which she would hesitate to discuss with most other people. Gabriel apparently perceived that relationship, and perhaps sensing that comfort level between the two friends, has on various occasions implied that her attraction to Jaime may be greater than platonic.

Jaime, knowing Mary's fondness for Cuban coffee, asked her if she would like some espresso, or perhaps café con leche, the inverse of the American coffee, a cup of hot milk with a shot of espresso.

Mary was unsure as to what she really wanted to accomplish, other than perhaps having a shoulder to lean on, and a good friend with whom she could share the romantic challenge that she was facing. She justified her visit to Jaime's apartment with the self excuse of wanting to confirm whether or not the other members of the gang agreed with the planned get together for Dina's birthday this coming Sunday afternoon. However, she knew quite well that the real reason for the visit was to be and to talk to her dear friend and confidant. She was depressed and needed a compassionate ear with whom she could share the burden and frustrations associated with a souring romantic relationship. Mary raised her sad face and made eyes contact with Jaime. Her eyes were moist and lacking the usual brilliance, reflected by their penetrating light brown pupils. Jaime needed no explanation, he knew that his friend was emotionally distressed and needed his attention.

Jaime suggested that, since it was Friday evening and since there was no work tomorrow, perhaps, they should begin celebrating the weekend with a Cuba Libre, thinking that, hopefully, having her favorite drink, the Cuban rum and coke, will help her relax a bit and motivate her to share whatever issue she is having difficulty dealing with and is emotionally defeating her usual "happy-go-lucky" attitude. Mary forced a half smile and told Jaime that his suggestion was perhaps just what she needed and that a Cuba Libre could be the trick to free her from an issue that she wanted to share with him. Jaime returned the smile, and took two tall drinking glasses from the shelf, over the sink.

As he began to gather the drink's ingredients, Mary got up and stood next to him trying to learn his trick making her favorite spirit. She asked him to explain, as he goes, how to make his Cuba Libre drink. Jaime told her that it is very easy to make, as long as you have the right ingredients, and make sure to use Bacardi Rum.

Jaime proceeded to explain how to make a Cuba Libre. He showed Mary the Bacardi bottle of rum, the lime, and the coke, and instructed her to prepare the drink. He told her to put four ice cubes in each of the glasses. Once that task was completed, pour rum to taste, but not to overdue it. He suggested that she use the height of two horizontal fingers as the measurement for the right amount of rum. He then told her to squeeze a quarter of the lime into each glass and to drop the spent lime pieces inside of each glass. He instructed her to fill the glass with Coca-Cola, to stir gently and briefly, and, finally, to add 3 or 4 of the washed mint leaves to the mixture as garnishment. He then concluded the instruction with "enjoy"!

Jaime picked up one of the glasses and gave it to Mary. He took the second glass, lifted shoulder high and offered a toast to the honorary Cuban for a job well done. They both sipped their drinks. Satisfied with the flavor and the rum strength, they returned to the kitchen table and sat down on the taburete next to each other. Mary's normal warm smile had partially returned.

Jaime, wanting to make it easier for Mary to share her concern, inquired about the status of the get together. Mary told Jaime that every one was in agreement for Sunday afternoon except for Dina, whom she had to contact tomorrow morning. She then said she will mention to Dina, that you are making chicken with rice. She further stated "Dina never turns down your chicken with rice".

Mary glass was already two thirds empty, a fact that surprise Jaime. Although she likes the Cuba Libre drink, Mary generally "nurses" her drinks and at most has a second drink, which she never finish during an evening gathering.

Jaime told Mary that he is looking forward to Sunday's gathering and suggested that she will need another drink, since her glass was almost empty. She looked at her glass, brought it to her beautifully color decorated lips, and gulped down the remaining elixir.

Jaime got up and began preparing two additional Cuba Libres for her and himself. As he mixed the ingredients, with his back to Mary temporarily, he asked her how she was doing. He asked if there was anything bothering her and then told her that his ears were available for her if she needed it. He further stated that she appears to be carrying a serious burden and that, perhaps, it might be helpful to give it an outlet rather than keeping it imprisoned and fermenting within herself, and possibly getting out of control.

He turned around with the two replacement glasses, and noticed that tears had escaped from her gorgeous eyes rapidly rushing down each of her cheeks, as if trying to hide before being discovered by Jaime. Her eyes were closed as if wanting to conceal her pain from her friend. Her head moved down slowly both of her hands moved rapidly towards her face to provide support, to shelter the expression of grief accompanying her now unbridled tears.

Jaime placed both drinks on the table in front of her, sat next to her, and gently lifted her head with his right hand, which he placed underneath her lower jaw, hoping to make eye contact. She lowered her hands, looked at Jaime and sobbingly told Jaime "Gabriel does not love me any more". Jaime asked her, "why do you feel that way?" Mary responded, "things have changed". Mary Richards fixed her eyes on Jaime's once again and, unexpectedly, hugged him with an intensity and needfulness never before experienced by Jaime. Jaime returned the hug with his left arm, and with his right hand caressed her fragrant and beautiful brunette hair. They both hugged silently, and the longer they continued sharing the comfort of their mutual affection and warmth, the less they were willing to cease its rewards.

Jaime, resisting the natural impulse and its potential consequences, began to disengage from the physical expression of compassion and understanding. In a tone, sharing his concern and desire to help, asked, "why do you feel that Gabriel does not love you anymore?". Mary picked up her glass and continued drinking her Cuba Libre at the same pace as before. Jaime reminded Mary to take it easy with the drink, that the name may be Cuba Libre, meaning free Cuba, but that if the liquor gets a hold of you, the only thing that you will be free of is your self control. Mary smiled at Jaime and told him, "Jaime, this is one of the things I like about you. You are always looking out for me. Besides, I would not mind loosing my self control with you"

Jaime smiled and proceeded to focus the conversation on the relationship problem which was grieving Mary, while continuing to consume the volatile concoction. He asked her to explain the rationale that is leading her to the conclusion that Gabriel doesn't love her anymore. Mary told Jaime that during the last three months Gabriel's behavior towards her has been changing and she has been feeling ignored. He has been visiting her less often than before. When they are together, he is often more interested in the basketball or baseball games than her. She added that they used to talk about their future together and now, when she approached the subject, he changes the conversation as if not interested in our future.

Mary drank the last drop of her second Cuba Libre and held her glass upside down, hinting her readiness for another round. Jaime got up to prepare another set of drinks. As he mixed the third round of Cuba Libre, Jaime asked Mary if it is possible that Gabriel had gotten a part time job or maybe if he was taking night courses, thus having less time to get together with her. Jaime and Gabriel, although members of the "gang", have not really connected very well and have not socialized outside of their group's get together. Thus, Jaime feels ill equipped to know what is going on with Gabriel, and respond accordingly to Mary's grievance. Mary told Jaime that neither was true. Gabriel did not get a part time job nor is he attending evening classes.

Jaime returned to the table with the fresh drinks and sat across from Mary. It was a premeditated and defensive move against the forces of temptation, nourished by the weakening resolve induced by the increasing liquor consumption.

Mary did not say anything to Jaime, but she wanted him next to her. She was disappointed that he sat across the table. She told Jaime that Gabriel no longer shows the passion for her as he did before. She said "I long for Gabriel's caressing and his physical desire of me". She added, "I feel that Gabriel is looking for an excuse to break up". Mary briefly hesitated before sharing that last night Gabriel, again, implied that my interest on you may be greater than a platonic relationship. She hesitated once again, and asked herself if she shared Gabriel's implication purely for

Seeking the Future

openness sake with Jaime, or if she shared it as a trial balloon to determine his reaction. She concluded that both reasons were most likely applicable.

Jaime was very surprised by Mary's assertion of the status of her relationship with Gabriel. He was under the impression that everything was "wine and roses". Perhaps, he thought, they just had a lover's quarrel and Mary is allowing a self fulfilling prophecy to become reality. His thoughts continued, "in any event she is a very attractive women that could knock any guy of his feet, including myself."

Jaime was trying to keep up with Mary's Cuba Libre consumption. At the same time, he was trying to help his friend deal with an apparent, broken, amorous relationship. After almost three Cuba Libres Jaime's mental agility was decelerating, since he is not much of a drinker.

Jaime looked at Mary, told her to be patient with Gabriel and to find the right opportunity to discuss her concerns regarding the future of their relationship. He told her to do her best to have a open and amicable discussion, absent of any animosity or blame placing. He emphasized that he was sure that they will be able to right any concerns and move forward with a happy and growing relationship.

Mary looked at Jaime, acknowledged his recommendations, and told him, "Jaime you always find the right words to put my mind at ease. That is why I love you so much". She got up from her taburete, walked around the table, a bit insecure from the effect of the rum, sat next to Jaime and gently kissed him on his lower cheek next to his lips.

Jaime also was carrying a burden which he needed to share, and perhaps this was a good time to unload it from his conscience with his good friend Mary. Since Vincent's killing, he has wanted to share with Mary, a secret that has become burdensome and somewhat conflictive, his moral values, to share a break a promise. He had given his word to his friend, Vincent, not to share his terminal illness with Dina or any one else. Yet, he feels that it may ease Dina's pain to know that destiny had already dictated the end of Vincent's life. And perhaps, the Ferry Boat tragedy may have been a God sent gift, which saved Vincent and Dina from the agony and suffering associated with his life slowly fading away as the vicious disease gradually and methodically destroys each human cell, protecting his being, and eventually life itself.

Jaime looked at Mary without saying anything for a moment, then asked her for advice on how to best handle an internal conflict. He shared with her that Vincent had contracted an advanced, untreatable, and terminal bone cancer condition. He also told her that the doctors' prognostication was a life expectancy of less than six months.

Upon hearing Jaime's confession, Mary finished the remaining drink in her glass, hugged Jaime and began to weep quietly. Jaime gently held her shoulders and slowly moved her body away from his until he could see her eyes. He then asked her whether or not he should share that information with Dina. Mary, without giving it much thought, perhaps due to the liquor effect, told Jaime that it was ironic that the loving couple kept such significant and impacting secrets from each other; Vincent keeping his onerous health condition from his loving wife, and keeping the fact that she was carrying his child from him.

"Oh no" were the only words that Jaime could muster upon hearing the unsuspected news. Considering that having a child without the father will be a significant challenge, both economical and emotional for his dear friend, Dina. He then realized feeling a moral responsibility, that because of his close friendship with Vincent, to be supportive of, Dina and the expected child. An additional and unexpected responsibility now weighted on his shoulder, he thought.

Jaime, justifying his good friend's action of not disclosing his health condition to his wife, explained that Vincent intended to tell Dina. He related that their trip to Coney Island was planned to provide the setting to come clean the sad news. They had such a wonderful time that Vincent did not want to spoil it by telling Dina that he was likely going to die within six months from cancer.

Mary told Jaime that Dina also wanted to share the news with Vincent but she wanted to wait until he joined the armed forces because she did not want her expecting condition to have been an impediment to his plan. She said, also, that Dina knew how important it was for Vincent to serve his country, and that she did not want the baby to have been the obstacle for the fulfillment of that dream.

Jaime found himself needing another drink. He got up and followed the same procedure as he had done the previous three times. This round killed that bottle of rum. Fortunately, he had another bottle remaining to "be tackled", if circumstances required it.

Jaime brought the two new full glasses of Cuba Libre to the table, looked at Mary and waited for her response to his dilemma. He looked at him and said, "I guess you do want my opinion?" He replied, "Indeed, I do". She thought for a brief moment and told him that Dina should know about Vincent's bone cancer. That it may help her better deal with the loss of her love. Jaime nodded in agreement.

They both continued drinking their Cuba Libre as if trying to find an escape from life's reality, or perhaps, to neutralize the inhibition, which was blocking an increasingly boiling desire to satisfy their mutual carnal appetite.

After finishing the fifth glass of an extra strong Cuba Libre prepared by Mary, they both got up from the table to refill their glass again. Mary's glass slipped from her hand hitting the the tiled floor and breaking into many small pieces. Simultaneously her legs' muscles, weakened by the high doses of alcohol, something that she is not accustomed to, surrendered their role and she began to fall. Jaime, ignoring the slowness of his motor movement, quickly captured her body and prevented it from crashing onto the floor over the broken glass. In the process of holding her body, to save her from falling, Jaime held Mary close to his body. She threw her arms over his shoulders and, as if rewarding Jaime for saving her, she passionately kissed him on the lips. Jaime responded with the same passion.

The many Cuba Libres, which they had already consumed, had mitigated any inhibitions, which may have existed between the two friends freed this couple's physical desire and drive for sexual fulfillment. They both pursued this new and mutual adventure with all the energy and passion their young body and strong hearts could muster until the combination of alcohol and pleasure surrendered their body into a deep and restful sleep.

Next morning, the sound of the truck's horn, crowding the earlier silent street, simultaneously awoke Mary and Jaime and, fleetingly they looked at each other as if asking what have we done?. The splitting headache, from the Cuba Libre's hangover reminded them of the night before, and prompted both to acknowledge to themselves what had happened. Jaime began to apologize to his her. She, on the other hand, placed her index finger on his lips and told him that there was no need for apology. She lightly kissed his lips, told him that she had a wonderful time, and what happened will remain between them.

Jaime returned the kiss, delivering it with passion and desire. Mary told him that she had to return to her apartment before Gabriel calls her, as is customary on Saturday mornings.

She gathered her garments; thrown throughout Jaime's room the evening before, and quickly exited the bedroom to get dressed as Jaime admired her beautifully shaped body as never before, and possibly as never again.

A few minutes later, Mary returned to the bedroom, fresh, radiant, and with a smile projecting complete satisfaction and fulfillment. She kissed Jaime on the lips and quietly exited his apartment.

As Mary crossed the street and briskly walked towards her apartment, she began to experience a bit of compunction for what had happened the night before. The feeling of satisfaction and fulfillment was gradually replaced by regret and guilt. Their action was not only an infidelity to Gabriel, but also betrayal to her values.

She continued dwelling on her self guilt and searching for an acceptable justification for their actions. Mary rationalized that the blame was to be assigned to Bacardi's Rum and its power to erase inhibitions and cause uncontrollable behavior. In her mind, she and Jaime were innocent victims of the spirit's powers.

Jaime, recognizing his demanding agenda for the day, got up, showered, and dressed in record breaking time. He decided to get a cup of black coffee at the corner deli instead of delaying his tasks by making breakfast at home. He needed to deal with the remaining emotional and physical consequences from last night's adventure, confirmed by the splitting headache from the tropical sugar cane bi-product, that he and Mary liberally, and abundantly, indulged together last night.

After drinking his black coffee and experiencing a slight relief from his hangover, Jaime called Silvia to confirm the late afternoon movie date and to coordinate their meeting place. Silvia was happy to hear Jaime's voice and told him "I am glad you called, I am very much looking forward to our getting together this afternoon". After hanging up with Silvia, Jaime took a mental inventory of the ingredients needed to prepare the Chicken with Rice. Since there will be six people, including himself, he needed to add extra rice. He did not have enough rice at home. He did have the necessary condiments: oregano, ground cumin, ground white pepper, pimentos for garnishing, and a can of peas for color and flavor. He needed to purchase rice, olive oil, onions, garlic, red bell peppers, a fresh tomato, red vinegar, tomato paste, and saffron in addition to the fresh killed chicken.

Jaime walked through the open market and purchased the needed ingredients, except for the fresh killed chicken he normally buys at the butcher across the street from the corner deli. He began his six block walk, carrying the bags loaded with all the "goodies" needed to prepare the Chicken with Rice and fried bananas.

Jaime finally reached the Polish butcher, his arms a bit strained by the weight of his purchases. The butcher greeted him with a heavy and different accent, and with a sincere welcoming smile. Jaime always has enjoyed walking into Benny's Butcher Block. The smoked Kielbasa and the Kiszka, the black colored blood sausage, hanging from the racks, always delights his vision and awakens his appetite. In addition, they reminded him of similar products in his homeland, in particular the Kiszka, which is very similar to the Morcilla, a delicious blood sausage, which his mother prepared on special occasions.

Benny wrapped the chicken with the white waxed paper, which he generally uses, and handed it to Jaime's order, to be added to the bag holding the other purchases. After paying for his merchandise, Jaime returned home to begin preparing the promised menu for tomorrow's get together.

As he began to gather all the ingredients, Jaime, once again, reviewed all the items required and realized that he did not have any beer. The malt beverage is a key ingredient that gives the dish a tangy and distinctive flavor. Jaime, once again, left his apartment to purchase a very important component of his popular chicken with rice recipe, the beer. Upon his return, he will get all of the ingredients ready to be prepared tomorrow morning, after he returns from Church.

Jaime decided to go to the local corner bar and purchase a bottle of Ballantine Ale, a brand that he has usually purchased, for it was his friend's favorite beer. As he thought of getting the beer, and of Vincent, Jaime recalled that almost every time that he offered Vincent Ballantine Ale, he would be reminded that it was brewed almost a stone's throw away in the Ironbound section of the Eastern most part of the city of Newark. He smiled, having remembered his friend's idiosyncrasy.

Mary Richards was at home most of the day taking care of her domestic duties and talking to her friends on the telephone. She called Dina, and mentioned that she and Gabriel will pick her up with his car and take her over to Jaime's apartment tomorrow afternoon. She had not discussed her plan with Gabriel, but she was confident that he will be agreeable with it.

Gabriel is expected to arrive at Mary Richards', and go to the movies to watch Captain Blood later in the afternoon. This movie is a remake of one of Wagner Brothers silent films.

Yesterday, when Gabriel expressed his annoyance at having to change their movie plan, Mary Richards suggested that they go to the movies early Saturday evening instead.

Gabriel called Mary Richards an hour before it was time to pick her up and profoundly apologized to her for having to cancel their date. He told Mary Richards "darling I am not feeling well. If you do not mind, let's postpone going to see the movie until next Saturday". Mary Richards asked " is there anything that I can do for you? Why don't I come over to your apartment and keep you company?".

Gabriel responded negatively to Mary Richards' suggestion and justified his reaction by explaining to her that he would be fine, that he does not want her to be exposed to whatever virus has affected him. He also told her "Darling it will be too much of a hassle for you to come way up town to my place. It is really not necessary". Mary Richards told Gabriel that she understood his. She told him, "make sure that you take care of yourself and call me if you need anything". She added "I love you very much and will miss being with you tonight" Gabriel responded with a somewhat detached tone "I understand. I will be fine, don't worry", and hastily hung up the telephone, as if wanting to escape. The cancellation of their date, Gabriel's excuse, and the aloofness of the telephone exchange reinforced Mary Richards' negative perception regarding the future of her relationship with Gabriel. Her female intuition continued to sway her consciousness to believe that another woman has diverted Gabriel's attention and affection away from her. Gentle tears dripped from her eyes as the feminine combativeness and revengefulness characteristics were awakened within her soul. "I will not forgive him for this", was the message engraved in her unforgiving, cerebral database.

Without much hesitation, Mary Richards picked up the phone one more time and called her friend Dina. She has sought, in the past, Dina's council regarding her intuition and concerns about the direction that her relationship with Gabriel was taking. Dina has counseled Mary Richards to be patient and that, perhaps, her inferences regarding Gabriel's behavior may have been wrongly perceived. Dina has told Mary Richards, on various occasions, that when she has seen Gabriel and her together, Gabriel has always demonstrated a high degree of affection towards her and an apparent genuine devotion and enjoyment of her company.

After Mary Richards related Gabriel's date cancellation and the absence of the customary warm and anticipated lover's telephone exchange, Dina exerted herself trying to ease her best friend's love created an emotional crisis.

Mary Richards listened to Dina's calm and conciliatory rationalization of Gabriel's behavior, and thanked her for her understanding. Then, Mary Richards asked her friend Dina for a favor. Mary Richards had decided, while listening to her friend's conciliatory effort, to go to see the film Captain Blood, starting the new and sexy English actor named Errol Flynn, this afternoon. "To hell with Gabriel", she thought.

Dina, unaware of Mary Richards' decision asked her, "What do you need?", Mary Richards responded, "Let's go to the movies now". Dina, caught off guard by the surprising request, hesitated before answering. She told Mary Richards, in a sympathetic tone but convincingly uncooperative, "I cannot go to the movies; I just buried my husband a week ago!"

Mary Richards was ready for Dina's response. While calling Dina she rationalized her reaction and composed a response to counteract it.

Mary Richards told Dina that she understood and shared her feelings. She said to Dina, "It will be very good for both of us to get out of the house and find and outlet from our mutual grief." Mary Richards mentioned to Dina that she is sure Vincent would have loved to see that movie and that, besides, the movie was an adventure and not a musical or a comedy. Mary Richards persisted, up to the point of begging her friend to accompany her. Dina was unable to continue declining Mary Richard's pleading and agreed to accompany her to the movie. She asked Mary Richards what was the name of the movie, where it was playing, and at what time.

Mary Richards responded that it was Captain Blood, starting the new sexy English actor, named Errol Flynn. The movie is playing only at the Liberty Theater, located at 228W 42nd Street, near Eighth Avenue. The movie was starting in an hour and a half.

The Liberty Theater was in the heart of Manhattan's entertainment center, which was coincidentally, halfway between Gabriel's and Mary Richards' apartment.

Dina recognized that they had to get going if they were to get to the theater in time. She told Mary Richards to get ready, that she will take a taxi and pick her up at her apartment on the way to the theater.

Mary Richards began the task of freshening up, a very easy process for a young women with a smooth and velvety like complexion, framed by a shinny and soft brunette color, head of hair, resting on the back of her upper shoulders. Her naturally light caramel colored lips, enhanced by a bright red lipstick together with her light brown eyes, completed the facial image normally seen on the "silver screens".

Dina arrived at Mary Richard's apartment, a bit sooner than expected, since traffic was lighter than usual. She asked the driver to please blow the horn three times to signal her friend that hey had arrived, and she was waiting in the taxi for her. waiting for her. Mary Richards grabbed her pocketbook, the apartment's keys, and rushed out of the house, as if she was the little girl of past years rushing to catch the ice cream man before he could turn the corner.

The ride up Broadway Avenue was as Dina anticipated. The trolleys, vehicles, and horse-drawn carriages' traffic was quite heavy as they got closer to the theater. Fortunately, not as heavy as it would have been during a weekday. Dina felt comfortable that she and Mary Richards will reach the theater district in sufficient time to purchase the tickets, purchase snacks and find the assigned seat.

It was quarter to five when the two young women reached the theater and joined the queue to purchase their tickets. The ticket line wrapped around the block when the two friends joined it. As they got closer to the ticket booth, a quarter of a block away, Mary Richards spotted Jaime getting tickets from the ticket clerk, and then walking to and joining an attractive young women who, apparently, was waiting on the side of entrance for him. Immediately, two thoughts became predominant in Mary Richards mind; to have found out the reason Jaime did not want to hold

Seeking the Future

the "gang" get together today and her secret desire wanting to be the young lady accompanying him to the movies.

Mary Richards turned to Dina, pointed to where Jaime and his companion were standing. She remarked to Dina that she hoped that Jaime will not get too tired tonight to make the Chicken with Rice tomorrow. Dina focused her attention to where Mary Richards was pointing, and saw Jaime and a young women standing there waiting to be let into the theater. Dina unsuccessfully waived at Jaime, hoping to catch his attention.

The two friends finally reached the ticket booth, with two minutes to spare, before lights out. They entered the theater and choose the right, red carpeted isle in search for two adjacent seats. The theater's seats were almost completely occupied, and Dina spotted two seats in the middle section, three quarters of the way back from the silver screen. Dina and Mary Richards felt fortunate to find such good seats. They hurriedly walked to take possession of the empty seats, excusing themselves from the patrons already comfortably settled and enjoying their popcorn treat.

Once sitting down, Mary Richards began to scan the audience, trying to locate where Jaime was sitting. Dina, not having been at the Liberty theater before, was admiring the velvet, dark blue curtains decorating the side walls of the theater and the magnificent crystal chandelier hanging from the ceiling's center.

The enjoyment of the décor, highlighted by the chandelier's beauty, was tempered by the recollection of a horror movie which she recently saw, together with Vincent, depicting an opera scene where the cable of the chandelier detached from its anchor, and fell on the helpless audience.

Mary Richards, after carefully checking the audience, in back as well as in the front, spotted Jaime and his companion sitting on the two seats next to the left isle, two rows forward. Her eyes focused alternated between the previews being shown on the screen and Jaime's silhouette.

Dina continued admiring the building's aesthetics and decorations. She especially liked the dark blue velvet curtains framing the guilded pillars and equally spaced guilded and crystal wall lamps. Dina was engrossed on the enjoyment of the theaters pleasantness. She decided to visually visit the entire theater area one more time before the lights were completely deemed.

As Dina turned her body to the center rear of the theater, from where the projection lights originated, and began to admire the fine workmanship combination of wood carvings and painting, she instantaneously froze. Sitting on the middle of the last row, against the rear wall, was Gabriel with another woman. Dina felt a dagger of betrayal penetrating her heart, as is it was she who had been injured, and as if it was she, whose trust had been severely violated.

Gabriel had wounded Mary Richards through Dina. By his action, Gabriel has placed a moral burden on Dina at a time when her strength has been exhausted by destiny's treachery when it took away her love.

The newsreel began with pictures of civil unrest in Spain and long lines of unemployed men applying for a few openings at the Bayonne Naval base. Dina turned back towards the movie screen, and tried to focus her attention on the images projected on the screen.

Mary Richards continued alternating her sight between the newsreel and Jaime's back until Dina whispered, "what are you looking at?" She responded that she had spotted where Jaime was sitting and then focused her sight on the silver screen. Mary Richards continued for the rest of the showing, looking at Jaime and his companion, utilizing her peripheral vision to avoid further disclosing her interest on the unaware couple.

Dina's show enjoyment was also diminished and partially disrupted by the internal conflict she was facing. Should she ignore what she has witnessed and shelter her dear friend from the pain that her knowledge will cause and the impending breakup of her relationship with Gabriel, as a sure consequence? Or should she immediately share her discovery and protect her friend from possibly a greater future grief?

Halfway through the movie, depicting the hero overcoming the power of the evil character, Dina decided that Mary Richards had to be told. She concluded that it would be a violation of their sisterhood not to forewarn her about the treachery perpetuated by Gabriel.

As the movie stopped for a short intermission to allow the projector operator to change reels, Dina whispered to Mary Richards, "Don't look now, but promise me that you will not say or do anything!" Mary Richards, puzzled by Dina's mysteriousness, quickly responded, "Surely, I promise!"

The two friends' isle had emptied as all the patrons had exited to the lobby to purchase refreshments and relief their organs. Dina got up, grabbed Mary Richards' arms and asked her to accompany her to the ladies room. As they began to walk towards the exit, Dina whispered into Mary Richards' ears, telling her to look at the couple "necking" on the middle of the last row of the center section, against the back wall. Mary Richards, somewhat curious about Dina's secretiveness, looked were instructed and saw a couple "necking". The fellows face was partially hidden under the girl's long blond hair. The dimmed lights made it difficult for Mary Richards to recognize the subject.

Mary Richards looked at Dina with an interrogatory looked and asked her, "What do you want me to see?" Dina responded, "look again". Gabriel had finished nibbling at his companion's left earlobe, and was targeting the taste of her lipstick. Mary Richards turned her head towards the rear wall, as instructed by her friend, and immediately recognized her treacherous boyfriend. She pulled her hand away from Dina's hold and walked briskly towards the rear wall, with Dina following four steps behind.

Gabriel, fully focused on his desire to conquer his new

friend's inviting moist lips was oblivious of the torment that was approaching. Mary Richards rapidly entered the last row. Before the couple, intensely distracted by their mutual physical attraction could realize that they had company, Mary Richards stood in front of him. Gabriel, thinking that a patron was trying to return to their seat, moved his body and looked up. As his head moved up to make eye contact with the patron's face, Gabriel recognized who it was. His face turned equally pale to the shade of silver screen. His vocal cord could not create an audible sound. Likewise, Mary Richards could not put together the desired combination of words that would carry a strong enough potion of the venom that she was feeling for Gabriel, and which she wanted to discharge at this moment. Mary Richards looked at Gabriel with an incomparable disdain. If her eyes could only project the power of the hate and antipathy that she was feeling at the moment, Gabriel would be turned into ashes. She raised her right hand, swung it back, and using all her physical strength, fueled by witnessing a lover's betrayal, slapped Gabriel with such force that its echo reverberated throughout the theater. It prompted the remaining audience to turn around and witness the live human drama that was taking place on the back row.

Mary Richards walked away silently and joined Dina, who was waiting for her on the isle by the end of the rear row. They both walked into the lobby and disappeared into the ladies restroom so that Mary Richards could touch up her previously professional like makeup, partially washed down her cheeks by the many tears flowing from their reservoir. The last tears that, she promised herself, would be shed on Gabriel. All that remained for him in Mary Richards' heart, was absolute disdain.

Dina and Mary Richards would not discuss in great detail what had just happened in the theater, for they knew that curious, receptive ears in the lady's room, are always trying to tune into any "juicy" conversation. Dina discretely congratulated her good friend for what she considered to have been a very effective and well deserved response to a treacherous behavior.

Gabriel sat next to an empty seat for the rest of the evening, his "new adventure" concluded. From what had happened, and after talking to Mary Richards in the lobby, as she and her friend were returning to their seats from the lady's room, she was not seeking a "one night stand" and Gabriel's moral fiber based on what she just learned, was beneath her expectations and not worthy of her emotional involvement. The two friends sat down on their assigned seats, and uneventfully watched the second half of the film.

At the conclusion of the film, as Dina and Mary Richards followed the crowd rushing to exit the theater, they were spotted by Jaime. He grabbed Silvia's hands and tried to rush through the multitude with his date being pulled from behind. Jaime and Silvia managed to reach Dina and Mary Richards, as the two girl friends had quickly exited the theater's door to get away from the unwelcome noisy and pushing crowd.

The two friends were walking on the sidewalk, right below the theater's Marquee, when Jaime touched Dina's shoulder to get her attention. Dina stopped, turned around and realized that it was Jaime who had gently got their attention. Before she could say anything, Jaime's face filled with a genuine smile as he moved his face towards Dina's left cheek and exchanged the traditional greeting with his friend. Mary Richards also turned around and recognizing her dear friend greeting Dina, anticipated an equally welcome, if not more so, greeting from Jaime.

Jaime gently placed his right hand on Mary's by right shoulders, and lightly kissed both of her cheeks intentionally, projecting the identical attention that he shared with Dina. He then introduced his date, Silvia, to both girls. He followed the introduction with an explanation that Silvia and he both attend Evening School, trying to improve their English grammar, and both share the same English class.

Mary and Dina politely, but curiously, said hello to Silvia. Mary could not help herself any longer, and with a smile stated "I guess you both must do a lot of home work together." Silvia, recognizing the implication of Mary's statement, did no hesitate to respond with a measured smile, "Not really, but I would not mind!".

Silvia wanted to make sure that she conveyed, and Mary Richards understood her potential interest in pursuing Jaime.

Dina was aware that Jaime did not own a vehicle, and although she was not sure about Silvia, decided to ask Jaime and Silvia if they would like to join them for an after movie snack before returning home. She also suggested to both of them that, perhaps afterwards, they could return downtown in a shared taxi, if they were planning to travel in that direction when they finished their snack. Jaime asked Silvia if she had any objection to share a taxi with them when returning home. Silvia preferred not to sharing his attention with Mary Richards and Dina, a feeling which she kept to herself. She responded with a smile, "Yes, off course", in an effort to satisfy her friend and date's request. She continued to emphasize her positive response by saying that she had no objection. She then turned her face to make eyes contact with Dina before thanking her for her thoughtfulness and opportunity for them to get to know each other better.

The foursome began walking away from the theater while discussing where to go to share company and enjoy the anticipated snack. Silvia suggested that they go to a Horn & Hardart Automat. She shared, having been told by one of her teachers, that it is a very nice and reasonable place to snack and or eat at. Silvia further related that, according to her teacher, the restaurant chain opened the Time Square's first automat, an automatic food service promoted with the slogan "Less Work for Mom" over twenty years ago. Her teacher also mentioned that the automat was a very popular concept because it offered a menu of reasonably priced and good quality staples, such as macaroni and cheese,

Seeking the Future

baked beans, and a variety of sandwiches, hot meals, and delicious desserts, as well a hot and cold drinks without having to wait for preparation. Jaime interjected and said that he had read a recent article acknowledging the success of the Automat concept during these economic depression years. He further shared that according to the article, the self service approach, displaying the hot and cold fares in individual cubicles with glass doors, thus providing self access for the consumers, after depositing the required number of nickels, was readily accepted.

The competitive pricing facilitated by, reduced labor costs, resulting from order taking and serving staff reduction, facilitated by providing customers the ability to choose their food and helping themselves by removing their selection from the individual glass cubicles, after inserting the required payment on the provided slot, together with the curiosity of experiencing the novelty like characteristic of the concept, contributing to its success. The group decided to follow Silvia's recommendation, and accordingly proceeded to their snack destination.

Once they arrived and entered the Horn & Hardart Automat, each took a metal tray and placed it on the silver metal rails, running parallel and waist high, along the far wall in front of the glass cubicles, where the food was on display awaiting for its hungry consumers.

The offerings were grouped by categories and identified with a large letters sign about each section: Sandwiches, Pies, Pastries, and Beverages were at the far end of the display

The four skipped the hot food area and proceeded to the pastries section. They examined the appetizing selection and decided to have apple pie and coffee.

They had forgotten, or likely not realized before hand, the cubicle door opening mechanism required the insertion of coins, a sufficient quantity of which they did not have.

Jaime, asking his friends to wait by the area, walked to Automat's attendant and asked her to change three dollars into coins to purchase their snacks. The elderly lady quietly and quickly took the three one dollar bills in exchange for the coins that she handed to him.

Jaime, demonstrating his love for ice cream, intended to also purchase a dish of vanilla ice cream to compliment the warm apple pie, which he had selected. All but Silvia hoped the pie which they would be selecting would provide the same gratification as the unforgettable treat, which they had last summer when Mary's Mom made her famous apple pie during their visit to the farm.

Jaime returned to the front of the pie display section and began to deposit coins in the slot of each of the girl's selections. Once all four had taken possession of their apple pie and Jaime of his ice cream and pie, the group moved to the coffee dispenser to get a cup of the popular Horn & Hardart coffee. Once they finished their selection, they all walked to and sat at a nearby empty table. Mary Richards made sure she sat next Jaime, and near the glass window, which provided a memorable Times Square view, particularly for the many tourists that frequented the famous Manhattan destination. As they enjoyed their delicious and refreshing snacks, to satisfied their physical hunger, Jaime and his three companions were also rewarded with the enjoyment of witnessing the constant movement and incredible appearance diversity of the human souls purposely walking in many directions, many with firm destinations while others wondering in search of place and purpose. All the passersby, were surely engrossed in their own mission, their problems, their opportunities, their happiness, and or their pain, and most likely, oblivious of their fellow humans watching them from the many restaurants and store windows, or walking near by.

Few words were spoken as the four enjoyed their anticipated treat as they watched the crowd walk by. Jaime's thoughts began to fade away to times before, in the Cuban country side, where the only constant movement prompting attention was the Jasmines flower laden branches being caressed by the gentle tropical breeze, or the Mockingbirds proudly serenading their mates in a cool sunny morning. What a difference, he thought, between the bounty of nature's virgin beauty and the wave of humanity appearing to aimlessly be walking on the streets of one of the greatest world's metropolis.

Half an hour later, after fulfilling their craving for a sweet snack, the foursome exited the Automat and blended into the crow, becoming part of it and an
object of other people's sight and speculations as to their origin or destination.

The group walked to the north east corner of 47th Broadway where a line of taxi drivers patiently awaited their new fare. They got on board the taxi in front of the line and shared their destination with the driver. Once all the passengers were settled on their seats, the engine roared, adding its share of noise to the city's ongoing Hustle and Bustle. The driver proceeded South on Broadway to deliver his fare. The four of them could not have asked for a more beautiful spring evening.

*

The cool breeze entered through the open taxi's windows and filled their lungs with the fragrance from the matured tree blossoms. The lights from the street and from the slow moving vehicles reflected back from the shiny and recently light rain on the smooth black pavement The clanking of the street cars and the voices of the street vendors promoting their wares, provided a background symphony hard to replicate elsewhere in the world and unimaginably contrasting with the mostly and naturally darkened Cuban country side.

Jaime was extremely grateful for the evening company, not

only for sharing the ride downtown, but also for the fortune of being a young man able to enjoy the richness of one the most wonderful cities in the world, together with good friends, including the recent addition, Silvia. He thought about the critical economic conditions, which the city and the country currently faced, including the constrained economic prosperity and limited individual flexibility to achieve their goals. However, he is convinced that friendship, confidence on self, and in one's God, will dull the edges of the national economic challenges, and with perseverance and hard work, dreams can become reality.

Mary Richards suggested that they all go to Union Square Park and enjoy the gorgeous evening and the park atmosphere for a while before returning home. Everyone in the car welcomed the suggestion.

The taxi approached Union Square Park, where a famous statue of George Washington sitting on his horse, symbolically safeguards the park's surrounding. This, sculptured by Henry Kirke Brown, was unveiled in the mid eighteen hundreds and admired by many since then.

The taxi drove slowly around the beautiful Union Square Park as it approached the taxi area, smiling young ladies accompanied by their escorts, could be seeing slowly walking through the park's paths, holding onto their serious looking male companion's arms. The men were elegantly dressed in their light woolen suits while the ladies displayed their elegantly, attractive gowns, as if rehearsing for the Easter Parade traveling up Fifth Avenue.

The driver pulled up to the curve on the corner of 17th Street and Union Square East, and all the passengers exited the taxi while Jaime was taking care of the fare. They crossed the street, entered the park, and followed some of the elegantly dressed couples, which they saw earlier, walking and enjoying the refreshing spring evening breeze. Dina and Silvia grabbed on to each of

Jaime's arms as they walked. Mary had no other option than to hold on to Dina's left arm.

The three ladies and the one fellow, leisurely "paraded" thru the park while envious male eyes wished that they could be so fortunate as to be escorting three very attractive young ladies, which appeared to be enjoying each other's company and the beauty of the evening. Mary and Silvia smiled at all the gentlemen sitting on the parks sideline benches, while walking and enjoying the atmosphere.

Dina could not help herself; her thoughts could not remain in the present. The setting, the fresh air, and the satisfying natural warmth projected by Jaime's body, shared with her by their arms holding and caused by their body contact, transported Dina's consciousness to the days when she and Vincent, after being engaged, frequented Union Square Park to enjoy the evening, as she and Jaime were doing tonight.

Vincent would drive her to the park and they would go into Amelia's, a small, quaint caffe right across the street from the park and on Broadway, to have a light meal, followed by a slice of freshly made cheese cake, and to sip a hot cup of coffee. They savored the famous cheese cake at the same pace as they "nursed" their warm coffee, beyond a reasonable time while watching the romance effervescence of their young peers sitting on the benches, enjoying the cool early evening's new flowers perfumed spring air and accompanying wonderful celestial display.

Dina wanted to just close her eyes and remain in that current dream state, sharing those wonderful moments that she cherished with the love that she can not longer have. Jaime's voice, inquiring if she was cold, brought Dina back to reality. She responded that she was fine and thanked him. He then asked Dina if Union Square Park was named after the brave soldiers who fought and died during the civil war. Dina explained that it was not, that the name evolved from the multiple trolley lines of service that converged into this area and facilitated passenger exchanges. Thus, the reason for naming the park Union Square.

As the evening began to age and the crowd of park goers began to thin out, Dina suggested that it was time to return home. Jaime concurred. He mentioned that he had a busy day tomorrow and wanted to retire at a reasonable time. Mary, biting her tongue for she mischievously wanted to whisper the question – "are you really going to sleep early, or perhaps you just want to spend some "quality" time with Silvia"?, into Jaime ears.

The four of them, once again boarded a parked taxi at the location where they were previously discharged. Silvia asked the new taxi driver to drop her off at the Southeast Corner of 22nd Street and 2nd Avenue. He quickly responded, "Sure, no problem", as he spat out of the car window the excess dark saliva accumulated from continuously chewing the strong smelling Cuban cigar. A pleasant smell which reminded Jaime of his home, but, unfortunately not perceived as pleasant by the girl in the car. The mild tension projected by Mary Richard's expression subsided after she heard Silvia's request to be dropped by her location rather than remaining in the car with James.

*

Sunday morning Jaime got up an hour earlier than usual to begin preparation of the planned afternoon meal before going to church. He placed all the ingredients on the kitchen table and began to cut the chicken into small pieces for the Chicken with Rice, which he promised to prepare for Dina's birthday gathering.

Jaime placed the cut chicken back into the refrigerator after applying salt, pepper in addition to the sour orange juice which he sprinkled on the cut pieces before returning to his bedroom to get ready to dress for church.

Mary Richards decided to go to Jaime's apartment earlier than two o'clock, as planned. She called Dina and told her not to pick her up as they had agreed when they spoke about getting together early Sunday at Jaime's apartment. Her self justification was wanting to help Jaime get things ready for the gathering. The real truth being her desire to, again, spend some time alone with him.

*

The ingredients for the Chicken with Rice were already simmering and almost ready in the special aluminum pot, which Jaime always uses for his favorite dish. He carefully stirred the already aromatic mixture while carefully adding the light beer, before covering the pot and allowing the cooking process to reach perfection.

Jaime began to peel the perfectly ripen plantains imported from his homeland, to have them ready for frying immediately before serving the anticipated Cuban delicacy.

It was twelve forty five when the door bell rang. Jaime placed his knife and the plantain on the cutting board and walked to the door wondering who could be visiting, for it was too early for his friends to arrive.

He opened the door and his curiosity was satisfied. It was Mary, holding an apple pie with her right hand and a bottle of Bacardi with the left one. Before he could get a word out, she cheerfully greeted him with one word, "Surprise!" Mary leaned forward to kiss Jaime on his left cheek and almost dropped the pie. Jaime, realizing what was going to happen, told her "hold on, let me help you with that!" He took the pie away from her. Jaime grabbed the apple pie and then returned Mary's greeting by kissing her on both cheeks. He expressed his surprise at her early arrival and asked about Gabriel's where abouts.

Mary thought that Jaime, having been at the movie theater,

had witnessed the lover's quarrel scene and her slapping Gabriel, then walking away without saying a word. Apparently, Jaime and Silvia had exited to the lobby during the movie reel change break and did not witnessed what happened. Mary Richards was pleased that Jaime had not seen what had taken place. She would rather not expose him, at least not yet, to that aspect of her temperament.

She entered the apartment ahead of Jaime, and placed the Bacardi bottle on the kitchen table. She then said to Jaime that she wanted to replenish his supply of Bacardi considering that Friday night he was left dried. Jaime placed the apple pie on the table and, with a small grin on his face and remembering some of that evening's episodes, told Mary that it was not really necessary for her to do that, but that it was very thoughtful.

Mary's words, actions, and expression raised Jaime's awareness of her brewing desire, and that was out of the question. This was not the right time to repeat Friday's night episode, for he needed all his attention to be focused on the meal preparation. Furthermore, because of his background and costumes, he was not comfortable, nor did he like the role reversal which was taking place. Jaime is accustomed to the traditional male role of being the pursuer, not the prey. Mary Richards had changed the rules. He needed to gain control of the situation, for being the prey made him uncomfortable. Jaime considered the possibility that Mary may have interpreted the physical episode that took place Friday evening as an indication, or confirmation, of an amorous inclination. The reality is very clear. He appreciates her friendship and very much enjoys the social synergism generated by the group. However, the indescribable magical feeling, recognizable only by those in love, does not exist for her in his heart. What happened Friday night was nothing more than satisfaction of a primitive human behavioral need, made possible by the spirits' altering effect on rational thinking.

Jaime decided that the best strategy was to change the subject back to Gabriel. He asked Mary again about Gabriel's whereabouts. She looked at Jaime and tears began to slowly escaped from the sides of her eyelids. She moved her closed right fist over her colorful lips, and began a sympathy seeking sob. Jaime responded as desired, with an affectionate tone and asked her, "Why are you crying? What is going on with Gabriel?, Did you talk to him as we discussed?". Mary Richards had accomplished her objective. She had gained Jaime's complete attention, and had captivated his empathy with her demonstration of unhappiness.

Mary Richards reminded Jaime about their conversation regarding her suspicions of Gabriel's infidelity. She again explained about a number of canceled dates, and about Gabriel's aloofness when they were together. She felt that their relationship detachment grew more obvious, from week to week. Jaime interrupted her justification of the declining relationship perception and told her that perhaps, as he had suggested before, she and Gabriel should have an honest discussion about their relationship's future. She told Jaime that it was too late. That last night she found Gabriel in the movie theater with another woman. She told Jaime that she has never, in her entire life, felt so humiliated and betrayed. Mary Richards told Jaime that last night's movie theater's live scene was the end of Gabriel's and her relationship. Jaime asked "What, when and where did that happened?, We were at the same theater, at the same movie, and at the same time, but I did not see you or Gabriel have a fight. She responded, "It happened during intermission and perhaps you both went out for snacks".

Mary Richards locked her eye sight with his and responded, "I slapped and told him that we were finished". She then told Jaime that Gabriel will not be coming today.

Mary Richards looked at Jaime's eyes once again, and with a seductive and inviting smile, declared her freedom from her relationship with Gabriel. He responded "I am sorry for you both. It is sad that it had to end, and worse yet that it ended that way".

Jaime, anticipating that Mary may suggest that he make a Cuba Libre and, wanting to control the situation, told her that he was going to make some café con leche. She responded that she would rather have a Cuba Libre, but that it probably would be wiser to have the café con leche.

Jaime placed a pot of water to boil, put coffee in the Colador, the unit, holding the funnel shaped, cotton sock, sitting on a three legged wooden fixture attached to a wooden base. He added sugar to the container sitting below the cotton sock, and waiting to collect the caffeine laden brew, to be delivered by the poured boiling water. When poured into the cotton sock, the boiling water will bade the aromatic grounded coffee beans and extract the color, flavor and caffeine, which it had safeguarded for this moment. Jaime poured some of the espresso coffee on two demitasse cups. He handed one of the full cups to Mary, then took the second cup and toasted to happiness. The door bell rang as they began to sip and enjoy the dark and richly caffeinated brew.

Cathy and George had arrived and were warmly welcomed by both Jaime and Mary Richards. They brought two bottles of California Chablis, their contribution to the early dinner gathering. They came into the apartment and walked directly to the kitchen, joining Mary Richards.

Jaime took two additional demitasse cups from the kitchen shelf above the stove and offered Cathy and George the recently made Cuban coffee. They both welcomed the treat and the effect of the strong caffeinated potion. Last night was a very late night, as Cathy and George celebrated their first wedding anniversary. The four together toasted, with the espresso cups, many more years of happiness.

The three friends sat by the kitchen table as Jaime took care of the food preparation tasks ahead of him. Cathy, who had not talked to Mary Richards since last weekend, asked her when will Gabriel will arrive. Mary Richards looked down, and responded, "He is not, we broke up last night".

Cathy felt somewhat uncomfortable for having asked the question, under the circumstances. She told Mary Richards that she was very sorry to hear about it. She further shared the though that, perhaps, viewing what happened from a positive perspective, it may better that it happened now rather than later when the relationship may have been more complex.

The focus was then changed to Dina. The four friends wanted to make sure that Dina had as nice a time as possible. They felt that Dina recognized that they are all available if she needed any help. But more impacting, they really want to help her construct a bridge that will take her to a road full of sunshine, away from from the current one. A road full of emotional lows, which, from time to time, drowned her spirit into the murky waters of desperation.

Cathy and George wanted their friends to be aware of their plans as well. Both Jaime and Mary Richards knew that George had lost his construction job a week after getting married, and that Cathy's work schedule had been reduced to four days a week. Thus, the newly wed couple was having a very difficult time making ends meet. Fortunately, Cathy's parents were able to help them with the rent for a limited period of time.

George mentioned that Congress had passed the Emergency Relief Appropriation Act, known as WPA, in mid April. A project spearheaded by President Franklin Delano Roosevelt, which will finance construction projects primarily in rural areas. He explained that the funds began to flow and constructions projects are being started. Cathy added that one of George's engineering classmates, who has a small construction company in the Blue Mountains foothills, had received a significant contract from the WPA to build a reservoir. George's friend contacted him with a job offer to coordinate the engineering design activity. George shared he has accepted the job and will depart for Virginia tomorrow afternoon. Cathy will follow him in two weeks, after she gives notice to her employer on Monday, and takes care of the logistics associated with the apartment and with the moving tasks. Mary began to cry. She walked over to Cathy and gave her a loving hug. She told Cathy how much she will miss her, but that she was very happy for them and for the great opportunity which they have. Jaime shook George's hands and expressed his hope that all his dreams will become a reality. He added that with the State of the Economy, it was wise for him not turn down that opportunity. He also said that they will be missed. Jaime then commented out loud that their "gang" was shrinking quickly from a "gang" of seven to a "gang" of three.

The four friends began to reminisce, as they drank the remaining coffee, about the highlights of their friendship, and the good times which they spent together,.

It was almost two o'clock and Dina was expected momentarily. Cathy and Mary helped Jaime set up the table, while George opened the Chablis. Three knocks, on the door, were heard from the kitchen, signaling Dina's arrival. The three knocks, rather than using the door bell, have become Dina's arrival "trademark."

The four friends walked to the door to greet her. They all expressed their pleasure at seeing her and wished her a healthy belated birthday. Dina expressed her gratitude to each of her friends with hugs and kisses. Dina would have preferred to skip this gathering. The depression, caused by her loneliness and insecurity from the loss of her love, was winning the battle over her spirit. However, she could not turn down her friends, for they have always been with her when she needed them most. Besides, getting out of her lonely apartment was probably a good thing she thought.

The five friends sat by the table and Jaime announced "Dina, you arrived at the perfect time." He said with glee, "The food is ready!"

George poured the Chablis into the five empty wine glasses. He picked up his glass to make a toast. He said, "Dina, to you. May health be abundant, may the future be bright, and may happiness once again flourish in your life" All five raised their cups in solidarity with George.

Mary raised her glass and said, "We just found out that George got a job in Virginia, let's drink to good fortune, much happiness and many children, now that they will be able to afford them." They all joined in, and drank to her toast.

Cathy raised her cup and toasted Jaime for preparing such a deliciously looking meal. Again they all supported Cathy's toast.

As is customary with the "gang", they all have to make a toast. Dina picked up her glass and said, "To my dear friends, thank you for remembering my birthday. But above all, thank you for your sincere friendship I love you all!" A "hip, hip" chorus followed.

Jaime raised his glass, looked at Dina and speaking from the bottom of his heart said, "Dina, we love you, and we are here for you. We know that these are difficult times for you. Indeed for all of us. You lost your great love and we lost our great friend." Jaime's voice began to sound very emotional. "Together we will get through this difficult period. Life has to go on." He continued, looking up to Heaven "Vincent, may you have found the peace and happiness which you deserve in God's Kingdom". Watery eyes became the norm for the moment. They all raised their glasses as high as they could reach and toasted to Vincent.

The fried plantains were finished and placed by Jaime on the center of the table, followed by the Chicken with Rice pot, which fragrance awoke the friends taste buds, garnished with French style petit poi and strips of Spanish pimentos, forming a perfect circle, providing a contrasting color, and enhancing the visual satisfaction.

The five friends began to eat and drink, satisfying the buily up anticipation for the Latin gourmet treat. While eating they discussed a "buffet" of issues ranging from the hardship brought about by the depression era, including Cathy and George's relocation, as well as the new film playing at the Liberty Theater, called Captain Blood which some of them enjoyed the night before.

By the time the conversation subjects had been exhausted, the entire pot of Chicken with Rice, the plate of fried plantains, and the crisp lettuce salad had been totally consumed. This was gratifying, not only for the chef, but more important, satisfying the digestive system of all that enjoyed it.

Before Dina arrived, the four friends had decided to skip singing Happy Birthday. The girls proceeded to clean the table and wash the dishes while Jaime made some American coffee and George cut the apple pie and the birthday cake.

As usual, time passed unnoticed when the "gang' gets together. It was already almost six in the evening. Cathy and George announced that it was time them to go home, for they had much to take care off before his trip to Virginia tomorrow afternoon. They both got up and walked to were Dina was sitting and simultaneously hugged and kissed her. George told the gathering that he was not sure when they will have the opportunity to get together in the near future. He suggested that perhaps, before winter comes, they all can get together in their new home in Virginia. Mary Richards embraced George and then Cathy, followed by Jaime. The three remaining members of the "gang" walked the departing couple to the door and sadly bid farewell to their dear friends. They returned to the kitchen, sat down, looked around at each other and commented how rapidly the "gang" had shrunken; the three of them were now the "gang".

Dina was getting tired and decided that it was time to go home as well. She looked at Mary Richards and told her that she was leaving and that she will be glad to drop her home. Mary Richards thanked Dina and suggested that she will stay a little longer to help Jaime clean up.

Dina was puzzled by Mary Richards' desire to stay at Jaime's, and by her lame excuse. The three girls had already cleaned all that needed to be done. The table was emptied, the dishes and pots were washed, dried and put away, and the floor was swept. That decision caused Dina to wonder if there was another motive for Mary Richards to have wanted to stay alone with Jaime. Dina has known her since high school, and knows that there is always a reason behind her actions.

Jaime, suspecting that Mary Richards was desiring a repeat of Friday night's adventure, based on her behavior and comments when she arrived, and preferring not to encourage it, responded to her comments, "Mary everything is as clean as it could be, there is really no need for you not to take advantage of the ride."

Mary Richards wanted to, and intended to remain with Jaime for the rest of the evening, and perhaps encourage him to desire her as much as she desired him. Unfortunately, she could not come up with a convincing argument to justify giving up the ride offered by Dina. She did not want to disclose to Dina, her true motivation at this time. She then, and regretfully, agreed to depart with Dina.

Dina got her sweater from the bedroom and when she turned around she noticed that Mary was hugging Jaime closer than would have been expected, and was kissing him on cheek scarcely away from his lips.

As Dina walked, in deep thought towards Jaime to say goodbye, Jaime asked her if she was okay. He told Dina "You appear to be in another planet." She responded that she was thinking about Vincent. In reality, she was pondering about Mary Richards' behavior towards Jaime and surprised at her own sensitivity being awakened by that behavior.

Dina knows her good friend quite well. She knows that Mary Richards is aggressive and vigorous when pursuing a target, regardless of existence of amorous justification or lack thereof. Dina cares for both of them very much, and does not wish either one to be hurt.

Dina kissed Jaime as she normally does and thanked him for the wonderful Cuban cuisine. She told Jaime that today's Chicken with Rice was better than ever before. He responded, "It was prepared with lots of love!" The girls walked to door without saying a word. Jaime opened the door, wished them a good evening, and closed the door behind them as they walked down the slate steps.

Dina was thankful that she was able to park her car only one quarter of a block away. The early evening was approaching. The sky was completely covered with cumulus clouds, pregnant with moisture. Rain drops began to unexpectedly attack the young ladies as they walked down the steps, forcing them to run to the car in search of shelter. Mary Richards anxiously prompted her girlfriend to unlock the car, while Dina struggled with the wet keys. Finally, the welcomed click of the lock mechanism was heard and both fugitives of nature's wrath found shelter and comfort from the environment while sitting in the car.

Dina turned on the radio already tuned to ABC's station and began to listen to the beautiful piano melodies broadcast live from the studio, where her mother played the piano every Sunday late in the afternoon.

Both friends remained quiet in the car as they traveled thru the wet New York City streets, sometimes having to avoid the pot holes filed with water and other times having to drive partially onto the sidewalk to protect the engine from the deep water puddles.

Seeking the Future

When the music stopped for a commercial break, Dina, no longer able to withhold her curiosity, asked Mary Richards if she was trying to "conquer" Jaime. Mary Richards hesitated before replying. She needed time to strategize how much details she wanted to share and how she was going to respond to her friend's questions.

Mary Richards decided to play the "innocent" role, one whose actions could be misunderstood or misread. She decided to answer Dina's question with another question, hopefully prompting a response that would disclose the premise behind Dina's inquiry. She responded as if surprised by the question tone, "Why would you think that?". Dina answered, "Come on, Mary Richard, We are friends." Mary Richards replied, "I know, but why would you say that?" "All right", responded Dina. "We have been friends for a long time and I know you very well. I noticed how enticing you were when you hugged and kissed Jaime. It was clear that you were encouraging him." Mary Richards smiled and explained to Dina that there was really no basis for her speculation. She then asked, "if indeed you were right, why the concern?". Dina responded, "Because you are a dear friend and so is Jaime." Then she explained that the last thing she would like to see is for either one to get hurt and find herself in the middle of a feud between two dear friends.

The radio commercial finished and the piano melody began once again. Dina's favorite melody, Siboney, composed by by Ernesto Lecuona in 1927, a Cuban musical eminence. A melody that her mother has played for her many times at home, was filtering thru the radio's speakers.

Dina sang the music's lyrics to herself, "Siboney, I love you, I die for your love   Siboney, to the singing, to sleep of the palm tree, I think of you   Come to me, that I love you and all treasures you are to me   Siboney, to the singing, to sleep of the palm tree I think of you" accompanying the sound of the piano keys played by her mother and broadcast from the studio as she continued driving to her destination.

*

It was Monday morning, and Jaime, as usual, arrived at his place of work before the bell rang. After checking the daily production schedule and ascertaining that all the parts and supplies have been adequately distributed to the production lines, Jaime informed his assistant that he was going to be "off the floor", at a meeting with the Plant Manager.

Jaime entered the conference room with his boss, Mr. Smith, and was very surprised at the number of people that were participating in this meeting. He had anticipated that the meeting was only going to be with Mr. Smith, the President, and, perhaps Mr. Wilkens, the General Manager.

The meeting turned out to be a general management meeting. All middle and top level managers were participants, including the company's president, Mr. Silver. Once all of the attendees had settled on their chairs and the meeting was called to order, Mr. Silver, who was sitting by a table situated in front of all the attendees together with Mr. Smith and Mr. Wilkens, who sat on each of his side, began his presentation.

At this morning's very important, regular factory monthly management meeting, the participants were to discuss the planned production levels and manpower "loading" requirements for the next two weeks. Generally, the plant General Manager provides a brief overview of order status and production requirements before dealing with the "nuts and bolts" of the production mix and levels, as well as related issues. During the last month's meeting, the plant's General Manager shared the fact that the company has been struggling, trying to survive the consequences of the weak economic conditions, resulting from the aftermath of the "Crash" and the ensuing economic depression. He further shared that company has reduced the level of operation, consistent with product demand. The organization's current work force is approximately fifty percent of what it was before the "Crash" and there was no relief in sight. The employees' reductions had encouraged the remaining employees to consider the idea of unionizing the company production departments manpower. He stated that the possibility of a Union representing the work force will present additional challenges for the management team, already overwhelmed with the task of assuring the company's survival.

Today's meeting began with a brief presentation by the company's president. He began, "Good morning ladies and gentlemen. This, my unscheduled meeting presentation, has been called to provide all of you with the latest update on the company's economic condition. We recognize and appreciate the important role which everyone of you has played, helping us deal with the challenges faced by our company's consequences of our nation's, and, indeed, the world's dire economic condition, resulting from the aftermath of the "Crash". Our tasks would have been significantly more difficult without your support."

Mr. Silver stopped, and sipped some water from the glass on the table immediately in front of his notes. He was not thirsty, perhaps, caused by the incredible pressure, which was exposed by the company's condition and challenges. His intent was to give the audience time to digest what he had just said and to anticipate the message to follow. Mr. Silver continued, "I wish that I could declare that the worse is behind us and that we see 'the light around the corner.' However, that is not the case. We have not 'seen the light around the corner' as of yet. Thus the reason for this unscheduled presentation." Again, Mr. Silver paused. He was having a difficult time selecting the words for the right message that he intended to deliver.

Mr. Silver's career has been exemplary. He began to work with the company in the warehouse, "green" out of college. During the last twenty five years, Mr. Silver has risen "through the ranks", always recognizing the important role that each employee played in the success of the organization. The economic slowdown brought about by the "Crash", has forced Mr. Silver to "cut back" the manpower level on a number of occasions already. This requirement, imposed by his responsibility as the Company's President, to assure the company's survival during these perilous economic times, has been the most emotionally challenging experience which he has had to deal with during his long business career.

Mr. Silver continued, "Our sales levels have been below plan, thus, creating a situation wereby our production capacity has significantly exceeded product demand, thus causing excessive build up of The Warehouse's Finished Goods Inventory. As you all are aware, Labor costs represent fifty five percent of our total production cost. This critical operation situation leaves us with no other choice than to implement an immediate labor cost reduction program. This plan, which is to be executed this Friday, is two fold; the layoff of ten percent of our manufacturing personnel, including production labor, factory staff, supervisors, and administrative personnel, and a ten percent reduction of all salary staff, including myself. Hopefully, this action will yield the needed results. If not, further action will be needed in the future to assure the company's financial viability.

Mr. Silver provided a moment for the meeting's participants to digest his directive, and to observe their general reaction. Silence permeated the room. Mr. Silver continued, "It is certainly my hope that this is a short term requirement. Nonetheless, we will need to be prepared to deal with future challenges and assure the company's survival." He took another drink of water and let his eyes travel and make visual contact with many of those, present hoping to infer their reaction to the challenges that he had shared. Before concluding his unwelcome dictate, he provided the attendees the opportunity to ask questions if they had any. Silence was the only reply to his query. Recognizing that questions will not be asked, he closed the meeting, sharing the following statement with the employees who participated, "Again, I thank you for your past and continued support. Together, we will overcome these obstacles, and we will move the company forward. Thank you!" Mr. Silver excused himself and left the meeting room.

Mr. Wilkens, following Mr. Smith's presentation, announced that the personnel manager will this afternoon coordinate the preparation of the list of personnel that will be subject to layoff, with production management and supervisory staff. He then thanked all the participants for their attention and cooperation and instructed all those present to return to work.

As Jaime returned to the factory, he reviewed the effect of what a ten percent pay cutback will have in his life style. He was pleased with himself, that he had been saving twenty percent of his pay trying to build a capital reserve to purchase land when he returns to Cuba. He had managed to save $2,350.00, a sum that will provide some security should it be necessary to use as a "fall back", if needed. He then rationalized that, since he just received a five percent increase consequence of his promotion, the effect on his available discretionary moneys is only five percent, which will not be as financially painful. By reducing his savings to fifteen percent, he will be able to neutralize the impact of the ten percent "cut" on his discretionary cash. Jaime smiles lightly, as if in a self congratulatory manner.

Jaime arrived at his desk and began to review his department's personnel list to select the names of the candidates for layoff. He concluded that he had to eliminate one of the lines, including a line supervisor in order to comply with management's requirements. He decided that the most equitable selection method was following seniority as the criteria. He identified the last eight line workers and the one supervisor hired as the candidates for layoff. The list include Mary, the young lady who had continuously made advances. As he saw her name on the list, Jaime considered the layoff requirement and his selection method to have been an ironic way of dealing with the challenges of a "female" "advance" in the work environment, which against his self management, imposed rule.

When Jaime arrived at home that evening, he was exhausted, both physically and emotionally. His first day on the job was very challenging from both perspectives; adapting to his new responsibility while simultaneously having to comply with the labor reduction dictated. He had to deal with the undesirable task of selecting people who will loose their jobs. Albeit, hopefully temporarily. Indirectly, he was responsible for the personal economic struggle, which some of the people that he worked with, will be facing. This caused a heavy burden for conscience.

*

As he sat by the kitchen table, he thought that leadership often is judged by the perceived glamour and economic rewards that accompanied it, and that it is rarely professed for the significant responsibility and heavy burden, an integral part that it entails.

Jaime was emotionally drained and too tired to prepare dinner. He needed to be with a friend who may help lighten the remaining part of the day's challenges. He decided to call Dina, his good friend, and find out if she already had dinner. Perhaps they could go to a diner near her apartment and have a hamburger and fries or something else. Getting together with Dina will give him the opportunity to discuss various issues he wanted to discuss with her alone. He wanted to share Vincent's secret with her.

Jaime felt strongly that Dina should know about Vincent's terminal cancer condition, even though his friend asked him not to do so. He is sure, that under the circumstances, Vincent would think otherwise and, thus, forgive him for violating his cofidentiality commitment.

In addition to sharing Vincent's secret, Jaime wanted to update Dina on his sister, Angelina, planned arrival from Cuba. Prior to Vincent's death, he and Dina had offered to host Angelina in their apartment while she was visiting. They felt that Jaime's apartment was too small for another bed and that he will most likely would have to sleep on the living room's small couch, if Angelina were to stay with him. Jaime wanted to confirm with Dina if the offer was still valid in order to plan accordingly.

Jaime left his apartment and walked to the corner Deli to call Dina. He waited while the operator connected the call and the telephone rang. After the fourth ring, Jaime was becoming disappointed and began to think that Dina may not be home. A sense of emptiness began to overcome his mood. Soon after, he heard Dina's usually cheerful telephone greeting, "This is Dina. How may I help you"? He smiled as he thought that she sounded a bit like the telephone operator.

"Good evening Dina", responded Jaime. He proceeded to ask her if she already had dinner. She told Jaime that she had not eaten as yet and really did not have any desire to eat by herself tonight. Jaime suggested that they go to the Greek Diner on the Avenue, two blocks away from her apartment. Dina welcomed the suggestion and told Jaime to meet at her apartment right away.

As Dina waited for Jaime, she once again experienced a sense of anticipation that Jaime's presence will help, at least temporarily, fill in the emptiness that she was carrying in her heart. Yesterday, while at his apartment, she felt very comfortable and was absent of that emptiness and loneliness that has prevailed, in her recent life, ever since Vincent's death. It was a welcome feeling, reminiscent of life before her love was unexpectedly taken away from her.

Jaime was anxious to share company with a friend, with whom he could be himself, and who understood him without reservation. A friendship much needed this evening after the unexpected emotional and physical challenges he faced at work today.

Anxious to not waste any time, he decided to take a taxi and shorten the time that it would have taken him if walking to Dina's apartment, as he has done many times before. As the taxi reached Dina's address, Jaime paid the driver, exited the cab, and quickly walked up the steps. The door opened, coincidentally as Jaime was reaching for the door bell. Dina greeted him with a welcoming smile, usually reserved only for someone she loves.

They hugged briefly and kissed each other on the cheeks. Dina asked Jaime to come into the apartment. He followed her into the living room. She asked Jaime what he would like to drink. He responded that he was starving and suggested they go to dinner. She was very receptive to his suggestion and asked Jaime to give her a minute to get a sweater.

Dina returned to the living room. She had put on a tight fitting, brilliant red pullover that highlighted her young and appealing shape, and contrasted nicely with her gorgeous blond hair. Jaime admired his friend's appearance and did not hesitate to express to her how nice she looked. He told her that the sweater was an excellent choice and that it looked great on her. She smiled with satisfaction.

Dina enjoyed the compliments, particularly since it reminded her of Vincent's similar reaction to the same sweater. She remembered the last time that she wore it, when going out for a walk with Vincent, the sweater became the catalyst for romantic interlude, instead of a walk in the park.

The recollation of that romantic episode of Vincent's love , and of the reality that it was all forever in the past, diminished Dina's eye's brilliance and erased the glee, reflected by her smile, when she welcomed Jaime.

Jaime recognized Dina's mood change and, without hesitation, apologized if he had said something that saddened her. She responded, "Jaime, not all. At the contrary, I needed to be complemented. It is just that you sounded so much like Vincent!" Then she follow with, "Don't worry I am fine". Dina grabbed the keys from the living room table, took Jaime by the arms and told him, "Let's go".

The two friends walked down the street holding hands and enjoying the early evening in the city. Young girls were playing "Hop Scotch" on the sidewalk, forcing the couple to temporarily walk on the street, while the older boys played catch in the middle of the street, sporadically interrupted by incoming traffic.

Dina and Jaime did not speak much as they walked to the diner. They appeared to be very gratified just holding hands and enjoying the comfort and warmth they shared as they walked alone to the Diner.

They reached the Diner and asked to be seated in a booth by the window. They were taken by their greeter to their seats. They sat across from each other in a booth by the window, as requested. The Diner was not very full, being a Monday night and early evening. Their waitress approached the recently arrived guests and greeted, "Hello, folks", provided each a two pages plastic covered menu, and with a professional, customary smile, asked the new guest what they would like to drink. The couple immediately told the waitress that they were very hungry and that they were hopeful that the food would not take too long, she responded, "No problem, honey!. We are pretty slow. Your food will come out quickly". She asked if they were ready to order and they responded that they needed a few minutes. The waitress responded, "I will be right back", andreturned to the kitchen.

A few minutes later, the waitress, dressed in a gray stripped uniform, somewhat similar to the Coca Cola advertising found in the newspapers, returned with two glasses of water and placed them in front of each of two new guests.

Dina looked at the menu trying to decide what she was going to have. Jaime already knew, and told the waitress he wanted a medium cooked cheese hamburger with raw onions and fries. Upon hearing his order, Dina stopped searching the menu and told the waitress "give me the same, except hold the raw onion."

The waitress asked, "What would you like to drink". They both responded in unison, "Coke".

The waitress walked away towards the kitchen to place the order. Dina asked Jaime how was his day at work. Jaime vacillated, he was not very eager to revisit the day's events. At the contrary, he would rather forget about the day's challenges. Jaime shared the highlights of what happened at the factory, withholding company's confidential information. He provided a limited review of the special manager's meeting and the instituted current action plan, including the fact that he will have a ten percent pay cut and that some employees may have to be laid off.

Dina, expressing her concern about the effect of the pay cut for him and his plan, asked Jaime, "will you be able to manage?". He explained to her that he had just received a five percent promotion raise. He also told her that with the recent pay raise, and with a cut back in his weekly savings, the effect of the pay cut on his take home pay will be negligible, not to worry. Dina told him that she was happy that the job situation will not cause undue burden on him. He repeated that he will be fine.

Jaime wanted to change the conversation to other issues, which he wanted to discuss with Dina. He asked her how she was doing, and told her he was concerned about her.

Jaime placed his right hand over Dina's left one, looked at her beautiful but tear strained eyes, and told her "I will always be here for you!"

Dina thanked Jaime and told him that she knows that he is a good friend that she can count on. She told him, "I miss Vincent so much". Tender tears began to slowly drip from her eye lids, defeating her effort to not allow it to happen., "I feel so lonely in that apartment without him". Jaime responded, "I understand your feelings, I shared it to some extent. I too miss Vincent's friendship very much"

Jaime looked deeply into Dina's eyes once again, raised his left hand onto the table level and proceeded to placed it on top of the back of Dina's right hand. Dina smiled as if welcoming his gesture. He said, "Dina there is something that I need to share with you". When Dina heard Jaime's words, she felt the blood rush through her brain cells, followed by an insecured warm feeling irrigating every inch of her body's surface. She was not sure what was that Jaime wanted to share with her and asked herself, could Jaime possibly be developing the same feelings for her that has been secretly ripening within herself for him, having been oppressed in the past, and now resurfacing again since Vincent passed away? Dina responded, with a controlled yet anxious tone, "Please tell me. My ears are yours!"

Jaime began, "Dina, I have been struggling with a difficult burden ever since we buried Vincent. You know that he was my best friend. I believe you also know me well enough to recognize that I am a man of my word. I have been wrestling with a promise that I made to Vincent, a promise that I feel that I have to break ". His unexpected and not quite understood statement baffled her. She had no idea what Jaime was talking about, but her curiosity level became somewhat intense. Even so, it did not sound that it was what, perhaps, she was subconsciously hoping for. Wanting to satisfy the raised expectation, she told Jaime, "Please tell me. Tell me what is bothering you?"

Jaime took a deep breath and reminded Dina about their trip

to Coney Island. She acknowledged and asked Jaime. "What does the trip to Coney Island have to do with what you want to share?" Jaime responded by explaining that Vincent confided with him that he planned the trip to find the right setting, and being along with her, to share the very bad news which they will facing in the near future. She alarmingly interrupted, "What bad news?" He then openly shared, with much hesitation, the secret that he promised to not reveal. He told Dina that the doctor who performed his physical exam required prior to military service induction had discovered his being inflicted with an advanced and untreatable terminal bone cancer condition. He told Dina that Vincent went for additional tests, and that those results also confirmed the original, terminal, cancer diagnoses

Dina looked at Jaime shook and with disbelief and an emotionally hurt voice asked "Jaime, why did Vincent not tell me"?. He responded that Vincent tried many times, including during their weekend at Coney Island. He added that Vincent loved her so much, that he could not find the courage to share information that, he new, would cause unmeasurable pain for you, and fill your with extreme sadness.

Dina looked at Jaime and tears began to escape from her already moist eye lids . She placed her forehead over her coiled arms lying on the table and began to sob quietly. Jaime got up and sat next to her. He put his arms around her shoulder trying to comfort her while she drained her tears ducts. He told her, he was sorry he felt that it was necessary to share this information with her, that he thought knowing the destiny had already prescribed Vincent's short term future. Knowing what was ahead may have helped make it easier for her to deal with the horrendous shooting, which destroyed his life, a sad and unforgetable event which may have saved him from the extreme pain and suffering, he would have experienced during his final days and weeks as he battled the undefeatable desease.

Seeking the Future

Vincent returned to his side of the table and, again, held Dina's hands hoping to ease her pain and express his empathy. Dina looked up, and her moist, blue eyes focused on his likewise moist brown eyes. She shared with Jaime, "It is ironic. Vincent passed away while we both were kept a secret from each other."

Jaime was now the one with the puzzled look on his face. He asked, "Dina, what do you mean by that statement?". She responded that Vincent died not knowing that a fruit of their love had sprouted and was rapidly growing within her. Jaime extremely surprised, and happy to hear that Vincent, although departed, will continue to live through his child. He got up from his booth seat and once again began to walk around the booth to hug and congratulate Dina.

Dina stopped Jaime as he approached her and, with one word; "wait!". He momentarily stopped at her command and waited for the other words to follow. She then said "There is no child". He responded, "But you just told me that, 'a fruit of your and Vincent's love has sprouted". Dina answered "Yes, Jaime, but what I have not told you was that I lost the child that dreadful night when Vincent was shot." Jaime returned to his seat, sat down feeling the excessive moisture bathing his Iris and again reached to hold Dina's hand. They both sat quietly digesting what had just been shared.

The waitress arrived with the two hamburgers, the fries, and the two tall glasses of Coke. She placed each plate and drink in front of the two patrons and moved on to the next table, to take care of another couple that had just been seated.

Both Dina and Jaime hesitated to tackle their meal. The conversation spiritually drained them and diminished their appetites. Finally, Dina insisted that they eat their burgers and fries before they got cold. As they began eating, their hunger was awakened and the dishes were left clean.

Jaime asked the waitress for the tab. They walked to the middle of the dinner where the cashier counter stood next to the exit door. Jaime handed the check and a five dollar bill to the cashier, who efficiently entered the amount tender. The cash register recorded the transaction, provided a soft ring feed back, and opened its drawer allowing the cashier to deposit the five dollar bill in the appropriate slot and retrieve the one dollar and fifty cents change, which she gave back to Jaime. He took one of the quarters and deposited it in the tip's container, sitting next to the cash register. After telling the cashier "Good Night", they exited the diner with the satisfying fullness they had anticipated. The two close friends began to walk back to Dina's apartment. It was a clear night. The sky was pregnant with stars, but it was a bit colder than they both had anticipated. Dina held her folded arms in front of her chest, trying to shield herself from the cool breeze, thus motivating Jaime to take off his jacket and placed it on Dina's shoulders to provide her additional warmth. The walk back was not as leisurely as the walk to the dinner, as the coolness in the air encouraged both choose a brisk walk, rather than otherwise. The two friends were both looking forward to getting back to the coziness of Dina's warm apartment and be sheltered from the penetrating, cool, spring breeze. They arrived at the apartment, and Dina invited Jaime to come in for coffee. He accepted without hesitation. Indeed, he wanted to spend more time with Dina and to ask her about his sister Angelina.

Dina unlocked the door and they both entered the apartment and proceeded to the living room. Dina returned Jaime's jacket, which he put back on trying to recover the lost body warmth. She then told Jaime she was going to make coffee and he should come to the kitchen with her so that they can continue talking.

Dina added coffee and water to the percolator and placed it on the stove. Jaime took advantage of this opportunity to inquire about Dina's desire, as per a previous conversation, to host his sister when she arrives from Cuba for a two week visit. Dina responded, confirming that the offer has not changed. She told him that Angelina will be more than welcomed in her apartment for the two weeks vacation and as a matter of fact, she was looking forward to it because that will give her an opportunity to learn a little more Spanish. Dina also mentioned that she is looking forward to Angelina's arrival since it will give him another reason to come over more frequently. She added that she enjoys not only his company, but also his impresive cooking abilities.

Jaime thanked Dina for making it easier with Angelina's accommodations and asked her, in a kidding way, if she was hinting for him to prepare a meal in the near future. Dina responded that her kitchen will always welcome him. Any time he wishes, he can come in to prepare one of his delicacies. She pondered and further said, "Actually, I have no plans Friday night. Would you like to come over?" Jaime responded, "Yes, I'd love to."

The two friends picked up their cups of coffee and returned to the living room to listen to the radio broadcast. They both sat on each end of the sofa and listened to the Long Ranger, Jaime's favorite radio program. During the program broadcast there was little conversation as both listened intensely to the story line while enjoying their hot cup of coffee.

At the end of the broadcast, Jaime got up an told Dina that it was getting late and that he should go home to get ready for tomorrow's workday. Dina did not want Jaime to go yet, emphasized that it was still early. She followed that plea telling him that she still had some Bacardi Rum on the kitchen shelf and had an urge to share a Cuba Libre with him. Then, with a pleading look on her face and a bottle of rum, which she took from the shelf, in her hands, she requested her dear friend to make a drink for both, to share before leaving. She then said, "you need to show me, step by step, how to make it as good as you do it. You know that your reputation making Cuba Libre precedes you. "Then, her facial look quickly changed from the pleading look to one comparable to that of a young lady flirting with her male prey. Her mischievous smile remained in her face.

Disappointing his close friend, and perhaps because he was remembering how his last and recent Cuba Libre episode ended, he responded without hesitation, that if she did not mind he preferred to take "a rain check". He told Dina that he does not like to drink the night before work. He added that he would be happy to teach her to make Cuba Libre's on Friday, when he comes over to prepare the promised meal. Dina did not want to insist about his staying longer and sharing a drink. She told Jaime that she understood, and that she always admired his responsibility behavior.

They both walked to the front door, and she asked him as she opened the door, "what are you planning to make Friday?. Would you like for me to pickup some of the things that you need to prepare dinner?" Jaime told her that he had not decided yet, that whatever it is, he hopes that she will like it. Then realizing that Dina will likely feel better by picking something up, he said, "On second thought,could you pickup some limes for the Cuba Libre, if you do not have any. Dina responded, "Great, I will get some!"

They kissed their cheeks simultaneously, said goodbye, and Jaime began briskly walking to his apartment, passing the folks socializing on the neighborhood's sidewalk.

As he crossed the quiet intersections and walked pass the partially lit streets, Jaime began thinking about Dina's Cuba Libre comment. Jaime repeated to himself what Dina said: "You know that your reputation making Cuba Libre precedes you." He began mulling over the possibility that Mary Richards, her close friend, may be the source of that comment. He asked himself, if it is possible that Mary shared their last Friday "adventure" with Dina. He wondered, if indeed, this was the case, and what was Dina's motive for bringing up the subject.

Jaime preferred that what took place last Friday between Mary Richards and him remain private. He is very zealous when it comes to promises of confidentiality. Discovery of a breach of trust will most likely result in a friendship termination, as worse case consequence, or an arms length relationship moving forward as a best case scenario.

Jaime set aside, for the time being, the issues that preoccupied him tonight and began thinking about what dish to prepare for Friday. He remembered wanting to make Carne Ripiada with Congri and maduros, a typical Cuban dish, which is not very complicated or time consuming to make. Jaime remembered that, with his shorter week, he will be able to leave work Friday at noon. This will give him the opportunity to prepare the Congri (rice with black beans) and Carne Ripiada (sauté shredded beef) at home. He will take the prepared dishes to Dina's and fry the plantains there.

Dina stayed in the living room listening to soft, relaxing melodies with her eyes partially closed. The melodies transported her to memorable and cherished occasions with Vincent, intermittent with flashes of Jaime's smiling facial images.

Lately, Dina has been thinking a lot about Jaime and has been yearning to share his company as often as possible. These feelings have brought about an internal conflict for her. She knows that the growing feeling she has for Jaime is more than just friendship. However, she doesn't know if Jaime feels the same way about her. She recognizes Jaime's kindness, his caring and the fact that he always goes out of his way to be supportive. She wondered if his behavior is motivated by a sense of obligation to his departed dear friend or if there is a possibility that he cares for her beyond friendship and duty. Unexpectedly, she whispered a wish to herself, "I hope his caring is more than just friendship."

Jaime had arrived at his apartment in what appeared to be no time at all. The reality was that his preoccupation with Dina's comment about the Cuba Libre drink and the decision as what to make for Friday, made the walk appear shorter and faster than it would have otherwise been. He was glad to be at his apartment. It has been a very stressful day, except for the time that he spent with Dina. Jaime needed to go to bed early and "recharge for the new day".

Next morning, as Jaime began handling his duties at the factory, he had to deal with all the employee's questions resulting from a very active, informal, factory channel of communication network. The production personnel, much to Jaime's surprise, were already aware that another "cut back" was in process. The concern and anxiety to find out who will be the unfortunate recipients of the dreaded lay off action was the subject for the beginning of the day. Employees experienced that for most cases, the company has generally followed the seniority rule, but that it has not always been the case.

Jaime had already submitted the list of potential candidates for lay off, which he prepared at home early this morning. However, the official list is subject to review and modification by the Personnel Department and by final approval by the General Manager before it is given to the supervisors, and to the payroll department to prepare the termination pay.

According to the company operating policy and procedures, employees are notified about the lay off when they receive their pay check Wednesday afternoons. The supervisors cannot release that confidential information until the prescribed time. His inability, due to policy restrictions, to truthfully respond to employee's he supervises, inquiry regarding their work status was perhaps the most difficult aspect of the job for Jaime. During that time he faced and ongoing conflict between his personal principles and his job's responsibility. It was very difficult not to respond to pleading inquiries, particularly from those individuals which he respected and appreciated.

Mary, the young lady that has been trying to amorously pursue him, came over to his desk and asked, "Jaime, am I on the layoff list?" Jaime looked at her, without making eye contact for he was unable to look at her eyes without giving away what he knew, found himself responding, "the personnel department has not provided the official layoff list. Thus, I can not confirm or deny that you are on the list.". He, knowing quite well that because of her limited seniority, she had to be placed on the top of the layoff list. Hoping to partially prepare Mary, he added that the employees that will most likely be "cut back" will be those with the lowest seniority, as per company's policy. Mary looked at Jaime and shared her usual encouraging smile. She then handed him a note and asked him not to read it until tonight, to please promise! Jaime placed the note in his pocket and promised to not look at it until the evening, as requested.

*

Jaime was glad that the work day was over. It was a long and stressful day at the factory. The reverberating rumors, the anxiety and the tension on the floor made it very difficult for the line supervisors to maintain the programmed production levels. Thus, requiring that Jaime take aside and individually each of the line supervisors, which he manages and insisted that production personnel focus their attention on the job and minimize the "chatter" since the morning's production level was already way below set standards.

Jaime's walk to his apartment was therapeutic consequence of the particularly challenging day which he had. The walk provided him the opportunity, not only to unwind, but also to disengage from the work day challenges before reaching his apartment. Jaime enjoys arriving at his apartment with his mind clear and tuned to the personal tasks and leisure activities, which a bachelor deals with on a daily basis. His preference being leaving his job focus at work, for the most part.

For Tonight he is planning first of all, to have some of the left over Green Pea soup, which he generally enjoys and which he considers to more satisfying to his palate, when it is made on a previous day, read the newspaper, write a letter to his mother, listen to the Lone Ranger radio episode, and hear the news before going to bed. He is particularly concerned with the goings on in Europe and Asia.

Jaime had read in yesterday's paper the Nazis were considering a "Hereditary Health" court that could order abortion and sterilizations for those that the court considered not to be "good racial stock". They justified this action as a preventive measure against transferring their perceived hereditary "weakness" to future generations. This issue was of great concern for Jaime, for this proposal was clearly a Racist behavior, as well as another clear violation of individual rights. He worried where all of these onerous events will lead humanity to.

As Jaime turned on to his block, he noticed the kids playing on the sidewalk and a female sitting on his building's steps facing the opposite direction. Thus he was unable to recognize who it was. Seeing someone sitting on his building's steps was unusual, particularly during a cool late afternoon. The other building occupants, who all were retired and for the most on the later part of life's third and likely last stage, generally avoided nature's weather challenges until the warmer weather evens the odds and assures the desire and needed comfort. His curiosity as to who was seating on the steps, became his focus and he increased his pace to find out. Jaime was three houses away when he thought he recognized the rear profile of the person sitting on the steps. He was sure it was Mary Richards. He wondered why she came over without finding out if he was going to be home. He thought that it was a pleasant surprise to have some unexpected company, particularly having had such a horrendous and emotional draining day at work. As he approached the building's steps, he called, "Mary Richards!" She quickly got up, and with a cheerful smile, affectionately responded, "Hello Jaime, I thought that I surprise you, with an unexpected and unannounced visit for a little while." Jaime responded that it was nice to see her, and that he hoped that all was well.

Jaime invited Mary to come in to the apartment and she happily entered the small apartment's kitchen and sat on one of the taburete. He took his light jacket off, threw it on his bed, returned to the kitchen and sat on the opposite taburete on the opposite side of the table from where she was sitting.

Mary had already planned the evening and did not want to give Jaime the opportunity to derail what she had in mind. She told him that she had an urge for a fresh corned beef sandwich and a beer at Brendan's Irish Pub, on the Avenue, only three blocks away. She added that it will be her treat. Jaime counter proposed that they stay in the apartment and share the Pea Soup and the beer, which he had in the refrigerator. Mary responded that she really wanted to treat him to a delicious corned beef sandwich at Brendan's saying, "Come on Jaime, let's go out and have some fun!"

The quiet evening and the savoring of anticipated Pea Soup that he had in mind has to be postponed he thought. Additionally, he concluded that perhaps it would be better to go the Pub instead of staying in the apartment. Jaime rationalized that maybe they will each go on their way after they have the Corned Beef sandwich, and that will give him the time to listen to the radio episode that he wanted to hear escaping the day to day life's reality. He acceded to the request with the proviso that he did not want to return to the apartment too late. Jaime explained to Mary that he needed to write to his mother tonight before going to bed. He planned to mail the letter in the morning on his way to work. She agreed and they both left the apartment after collecting their jackets and Mary belongings.

Jaime and Mary Richards walked towards the Avenue, avoiding the children playing on the side walk. She firmly held on to his left arm as they walked to the Pub and shared a light conversation. Mary Richards asked Jaime how he was dealing with his new work responsibilities. Jaime preferred to not really think about work, nor about the issues that he had to deal with during the last two days. He told Mary that work is very slow and that the company is in the process of cutting back again. She expressed concern and understanding for what he was experiencing. She told Jaime that she hoped that his job was secured. She then shared that some people had been terminated last week at her job also. He responded that in today's business climate, very few jobs are secure, and added that the only thing that each person can do is to work as best as they can and hope the economy will turn around and the companies provide a concernless and secured work environment for everyone.

When they reached their destination, he opened the Pub's door for her and they both walked into the smoked filled and extremely crowded bar. Mary spotted a small table near the kitchen entrance and pointed it to Jaime. They walked around and avoiding bumping into the patrons, who were two person deep, standing in front of the bar and waiting for the bartenders to hand them a cold glass of draft beer, or perhaps a Boilermaker, a glass of beer and accompanying shot glass of whiskey, which is dropped to the bottom of the filled beer glass, and drank simultaneously by generally experienced "heavy" drinkers.

They both sat down at the last available table and Mary attempted to talk to Jaime. Unfortunately, the noise from the multitude made it almost impossible to have a conversation. Jaime began to get up to go to the bar and order a drink but Mary held him back, holding his hand, telling him that one of the bartenders will come to the table to take their order.

Mary shared that she could not stop thinking about the good time that they had together at his apartment the night of the Cuba

Libre. She waited for his reaction. He looked at her appearing confused, pretending, not knowing what she was talking about. He moved his face closer to her's, and apologizing, asked her, "Please repeat what you just said, I was unable to hear you", as if giving his friend an opportunity to reconsider the thought that she shared. Mary concluded that this was not the right moment, nor the setting to try to reignite the spark that will lead to another romantic moment which she wanted to replicate. She decided to wait until they return to his apartment later. Thus she responded, "It's ok. It was really not that important."

The bartender approached the couple and asked them what they wanted to drink. They both quickly, and almost simultaneously responded, "two draft beers, and two of the house special, hot Corned Beef Sandwiches. The house special included a large whole pickled cucumber, fries, and extra meat. The bartender thanked them for the order and told them the beer will coming right up.

Two tall beer glasses, filled almost to the top and covered with an overflowing beer "head", were placed on their table almost immediately after the bartender took the order. They both picked up their glass and toasted to health and friendship. Both drank almost half of the beer in the narrow glass as the cool brew satisfied their thirsts.

As they were about to finish their first beer, a young man exited the kitchen and approached their table, with two dishes loaded with the sandwiches, the pickles, and the fries the two of them had ordered. The Corned Beef, piled high approximately three inches high, between two slices of rye bread, was two high for Mary to pickup and take a bite. Instead, she began to eat her sandwich with a fork and knife. Jaime signaled the bartender, with two fingers extending from the top of his raised right arm, and soon, thereafter, two additional glasses of beer were delivered to the table for the awaiting pair.

The two friends quietly enjoyed their meal and the accompanying brew. Their limited conversation was not by choice, but rather consequence of a forced behavior brought about by the spirited and loud exchange taking place among all the patrons enjoying themselves in the Pub. The setting did not turn out as Mary had anticipated. Her game plan was to find a quiet table in the corner of the Pub and utilize the setting and the mood as a vehicle to explore and motivate Jaime's, and enhance their relationship beyond just friendship. She desired to upgrade their friendship to a romantic level. Based on his lack of reaction to her recent and somewhat aggressive moves, Mary concluded that Jaime's masculine ego is better satisfied when he perceives himself as the aggressor rather than the prey. Thus, she concluded that she had to diminish any barriers that may impede his self-perceived manly behavior from seeking an amorous relationship between them. By curtailing her own initiatives and providing him the wanted space to be the aggressor, Mary is now hoping to encourage Jaime to try to conquer her.

The two friends finished their Corned Beef sandwiches and decided, after the second beer, to escape from the smoke and noise in the Pub. Jaime paid the bartender, not ceding to Mary's objection when she claimed that it was she that invited him. They walked out onto the street with Mary acknowledging to herself, that arguing about paying the tab with Jaime was futile and inconsistent with her new strategy. Jaime and Mary Richards began walking, their lungs began to replace the smoked filled air from the pub with the fresh spring evening air. Their their ear drums adjusted to the melodic sounds of the city streets, a welcomed change from from the extremely noisy Pub atmosphere. She thanked Jaime for the dinner and jokingly reminded him that it was she who invited him. She asked if he enjoyed the Corned Beef sandwiche. He responded, "the Corned Beef was excellent, the beer very refreshing, but the best part was the company." He added that, "However, the place was too crowded and too noisy for my taste."

Jaime reminded Mary that she tried to tell him something at the Pub, which he was unable to hear. He asked her what was it. She responded that she was commenting on how much she enjoyed learning to make the Cuba Libre the other night, but more so, seeing him next to her when she opened her eyes in the morning. Realizing that her statement was more overt that she desired, Mary then tried to divert Jaime's thoughts, by asking him, "why is it called Cuba Libre.?" Jaime was thankful that Mary changed the subject. He preferred to leave that episode in the past. He then, welcoming the change of subject, told her that there are different versions regarding the origin of the drink's name. He shared that one of the most popular folklore is that after Cuba gained independence from Spain, three American sailors were having a good time in a Havana bar and one of the sailors was drinking Gin and Lime. When he finished one of his drinks, the bartender added another lime to the empty glass and moved away to get the Gin. A second bartender mistakenly filled the glass with rum and Coke. One of the sailors, having already downed various glasses of Gin and lime, and unaware of the accidentally prepared new concoction, raised his glass and toasted to "Viva Cuba Libre". According to the legends, thereafter bartenders adopted the name Cuba Libre for the newly concocted Rum and Coke beverage.

They reached the apartment and Jaime stopping in front of the stairs asked Mary how she was planning to get home. She responded that she was going to get a cab. Not wanting to leave as yet but following her new strategy, Mary, recognizing that Jaime had no intention of asking her inside, decided to take control of the situation. She asked Jaime, "Are you not going to invite me in for a nightcap?, what kind of friend are you?". She laughed lightly. This was precisely what Jaime was trying to avoid, at least for tonight. He reminded her that tomorrow was a work day and added that he thought that she was planning to get home early to get ready for work tomorrow. He then told Mary that it will be a pleasure to share a cup of coffee with her. He asked her to come in to the apartment for coffee before calling the cab. She responded that a cup of coffee would be magnificent and added, "Cuban of course". The two friends entered the apartment. Mary Richards sat on the taburete while Jaime heated the water and prepared the coffee ground to make them each an two espresso cup.

They both entered the apartment and proceeded to the kitchen. As Mary made herself at home sitting on the taburete, he began to prepare the promised espresso. He took a soup spoon from the drawer to measure the amount of grounded coffee that he was going to use, followed by grabbing a pot which hung above the stove, to boil the required water, the second key ingredient to fulfill his promise.

Mary began to speak, as Jaime was pouring the hot coffee into the demitasse cups. She asked him with sort of a childish or perhaps insecure voice, "Do you not like me?" Jaime brain cells accelerated, almost causing his pouring the coffee on to the small plate supporting the coffee cup. He thought that, as anticipated and justifying his effort to encourage Mary to go home earlier, her line of question was going to lead precisely to the subject that he was trying to avoid.

Jaime enjoyed and appreciated Mary's friendship, but in reality he had no emotional feelings for her beyond that. He considers her to be very attractive, friendly and a fun loving individual. However, Jaime has wanted to discourage her having any romantic expectation, to avoid affecting their current and long term friendship and knowing that for him, what happened recently did not represent anything other than unbridled human behavior. He recognized that their recent intimate episode may have significantly contributed to it causing behavior assumptions other than what it was, just satisfaction of normal and uncontrolled physical desire between two young adults. Having poured the coffee, Jaime turned around with a cup on each hand. He placed them on the table, one in front of Mary and the other across from her where he intended to sit. He sat down and proceeded to make direct eye contact with with her. Jaime responded, "off course, I certainly like you." He added, "You are a wonderful person and I very much enjoy your friendship and your values." Before Jaime could go any further she asked, "Do you love me?" Jaime quickly responded, "Off course I love you" then proceeded to explain that he loves her as one loves a sister, or a good friend.

Mary's expectations deflated emotionally, crumbled when those words, "I love you as one loves a sister or a friend" traveled through her ear's canals as a poisonous arrow, merciless and painfully wounding her unexpecting heart. Words only used when conveying the existence of an impenetrable heart shield in the "game" of love. Jaime reached across the table and gently held Mary's hands. He then told her that he would be lying if he were to tell her that he had any romantic feelings for her. She responded that he was certainly very romantic on the Cuba Libre night. Still holding her hands, and once again focusing his sight with hers, Jaime added that what happened that night was not love, or true romance. He further added, possibly trying to justify their previous behavior, that their better judgment was disabled by the excess tropical spirit, and that their physical drive and raw carnal desire triumphed. Trying to add a bit of levity to the conversation, he suggested with a partial smile the word "Libre", in the name of the drink, was not intended to be inferred as a guide for sexual behavior.

Mary looked at him with her now moist eyes and shared her belief that he has to feel something more than just friendship towards her. Then she said, " I can not understand why you are denying to yourself the true feeling that you have for me." Before he could respond, she added that she could not believe that his tenderness, and his caring, during their Cuba Libre night could have occurred as it did if he was so emotionally unattached.

They both remained as if frozen in time, silently sitting across from each other, possibly strategizing how to proceed from this uncomfortable and telling moment. Jaime wanted very much to shelter their friendship from being damaged, and Mary wants to safeguard her pride by not yielding to her prey's wishes. She placed aside her previous decision to allow him to exercise the initiative since the relationship challenge has moved to a different level.

Jaime responded to her amorous allegation in a very candid and sincere way, having concluded that the appropriate response would perhaps result in her rebuff, scorn and, maybe, the unwanted friendship loss. Nonetheless, he thought that this was the moment to curtail any false expectation of a love relationship, between the two of them.

He looked at her glassy eyes. They were beginning to fill with the "liquid of discontent", a technique sometimes used by the "fairer sex" to weaken their male prey's defenses. He told her again, that their physical episode during the Cuba Libre's night was indeed a physical response, encouraged by the Spirit's power to affect self control, devoid of any emotional motivation. He added that he will not refuse to acknowledge their physical adventure was a pleasurable experience when it happened. He stated further, that, in retrospect, he wishes that the episode had not occurred, for it caused her to infer nonexistent motivations. Jaime reminded Mary that male sex behavior and expectations are indeed different than women's. He told her, that he believes that in most cases the male specie is more likely than the counterpart to have the ability to participate in physical encounters without expectations and without emotional or romantic attachment. He further stated he believes that lack of understanding of that behavioral differential, between the two genders, may impede her acceptance of his lack of amorous motivation when they were intimate.

Mary looked at Jaime and asked him, in an aggressive and demanding tone, "When did you become a psychologist?" Then without any hesitation, but with a more conciliatory tone, she asked if there was someone else that he was in love with. Then she asked "are you in love with Silvia?" Jaime was not ready to respond to that question, from Mary, certainly not at this time, and particularly since he wondered if she may have shared part, or perhaps, their entire Cuba Libre episode with Dina. He has been very curious about how much of their intimacy episode she may have shared. He thought that the best strategy to get closure on the subject at hand was to change it. Thus, he decided to ask Mary if she shared their "escapade" with anyone.

Jaime's question prompted her to want to punish him. Since she had indeed shared the details of their sexual intimacy with Dina. She told him, that she did share everything with her best friend. She then followed up her disclosure, questioning why he was concerned about it since he knows Mary and her are very closed friends, who do not keep anything from each other. The effect of the disclosure was merely a confirmation of what he already suspected. Mary's acknowledgement served as another dagger, cutting off the unlikely possibility that he would develop a romantic attachment with her. Not only did she violated his trust, but also the implicit understanding to safeguard the confidentiality of what he now considers a one time, foolish, and irresponsible affair between the two of them. Particularly, knowing the potential consequence of said behavior to his deep rooted desire, if exposed. Integrity is one of the most significant qualities, in the hierarchy of female traits that Jaime highly values, in the quest for the eventual life time love companion, friend and partner. Mary, by her admitted behavior, has permanently disqualified herself from such consideration.

Quietness prevailed in the small kitchen. As the seconds ticked away, only the sound of the empty demitasse coffee cups being placed on the matching saucer could be heard.

Mary was furious with Jaime. He refused to acknowledge that he had romantic feelings towards her as she perceived, and certainly desired. This resistance prompted reinforcement, justification and correctness of having confided with Dina about their recent affair. It was an appropriate punishment for his undesired response to her expectation. The prey became unapproachable, she thought.

Jaime was experiencing mixed feelings. He was satisfied having confirmed his suspicion of Mary's inability and or willingness to keep their secret to themselves, an action which impacted his perception of her integrity and perhaps worthiness as a life time partner. Simultaneously, he had remorse at the fact that his perception of her and of the quality of their friendship had been altered for ever.

Jaime got up, took his cup and asked her if she wanted more coffee. She responded negatively, thanked him for the coffee, and curtly told him that she was going home. Jaime volunteered to go outside and signal a cab for her. She refused, stating that it was not necessary. She aggressively picked up her pocketbook from an adjacent taburete, almost knocking it down, kissed him on the cheek and proceeded to the door as he placed the espresso coffee cups and saucers in the sink. She opened the door and walked out of the apartment, closing the door behind her without further conversation.

Jaime was glad that Mary had departed. He hoped that after tonight's visit her expectations has been calibrated to reality. Jaime needed to unwind from the stress brought about trying to balance his desire to be sensitive with his friend, and the need to get closure of her unwanted expectation and desire to fertilize, her self perceived emerging love relationship

Mary did not take a cab as Jaime thought she would. She decided to walk home, unwind, and recover from her prey's romance refusal. She could not accept rejection and contention that her effort to romantically conquer him was for naught. She had been sure that the seeds of their relationship were ready to sprout and ready to blossom into the beauty and and the desired long term pleasure that love can offer, when adequately nurtured. However, after tonight's encounter, her desire to conquer was no longer the challenge. Her pride and her ego, nourished by the inner conviction of feminine irresistibility, had been hurtfully deflated by Jaime's rejection.

She walked through the quiet New York streets as if almost in a trance stage while revisiting every movement that took place, and every word that was thrown into the air in the small kitchen. She was trying to identify any and all evidence that could possibly negate rejection and that may help expose his true romantic feelings. As she turned the corne, she saw a couple embracing and kissing with a passion that isolated them from their surroundings. Mary Richards was envious of the couple and wished that it would have been Jaime and her. Her anger continued to brew.

As she proceeded with her walk home, past the romantically engaged couple, Mary Richards recalled asking Jaime if there was someone else. She also clearly remembers that Jaime avoided answering that question, thus implying from her perspective, that indeed there was someone else. She wondered who the someone else may be. She thought again that perhaps it was Silvia, the young lady he took to the movie last weekend.

Mary Richards made a decision to visit Dina tomorrow night and share her frustration about Jaime, asking Dina's impression about what had happened and her opinion as to whom Jaime may be pursuing.

*

Jaime was glad to be in his apartment alone. He needed to unwind, not only from the job's challenges, but, perhaps, more demanding from the social challenge imposed by Mary's aggressive pursut and his own effort to discourage it. He took his shoes off, walked to the refrigerator and poured a cool glass of milk to drink while listening to the radio, hopefully to help soothe the gastric cavity from the excess acidity generated by the challenging exchange with Mary. As he sat down by the radio, he remembered the letter he planned to write to his mother. He concluded that it will have to wait until tomorrow when he would be in a more favorable frame of mind.

As Jaime began to take off his shirt, a small piece of paper escaped from the shirt pocket and felt onto the floor. He had forgotten that Maria, the young lady working on one of the production lines which he managed, had given him and had asked him to wait and read it later, when she was not present. Jaime picked up the small note from the floor, unfolded it, and with some curiosity began to read its content. It was a short, nicely handwritten note, thanking Jaime for everything and expressing her hope that her departure from the factory will not mean a departure from his life. The note included her telephone number followed by her comment that she was available for him any time, day or night. She also told him that she will be very disappointed if she were not to hear from him in the near future. She signed it with a heart outline followed by xxx. Jaime smiled at Maria's persistence and of the likeness between Maria and Mary. He lightly smiled and placed the note on one of the kitchen's drawers, where he keeps all his important papers. Her overt expression, absent of confrontation, was well received and gratifying to his male ego.

*

Wednesday morning atmosphere at the factory was subdued. The "rumor mill" had already been cranked and most people were aware of the planned layoff. The line supervisors had to exert themselves to maintain the production tempo and to avoid unwanted negative behavior from the people who had been identified as candidates of the layoff.

Jaime was anxious for the day to finish so that he could once again escape and return to his emotional shelter, his apartment. Tonight he needed to be by himself and allow his thoughts to escape from the economic realities and related consequences at work, and from personal interaction challenges, relating to the upcoming job terminations to be executed in two days.

As the work day closed and Jaime exited the building, Maria approached him and captured his attention. Before he was able to acknowledge her, Maria asked him if he had read her note. She emphasized that she meant every word in it.. She then kissed him on the cheek and walked away. Jaime remained in place, surprised by her behavior and admiring her attractive figure, and purposeful seductive movements, as she distanced herself from him.

*

As the early evening approached, Mary Richards called Dina and asked her if she could use some company. Dina responded, as always, that she would be delighted for her to come over. Mary Richards told Dina that she will be over in about an hour.

Dina had already eaten her dinner, and was sitting in the living room reading the daily paper when the bell rang. She hurriedly got up and rushed to the door to welcome her good friend. They greeted each other at the door with the customary kiss, and then they both walked into the living room.

Dina had already prepared some refreshments including their favorite snacks, and had placed them on the living room's center table to share. They both reached for a cool glass of Coke, as they proceeded to sit down.

The living room is Mary Richards' favorite room in Dina's apartment. She very much liked Dina's, Georgian style furniture selection, which depicts a modern version of King George's furniture. She also likes the roominess, brightness, and openness which the two large windows add to the room's aesthetics.

Dina cheerfully shared how extremely happy she became, when she got her call about coming over so they can "catch up". She also told her, that they have not been spending as much time together as she would like. Mary Richards agreed with Dina that they should spend more time together and told her that she will make sure that they do that more of this.

Dina has been concerned as to how Mary Richards has been handling her breaking up with Gabriel and has been curious if any other romance was budding. She wanted very much to find out if anything was going on with Jaime without disclosing to her close friend the real reason for her curiosity. Dina asked Mary Richards if she had "gotten over" Gabriel. Mary Richards responded that her memories of Gabriel had been filed on the annals of her romantic conquests. She added that he ceased being a factor in her life that night, at the theater, when the palm of her hand impacted the side of his face. "Prompting me to discharge from my heart and emotions any and all feelings that I may have had for him." She added, "I am glad that it is all over'.

Dina, somewhat hesitant, then asked Mary Richards if she had any other romantic episodes with Jaime. That question changed Mary Richards' demeanor from a relaxed and joyful one, as she usually feels when together with Mary, to one depicting a female warrior wanting to castigate her victim for refusing to be responsive to her desire and fulfillment of her expectation. She has never held back any feelings from Dina and today was not going to be an exception. She told Dina that she was furious with Jaime. Dina asked her, "why?". She responded "I have never in my life been so humiliated by a man". Dina confused, curious and secretly pleased by the response asked, "What happened?" Mary Richards related that she was sure that Jaime was attracted to her. She said that his actions the night that they spent together, confirmed her belief of the existence of a romantic attraction. Yet, no matter how hard she tried to get him to acknowledge what she perceived to be his true feelings; Jaime continued to reject having any such feelings. She told Dina that Jaime claimed that their sexual adventure was indeed a physical reaction, devoid of any romantically driven motivation. She also told her that he had the nerve to lecture her on the difference between male and female sexual behavior. Showing her irritation, Mary Richards repeated Jaime's statement, "That he believes in most cases, the male species is more likely than the counterpart to have the ability to participate in physical encounters without expectations and without emotional attachment."

Mary Richards shared with Dina that she has gotten to a point that she can no longer stand Jaime and his rejections. She also shared, with Dina, her extreme anger with Jaime, which prompted her to ask him, "When did you become a psychologist?" At that point they both laughed and changed the subject.

Mary Richards' tale of her failure to conquer Jaime, her explanation of his rejection to her encouragement for a commitment to a romantic relationship and her new attitude towards him was gratifying and, to some extent, comforting to Dina. A behavior that confirmed, via self confession, her brewing and growing romantic interest in her close friend, Jaime.

Mary Richards has been planning to talk with Dina about the

need for her to move forward with her life and to contemplate developing new personal and potentially romantic relationships. She told Dina she was sure that Vincent would want it that way. Dina responded that she could not possible contemplate dating anyone so soon after Vincent's departure. She told Mary Richards that, in due time, and when the right person came along, she will deal with that challenge. However, Dina did not share with Mary Richards her growing interest and desire to develop a more intimate relationship with Jaime.

The two close friends spent the rest of their time together listening to music broadcast on the radio and paging through the collection of magazines, sitting on the bottom shelf of Dina's living room set's corner table, looking at the published variety of new clothes styles.

*

It was nine fifteen in the evening and Jaime was finishing the second page of a letter to his mother. He told her, as usual, how much he missed her and that he could not wait for his return home to embrace and kiss her. He shared with his mother that he was recently promoted at his job, but the economic situation was making things very difficult. He related that some of the employees at the factory would have to be terminated today because of the decrease in product demand. He shared with his mother that his friend, Dina, has graciously offered to accommodate Angelina when she comes to visit him. Jaime explained that his apartment is very small and that Angelina will be more comfortable in the spare room that Dina has in her apartment.

Previously, Jaime had written to his mother regarding his friends, in particular about Vincent and Dina. His mother was becoming acquainted with the couple via Jaime's letters. She was well aware of Vincent and Jaime's friendship. Jaime's recent letters shared the significant vacuum that Vincent's untimely death created for her darling son. Jaime's mother also was aware of Jaime's admiration for Dina. Whenever he wrote about Dina, Jaime described her beauty and admirable qualities, as a painter would depict a beautiful bouquet of flowers on his canvas.

Jaime continues to hope that he will be able to flight back to Cuba, when the time comes and had wished that Angelina could have taken a Pan American World Airways flight rather than traveling by steamship when coming to visit him.. The flight would have been a less onerous trip, but the cost relative to the Steam Ship line was unaffordable.

Jaime has been impressed by the publicity and great reputation Pan American World Airways has gained. The company began flying in 1927, with single engine planes from Key West to Havana. The company's vision and excellent business strategy execution made it an American icon and an air route pioneer over many oceans and Continents.

The trip to New York City will be the first time that his beautiful twenty one year old sister, Angelina, a Carnival Queen contest's first runner up, from the city of Santiago de Cuba will be traveling outside the country. Santiago de Cuba is the second largest city of the island, located in the eastern end of the island in the province of Oriente.

Jaime admired his sister's picture as he completes the letter that he was writing to his mother.

Angelina has been blessed with a natural beauty and a delightful presence envious by most of her contemporaries. She is bubbly, witty and has a captivating personality. Her dark, soft, and shiny Chesnut hair perfectly rests on her shoulders. Her brilliant dark brown eyes are complemented by the firey red lipstick, perfectly enhancing her moist lips. The natural beauty preserve by the photograph that Jaime is admiring confirms the reason why his sister was chosen first runner up during last summer's carnival beauty contest in Santiago de Cuba

Jaime was some what concerned about his sister traveling by herself. Fortunately, the steamship owned and operated by The Mail Steam Ship Company will depart from Santiago de Cuba to New York City with stops in Guantanamo and Havana, Cuba. The direct cruise from Cuba to New York City will make the trip that much less challenging for Angelina, particularly since her English language communication ability is quite limited.

The Mail Steamship Company owns twelve vessels including the SS Santiago, the ship which brought Jaime to the U.S. The ships sails from Santiago de Cuba every other Monday and are scheduled to arrive in New York City Saturday mornings. The weekend arrival is an ideal time for Jaime. It provides him with two days available to help Angelina get to know Dina, get settled in her apartment's room, and have a general orientation on how to get around New York City.

Jaime finished his mother's letter and placed it on the kitchen table to be sure not to forget to take it to the mail drop box in the morning when going to work. He is anxious for a response from his mother, providing the sail date and ship's name that will bring Angelina to New York City. Jaime is extremely excited with the thought of seeing his loving sister again in the very near future. There is much he wants to show and share with her. Thursday morning Jaime arrived at the factory earlier than usual, as he wanted to meet with the line supervisors to review the production schedule and the line loading. He anticipates that productivity per labor hour will be negatively affected by the employees' anticipated post cutback behaviors, since employees normally will slow down their production pace as an overt reaction to the manpower reduction. Jaime needed to communicate the need to maintain anticipated productivity levels and to motivate the employees to overcome the natural desire to reciprocate with lower productivity in response to their peers cutback. It was quite obvious by the solemnest in the production floor that the employees were struggling with a mixture of anger for their friends' job termination and concern for their own job security.

Jaime recognized and empathized with the employees' feelings and concerns. As manager he felt compelled to convey to his subordinate supervisors the importance of reinforcing management's justification and rationale for the pending cut back. He told them that, it was imperative that employees understood that the employment termination, as undesirable and painful as it was, had to be executed to assure the survival of the company and the retention of the remaining employees.

Jaime instructed the line supervisors that effective on Monday, he requires on a temporary basis, they provide him with mid-shift line production reports until the productivity level equals or surpasses the planned goals, adjusted by the planned manpower reduction that will be taking place Friday. This requirement added additional work load for all of the supervisory staff, including himself, but it was a necessary action to motivate employees as well as supervisors, in addition to overcoming the natural slowdown behavior caused by the employees' terminations.

It was a challenging week for Jaime and for the entire organization. As the days pass, employees accept and adjust to the realities of business conditions and gradually return to their normal, and acceptable production levels.

As the "five to five" warning bell rang, the employees began to finish their task and to clear their work station as they prepared to end another day at work. Excitement permeated the environment as the employees anxiously and rapidly moved around, gather their belongings, and quietly wait to rush to the time clocks as soon as the five o'clock bell brakes the waiting employee's anxious silence.

The bell rang and the employees, some walking briskly and others running, rapidly move towards the time clock as if the gates for a thoroughbred race had been opened.

Jaime was also anxious to depart, not only to seek refugee from the work day's challenges, but also to rush to the butcher and then to the market to purchase the meat, rice and beans for the promised Cuban meal which he was preparing for Dina tomorrow.

As he began to focus on the needed ingredients, Jaime thought of Dina and how much he was looking forward to be around her, simultaneously wondering about the impact that Mary's sharing of their intimacy will have on her behavior towards him. Thinking of her name alone triggers a magnetic desire to be by her, to enjoy looking at her sweet smile and to submerge himself in the pool of tranquility and satisfaction that her presence and companionship generates in his soul.

The walk to Benny's Butcher Shop was pleasant and relaxing for him. Particularly since it was a beautiful afternoon. The nature's magnificence was abundant at this moment. The sun was shining, the cool and dry breeze gently caressed his face and lightly moved his pitch black hair back and forth, as if it was responding to a tropical melody. Jaime could have continued walking and thinking of Dina, of his dear mother in Cuba, and of his good fortune being a young man experiencing the streets of New York, and enjoying the many gifts that this wonderful City had to offer him.

He arrived at Benny's Butcher Shop and was greeted, as always, with a welcoming smile, a "how are you today, young man" comment, and a genuine willingness to be of service. Jaime responded also as always, "Hola, Ben, I hope you are well and business is good". He waited for Benny's favorite expression and usual reply to his comment, "Young man, as long as health is good, business will take care of itself".

Jaime purchased the sheen beef for tomorrow's dinner and a small Kielbasa ring for his own enjoyment during the weekend.

He could not resist his palate's enticement of a fried kielbasa omelet, garnished with a sofrito (sauce) consisting of chopped onion, green papers, garlic, and green olives, fried with olive oil, pepper, salt, and a bit of tomato sauce.

As he purchases the ingredients, Jaime anticipated the pleasure of preparing the dish for Dina. Tonight he will make beef soup with the sheen beef, vegetables, and all other usual ingredients, for himself. Tonight he will also separate the beef from the soup, shred it, add condiments and place it in the refrigerator to take to Dina's apartment, for the final step; the preparation and mixing of the sofrito, somewhat similar to what his palate had urged him to prepare with the Kielbasa. However, in addition to the chopped onion, green papers, garlic, olives, fried with olive oil, pepper, salt, and tomato sauce, Jaime will add a small quantity of capers and raisins as well. Before leaving Benny's Butcher Shop, Jaime mentally inventoried the ingredients required for tomorrow's dinner. He realized that he has not considered desser. Thus, he decided to make Natilla (Custard). In order to prepare the Natilla he needs to purchase corn starch and vanilla extract at the local grocery outlet. Jaime knows he has the additional Natilla ingredients; sugar, eggs, and salt, and milk. He also decided to get additional milk, since the Natilla recipe requires four cups of milk, and that will pretty much take care of what he has left at home.

It has been quite a while since Jaime made Natilla, following the recipe that he learned from his mother at home in Cuba. He remembers that he needs two tea spoons of Vanilla extract, three quarter cup of sugar, three and one half table spoons of corn starch, three and one half cups of milk, five egg yolks, and one half tea spoon of salt. Jaime decided to make Natilla, because it is a fairly simple dessert to prepare. The five eggs, one cup of milk, and the corn starch are mixed well in a bowl and strained. The remaining ingredients, minus the vanilla extract, are also mixed well in a pot and placed on the stove over medium heat until it begins to boil. The heat is lowered and the mixture waiting in the bowl is added to the pot while rapidly stirring until it thickens. The Natilla is removed from the fire once it thickens and the vanilla extract is added, and mixed thoroughly. He reminded himself to let the Natilla cool down before placing it in the refrigerator.

Jaime arrived at his apartment, loaded with the purchases and ready to tackle the meal preparation for tomorrow's get together with Dina. He placed all the ingredients on the kitchen table, turned on the radio to one of the local music stations, and began executing his culinary techniques.

*

Dina had eating her dinner and was relaxing and reading Pearl Buck's novel, The Good Earth, recommended by her father, which she had began to read but had not finished as yet. The telephone rang and momentarily startled Dina, as she had been engrossed in the human kind resilience and its ability to deals with challenges and suffering, brilliantly described by the author. It was Mary Richards calling.

The two friends greeted each other. Dina expressed her satisfaction to hear her friend's voice and asked Mary Richards how she was feeling, and how things was coming alone.

Mary Richards, sounding very cheerful and with a somewhat victorious tone, responded that everything was fantastic. Dina told Mary Richard that she was very glad that she sounded so happy and that everything was going well.

"Dina", "I need a favor". Dina responded "what do you need, how can I help you?" Mary Richards hesitated, she then asked Dina to go out with her tomorrow night in a double date.

Before Dina was able to respond, Mary Richards bombarded

her with a series of superlatives, describing the fellow that she met yesterday at lunch. She told Dina that she felt in love at first sight. His name is Roger Martinelli, a very prosperous produce wholesaler.

Roger had asked Mary Richards if she had a girl friend that could invite to join them, and his friend for dinner, at a Little Italy downtown restaurant, tomorrow night. She added that it will be a fun night, and will give her an opportunity to get out of the apartment and to start getting her life "back on track". She appealed to Dina's friendship and loyalty by relating that he cooperation will please Roger and will enhance the potential of a relationship with him.

Dina was silent, absorbing Mary Richards request and strategizing how to best handle the rejection for her friend's plea. She has been anxiously anticipating tomorrow night's dinner with Jaime and she has no desire, nor intention to change this plan. She definitely does not want to disclose her motives for rejecting her friend's supplication, nor, does she want disclose her inner most feelings that she has guarded from all, except herself.

Finally, Mary Richards having exhausted all her persuasive arguments trying to convince her friend to go out on a blind date tomorrow night, decided to give Dina an opportunity to respond and hopefully yield to her request. Dina, although somewhat intrigue by the opportunity to go out on an unexpected social adventure, was very determine not to prolong the dialogue regarding the blind date.

She told Mary Richards that she was very, very sorry but that she had already made a commitment with a friend coming over the house tomorrow night, and added that she would not be able to forgive herself if she were to change plans and go out with her on a blind date. To further reinforce her position Dina said "I am sure that you would not appreciate it if I were to do that to you. Therefore, you would not want me to do it to someone else".

Mary Richards' enthusiasm was no longer as prevalent as when she originally called. Her voice reflected a degree of disappointment and the acceptance of the inevitable; her friend was not going to yield to her persuasion. It was of no use to continue trying to convince her. She concluded that her friend was not yet ready to explore potential romantic adventures and that, perhaps, it was to soon.

Dina recognizing her friend's acceptance of her rejection directed the conversation to Roger. She asked Mary Richards to tell her all about Roger. How did they meet? What does she like the most about him? What is his personality like? The response to the line of questioning from Dina returned her to the same level of excitement and sense of adventure that she had when she called and tried to recruit her friend. Mary Richards began, once again, to describe her new prey as if it was the greatest discovery and challenge that a women had ever made. Dina told Mary Richards that she was very pleased about her potential relationship and that she hopes that Roger will remain "the brilliant star in her sky conquest" for a long time.

The two friends chatted for a while longer and finally, after wishing each other a good evening, they said goodbye and ended their telephone call.

After finishing the call and placing the telephone on the holder, Mary Richards realized that her friend did not share with her, nor did she inquired about who was coming over tomorrow night. Dina has always been very open and has always shared with her what she does and with whom without being prompted. This raised her curiosity and she almost called Dina back to ask her.

Dina was pleased with herself at being able to reject Mary Richards request to go on a "blind" date without disclosing that Jaime was coming over tomorrow night to prepare diner for both of them.

She returned to the book that she was reading, and once more submerged herself into the captivating story which Pearl Buck wrote.

*

Friday morning was cool and drizzling. Nonetheless, Jaime arrived at the office full of energy and in a very jovial mood. Today there will be, to Jaime's pleasant surprise, an earlier than usual work dismissal, consequences of the layoff. Management decided to close the operation earlier than usual to diminish potential employees' negative reaction to the "cut back". Jaime welcomed the resulting shorter work day, for it provided additional time to be with and to be shared with the person, he definitely wanted to spend a lot of time with.

The daily tasks occupied and prevented Jaime from thinking much about the rest of the day. Before he realized it, the lunch time bell rang announcing the beginning of his much anticipated weekend.

*

A taxi stopped in front of Dina's apartment, it was a quarter past three. Jaime paid the taxi driver and slowly and carefully exited the cab, carrying a medium size cardboard box where the evening meal's ingredients had been carefully placed. The Natilla was already prepared, the meat was shredded and ready to cook, the black beans were being soaked in water since the day before, and the plantains, rice, and condiments were ready to be prepared in Dina's kitchen.

Jaime walked carefully up the steps, making sure not to tilt the box and spill the bean's water or disturb the Natilla. He rang the bell, and anxiously waited to see Dina's beautiful smile, to have an excuse to be close to her and to share her captivating warmth.

Dina was also anxiously awaiting Jaime's early arrival, having been phoned at noon time and asked if it was all right for him to come earlier since the company had an early work dismissal.

When the bell rang she stopped by the mirror and confirmed that her hair was in place and that her vibrant red lipstick perfectly framed the outline of her moist young lips. Once satisfied, she proceeded to the door to greet her close friend. The door opened and opposite Jaime was Dina in her fire red sweeter complemented by the vibrant red lipstick, which highlighted her soft blond hair, resting on her smooth shoulders. They looked at each other and remained silent and motionless for a moment, as if conveying their true feelings via a telepathic medium. Recognizing their unusual and unexpected reaction, they both began to talk simultaneously. Dina commented that the box looks very heavy and asked Jaime if he needed help, while Jaime tried at the same time, to express his admiration and compliments on how wonderful she looked and what a pleasure it was to see her. Once the couple overcame the moment of insecurity and unplanned, uncontrollable behavior, they continue greeting each other and exchanging the customary welcoming kiss.

Dina invited Jaime to follow her, pointing towards the kitchen, and told him to make himself at home. Dina followed, sat by the kitchen table and watched her dear friend carefully remove the pots and containers from the cardboard box onto the kitchen counter.

Jaime began the meal preparation while Dina kept focus on every movement he made. Whenever his eyes disengaged from the tasks he was performing and looked at her, he noticed that her eyes had been fixated on him. This behavior made Jaime somewhat self-conscious about his activities, while simultaneously providing him a certain degree of satisfaction.

Dina was curious as to what the fare of the evening was going to be and asked Jaime what he was making. He responded that, as promised, he was making Congri (rice and black beans), Carne Ripiada, (shredded beef), and Maduros (fried riped plantains). "Yummy, I cannot wait"!. "What about dessert?" she said, with a partial smile and mischievous look on her face.

Jaime experienced an unexpected inner sensation that revealed itself with redness on his cheeks, followed by miniature pebbles of moisture escaping on to his upper forehead.

Jaime hesitated before responding to the "What about dessert?" question. His respect and admiration for Dina restrained him from expressing the thought that had crossed his young mind, momentarily. He smiled at her and told her that the dessert for the evening was Natilla, which he prepared following his mother's recipe.

Having witnessed Jaime's unexpected cheeks blush, Dina smiled and responded "I cannot wait for the dessert", a response that further induced the continuation of the blush experienced by Jaime and a reinforcement of his innermost desire.

Jaime's reaction further confirmed Dina's suspicion that his feeling towards her were beyond platonic, a very comforting and desirable reaffirmation of her expectation and longing. Dina had considered that Jaime's friendship and loyalty to Vincent, and his moral values would prevent him from pursuing her, regardless of whatever feelings he may have towards her. She liked Jaime very much and enjoys being around him. She decided that she will have to be the protagonist if their relationship was to grow beyond what it is today and become what she secretly wishes it will become tomorrow. Jaime continued cooking and making light conversation while she listened, smiled and found ways to tease him. Jaime began to make the Sofrito for the Carne Ripiada. The kitchen air was impregnated with the aroma emanating from the frying pan. Dina's appetite was awakened, and prompted her to inquire how long it will be before dinner was ready. Jaime told Dina that the Congri will be ready in about an hour and the they will be able to eat. Dina responded, with a smile "you are starving me to death!"

Dina got up and walked to the Dinning room closet where she had stored a bottle of Bacardi Rum and a bottle of Coca Cola. She brought the two bottles to the kitchen, placed them on the kitchen table, and told Jaime "you made me a promise, now you have to keep it". Jaime looked back at the table and saw the bottles of Bacardi and Coca Cola on the center of the table. He remembered that the last time he was over her house, he had promised to teach her how to make Cuba Libre. He looked at her smiling and simultaneously challenging expression, highlighted by a mild blood rush, adding a pinkish tone to her lovely cheeks, and, perhaps, betraying her inner most thoughts and desire.

Jaime smiled and he too experienced the same sensation that caused blood rush and awakening of his physical and mental sensors. He said "a promise is a promise", and asked Dina to get two glasses with ice. Jaime checked the refrigerator and looked for limes. They were waiting in the refrigerator for him to squeeze and to extract its delightful tangy juices, a clear indication that she had anticipated and had carefully planned for this moment. As Jaime waited for the glasses with ice, he recognized the absence of his having any hesitation or natural resistance to the scenario that was evolving. Indeed, his inner most feelings, his desire and willingness to be a participant and not a protagonist. Dina placed the glasses with ice on the table and Jaime began pouring the ingredients into the glasses and instructing her on the necessary steps to make a good Cuba Libre.

As Jaime poured the rum into the glasses, he was careful to prepare a mild concoction. He explained to Dina that drinking Cuba Libre was akin to fishing. When fishing, if you let go too much string, the fish may swim away with the bait, the hook and the string. When drinking Cuba Libre, if you add too much rum to the mixture you may risk loosing not only your self control but also your inhibitions. Upon hearing Jaime's anecdote Dina smiled, picked up the bottle of Rum, and filled the remaining space in the glass with the sugar cane spirit. Each picked up their full Cuba Libre Glass, and the silence was broken by the sound waves of the clicking glass sides. Jaime raised his glass and Dina followed with her hands, the same trajectory, until both glasses were parallel to each other. Jaime toasted "to friendship and health". Dina toasted "To us". Once more the clicking sound momentarily pervaded. The two friends sat down and began to savor the tropical mixture, with the same delight as they pleasured the inferences from each other's words and actions.

The zestfulness of the moment, promoted by the delightful aroma of the Carne Ripiada, slowly simmering in the sofrito ingredients, awakened and enhanced the shredded meat flavor, and by the smell of the frying plantains together with the sweet and tangy Cuba Libre, created the perfect mood and the perfect setting for oppressed feelings to flourish and conquer what previously had been forbidden.

It was not long before the young couple ingested the magic brew, and provided Dina with the opportunity to demonstrate her quick learning ability by precisely following Jaime's instructions. The exception was her opting to mix a "high octane" concoction rather than the mild version suggested by Jaime.

Dina picked up both glasses of Cuba Libre that she had just prepared and walked around the table to where Jaime was standing near the stove. She handed Jaime his glass and made a toast with a very crisp and convincing "To us". Jaime's glass clicked Dina's and he repeated "To us" with the same tone and conviction. Dina pulled her chair to the side of the table were Jaime had been standing, next to his chair. She sat down and waited for him to finish stirring the rice and sit next to her. Jaime sat down and his unchallenged eyes penetrated hers, as if trying to reach and communicate with the most inner parts of her soul.

They sat silently, looking at each other. Dina lifted her left hand and slowly moved it towards his. As both hands took possession of each other, the couple experienced an instantaneous, but yet mild sensation traveling throughout their entire body, as if their hand holding had triggered a mild lightning like occurrence.

They both felt insecure, and yet gratified, by the experienced feeling of elation. Their vocal cords remained silent, as if numbed by what had just happened. Their eyes focus remained fixed on each other's.

They maintained their hands hold even tighter then before, hoping for a prolonged recurrence of such a satisfying sensation. Unable to achieve their wish, they finally released their hands and both lifted their glasses and again delighted themselves with the tropical mixture.

The room remained silent except for the sporadic taping of the pot's lids, against the edge of the pots as it dropped back down, having been slightly lifted by the steam escaping from the boiling rice and beans and from the sizzle of the frying Carne Ripiada being prepared. This was a perfect and unforgettable moment for the young couple. They both experienced an unplanned, but yet desired inner eruption of the restrained love that they have felt for each other. It did not matter whether the catalyst was the quiet setting, the aroma of the evening's fare, the enticing spirit, or all of those factors combined. What really mattered is the sprouting of that previously restrained inner feeling, not unlike the budding of a beautiful yellow rose in a sunny spring morning, yielding natural beauty and abundant fragrance. What really matters is the recognition of the mutual desire, the inner peace, and tranquility that its ultimate consequence will gift to the loving couple.

They both returned their almost emptied Cuba Libre glass to their lips, as if an excuse for each to wait for the other's words or deeds. This pause provided a very brief but nerve testing interlude before either, allowing passion to triumph, being overwhelmed by the moment, unbridled realization of previously constrained desire, or permitting their conscience to impede the eruption of their physical desire to indulge in a long waited and fantasized romantic episode.

The glasses no longer held the unrestraining potion, having been anxiously consumed by the couple. Their lips could not be further sheltered by the crystal. Thus, the couple slowly moved their glass holding arm away towards the table surface, until carefully placing the glassware on the center of the dinning table.

They focused their sight on each other's eyes, both fully resolved to fulfill their desire. Their hands began to move seeking each other. Once they reached their destination, fingers interlocked and Jaime gently pulls Dina's arms and her upper body towards him.

Dina's face slowly moved towards Jaime's. Their eye sights continued fixed on each other's, as if in a spell. Dina's lips are now fractions of inches away from Jaime's. Their breeding accelerates. Their passion and desire explodes and becomes uncontrollable as Dina's radian red and moist lips join his. Their hands quickly separate and their arms embrace allowing their hands to aggressively but tenderly caress each other.

An unexpected and unwelcomed telephone ring interrupted the beginning of a long time secretly restrained romantic exchange, now being liberated by the couple, whose previous close friendship and mutual admiration has now evolved into a much more complex relationship. The intensity of the passion encouraged Dina to ignore the attention prompting telephone ring. The ring's persistence and the aroma of the fried plantains which had reached the perfect frying point, forced Jaime and Dina to delay their amorous adventure and to pay attention to the pending call and the attention seeking fried plantains.

Dina proceeded to the living room to answer the telephone as Jaime went to the kitchen to begin removing the almost over fried plantains from the frying pan, and place them on a dish covered with a piece of brown paper bag, which he had waiting near the stove for that purpose.

Dina picked up the receiver and greeted the caller, with a tone which although controlled with much effort still projected a level of frustration with the call's un-timeliness.

The caller, Mary Richards, noticed Dina's tone. She asked Dina if she had awakened her. Dina replied with a more conciliatory tone, "No, why do you ask?" Mary Richards responded "Because you sounded annoyed when you answered my call" There was a moment of silence and Mary Richards asked "Are you ok?" Dina assured Mary Richards that she was fine and apologized if she sounded that way. She told Mary Richards that she was reading a romance story and the telephone rang just as she was reaching the climactic point of the story. Dina desiring to keep the conversation as brief as possible shared with Mary Richards how surprised she was by her call, since she was supposed to be have gone out in a double date. Mary Richards told Dina that the reason she called was because she was hoping to convince her to reconsider her decision not go on tonight's blind date with her, Roger, and his friend. She told Dina that all she needed to do was to say yes, and they will come by her apartment in half an hour to pick her up.

Dina turned down her invitation once again. She embellished her excuse by stating that her stomach was acting up, as has been the case in a number of occasions, since she lost both her husband,and the child which she was carrying. She then shared with Mary Richards that she canceled the commitment that she had for the evening.

Seeking the Future

Dina felt a combination of remorse and mischievousness as she told Mary Richards the harmless reading and ready to bed fib. The remorse was caused by having lied to her closest friend, something that she was not accustomed to doing. The mischievousness was triggered by her desire of indeed going to bed early, but not with her book. Mary Richards responded "It is too bad. You are going to miss a fun night!" Dina told her friend that she appreciated very much her concern and offer, and that perhaps another opportunity will come up in the near future. Dina thanked her friend and told her to have a good time, to take good care of herself, and not to forget to share all the details of her evening experience, next time they get together. Mary Richards, anxious to go, responded "see ya latter alligator!" and hanged up the telephone receiver.

As Dina entered the kitchen, Jaime quickly got up and pulled the chair immediately across from him for her to sit. While Dina talked to Mary Richards, Jaime had served the meal, had poured the wine, and had lit a pair of white candles that had been resting above the stove on individual candle holders. Dina eye sight lowered to the table top and saw the Cuban delicacies awaiting her taste buds. The aroma from the served dishes spilled over the side of each of the plates, and blended into a symphony of flavor, awakening and tantalizing the anxious palates. Jaime stood behind Dina's chair, waiting for her to sit down, to help her move the chair forward. She slowly turned her torso, ninety degrees to te left, followed by another slow ninety degree neck turn, until her eyes could capture his bright and gleeful brown eyes. Locking her eye's view with his, she shared how grateful she was that he came over and prepared the wonderful dinner, and how much she was looking forward to spending the evening with him alone. Before Jaime could utter the first words of this response, Dina tenderly placed her open left hand on back of Jaime's head, and slowly brought his lips to join hers. They passionately kissed, as if it was a prelude to the awaiting epicurean and romantic feast to follow.

It was nine o'clock Saturday morning. Jaime got up, being careful no to awaken Dina from her restful and dreamless sleep. He proceeded to the kitchen and began to prepare breakfast before she awoke.

The coffee was percolating and the bacon was sizzling in the frying pan when Dina walked into the kitchen in her burgundy satin house coat. The aroma from the coffee and the bacon had broken her contented sleep, a feeling that she was beginning to forget.

Dina's had freshened up before making her appearance at the kitchen's door. The room's invading morning sun rays reflecting from her back, framed her shadow on the opposite room's wall, accenting the physical beauty that she radiated. Her eyes, clear and bright, her cheeks highlighted by a natural pink blush, and her brilliant red moist lips, as inviting as the night before. But of greater import for her, the emotional burden which she has been secretly carrying, has been released akin opening the reservoir's gate and releasing the lake's overflowing waters.

As she appeared by the kitchen, he smiled in a way that caused her to wonder if life was always this good, or should it have always been so. He greeted her, "Good morning Darling! Are you hungry?" She continued her sensuous smile and responded', "I am starving!" Jaime replied, with a generous grin, "Bacon and eggs or me?" She smiled, and without hesitation said, "All of the above!" They both laughed childishly and sat at the table to enjoy the fried eggs and bacon accompanied with the always required Cafe con Leche, already waiting.

*

Four weeks had already gone by since Jaime and Dina had shared that unforgettable weekend that began innocently with the sharing of a Cuban meal, which he prepared in Dina's apartment.

The two close friends, who that evening crossed the boundaries of friendship and entered adventurous arena of intimate romance, could not find time enough to satisfy their mutual amorous desire. For Dina it was a new beginning. Life, once again, has a purpose, and now she has someone to share this purpose with. Her love for Vincent and for the fruit of their love will not be extinguished. That love will be sheltered in the deepest part of her soul, and will remain in her memory until no longer be. She now has a new love. Someone to dream with, someone to make her smile, someone to share the joys of life, and someone to help her face life's burdens, challenges, and opportunities. Jaime is likewise, elated that his friendship with Dina has blossomed beyond any immediate expectation and has crossed the boundaries leading into hopefully a long term, joyful and fruitful relationship.

During the last four weeks, life has been very different for Jaime. He no longer feels the loneliness that he felt before. He no longer yearns for his family in Cuba the same way as he did before. Yes, he misses them very much and can not wait to be with them again, longing for the love of family. But he no longer feels the emptiness and loneliness that he was experiencing in the recent past. Now, he has Dina, and while at work, he counts the hours before he can feel her warmth and enjoy seeing her smile.

During the last four weeks Jaime has, on occasion, found himself struggling with his conscience, as he remembers his best friend Vincent. He wonders whether his current relationship and blossoming love for Dina is an expression of disloyalty and a violation of the trust between two good friends, even though one has passed away. Jaime also questions himself, if his love for Dina always existed. If so, he wondered how it was possible for him to have been able to effectively conceal it from his friends, and, more important, from himself. Did any of them, or even Vincent, suspect the possibility of it's existence?. He pondered if, and how Vincent may feel, in the beyond, about this amorous development. Jaime self justifies his actions rationalizing that Vincent's love for Dina was endless. Thus, he will understand knowing Dina will be not only well taken care off, but also will be love with similar passion and care as if it were him at her side.

*

Jaime had arrived at the factory Friday morning, very anxious to attend to his responsibilities and complete his half day of work tasks, as required by his current schedule.

Today Jaime is extremely happy and excited. His sister Angelina's ship arrives tomorrow morning from Oriente, Cuba. He can not wait to see her, introduce her to Dina, and share with her the magnificence and beauty that the New York City Metropolis is. Two weeks ago, Jaime received a letter from his mother confirming that Angelina will be arriving the morning of the 15th of August at the New York City midtown pier. She will be traveling on the SS Santiago, the same ship that brought Jaime to New York City four years ago.

Jaime remembers, as if it was today, when he boarded the ship in the Port of Santiago de Cuba. It was the end of August and the eastern most city of Cuba was trying to cope with an unbearable heat wave that was only partially tamed in the early hours of the day when the Sun's rays bathed other parts of the world. The city dwellers often remained sitting outside their homes until one or two o'clock in the morning, waiting for the welcomed sea breeze to cool the night and allow them to enjoy the much needed rest without saturating the bed sheets with the body's cooling fluid. As he boarded the ship, at around nine in the morning, his shirt had already absorbed a significant amount of moisture escaping from his pores, as his body tried to compensate for the punishing heat with usual perspiration. The air was still and the scent of rum fragrance, escaping from the nearby Bacardi Rum factory, permeated the air and filled the lungs with an unforgettable aroma.

The Bacardi tradition began in the City of Santiago de Cuba in the year 1862 when the company was founded by Don Facundo Bacardi Masso. The original building that used to produce the Bacardi Rum was inhabited by fruit bats and, thus, the origin of the famous Bacardi trade mark logo

The Bacardi family played an important economic, as well as political role in the history of Santiago de Cuba. Don Facundo was exiled from the island by the Spaniards because of his anticolonial activities, and his oldest son fought on the side of the Mambises during the War of Independence from Spain. Emilio was subsequently named mayor of Santiago de Cuba by General Leonard Wood, representing the United States armed forces during the period in which the US had military control of the island.

The trolley cars unloaded their passengers. Some carrying their heavy luggage for the trip. Others carrying a heavy heart because of the oncoming separation from their loved ones, as they departed, just as Jaime was doing in what may possibly be their first adventure outside their paradise island.

Jaime remembers, once on board the ship, going on the shore side deck and waiving at his loving mother and two sisters who accompanied him for a final farewell. Momentarily, the joy of anticipating new experiences, and indeed a new life's adventure, was overcome with tempered trepidation about traveling to the unknown, and by the recurring desire not to part from those that he loves.

The ship whistle, followed by the black smoke, escaping from the smoke stacks and tarnishing the baby blue skies, interrupted the crowd's excitement. The sailors untied the thick ship's ropes from the dock's bollards and the tug boats slowly, and gently, moved the ship onto the Bay's channel. As the steam engine's pressure built up, and the speed of water displacement increase, the ship began its journey North.

The SS Santiago was primarily a cargo ship with accommodations for one hundred passengers. The cabin space was very restricted. There were four bunks per cabin, community shower and bathroom facilities, a small library, and a mess hall which could accommodate fifty people per sitting. The "chow" was for the most part very tasty. It satisfied both The Cuban and American palate.

The trip was uneventful until the ship arrived off the coast of New Jersey, near Atlantic City, and was hit by inclement weather. The breakfast that was being consumed was not retained for very long by most of the passengers, Jaime included. Large waves moved the ship in what appeared to be different directions simultaneously, complemented by unpredictable and punishing up and down motions. Jaime does not remember having prayed as much and as intensely before, as he did in the ship when it was traveling thru that storm.

*

After he finished work, Jaime rushed home to change and to meet Dina, who had taken half a day off work, to spend the afternoon with Jaime.

When Jaime arrived at Dina's apartment, she was already anxiously waiting for him. He rang the bell. Before he could ring again, Dina opened the door, greeted him with a broad smile, embraced him, and rewarded him with a sensuous kiss, as if they had been apart from each other for days. Jaime responded with equal intensity. The couple continued their loving greetings uninterruptedly as they closed the doors behind them.

Dina and Jaime had decided to go grocery shopping and to

Seeking the Future

purchase a token welcome to New York gift, for Angelina. After completing their shopping tasks, Dina suggested going to China Town for dinner. She shared having an urge for Chinese food. The word "no" was nonexistent for him and when it came to her desires, thus their destination became Chinatown. On their way downtown, they decided to go to the Lucky Moon, a restaurant which they frequented with the "gang of seven".

This will be the first time that they, either alone or with each other, will visit the Lucky Moon since Vincent's death. They both recognized that memories of times past may be awakened and, perhaps, cause diminishing of the anticipated mood as they dealt with resurfaced sorrow and, perhaps, unwarranted guilt, having filled his death-creating vacuum well beyond the close friendship that would have been anticipated. Nonetheless, they mutually concluded that sooner or later they needed to let the past remain so and that it was better, based on their new developed relationship, for it to be sooner rather than later.

They decided to take the trolley downtown, since they had finished their tasks earlier than anticipated.

It was a beautiful afternoon in the city, although a bit hotter than the couple would have preferred. A light breeze, from the west side of the island joined and was welcome by the weary passengers on their way home from a tiring work day. Unfortunately, every time the trolley stopped for pickup or discharge that pleasurable unplanned passenger dissipated it's presence. After a forty five minute ride downtown, including one change of trolley, the couple got off at Bowery and Canal Street. They walked approximately two and one half blocks to Mott Street, were the favorite restaurant was hiding below street level.

The restaurant facility was not luxurious, but the lack of ambiance was more than offset by excellent quality, attentive service, and reasonably priced cuisine. The restaurant had eight round tables, each covered with a bright red table cloth and surrounded by four plain wooden chairs.

The owner, Mr. Lee, recognized Dina, bowed to her more than once as a sign of respect while simultaneously and affectionately greeting her. Mr. Lee directed the couple to the corner table, the best location in the house. He assisted Dina with the chair and then asked her how she was. He told her that he missed their presence at the restaurant. Mr. Lee looked at Dina's eyes and said "Miss, Dina, it has been a long time since you visited my restaurant. What's happening. You no like my food no more?" Neither Dina nor Jaime wanted to dwell on the details as to why they had not returned to the restaurant for quite a while. Dina responded "Mr. Lee, we do like your food very much. That is why we are here this evening. Over half of our dinning group of friends moved out of town, and the remaining members of the group stopped getting together after that".

One of the waiters brought hot tea and filled the tea cups already set and awaiting the hot brew to delight the dormant taste buds. Once they both sat down, settled themselves on their seats, and zipped a very small portion of the very hot tea, Mr. Lee returned to their table following the undeclared protocol. Mr. Lee handling the waiter's duties for his favorite customers. They browsed the extensive Oriental food menu as Mr. Lee waited patiently for the couple to decide which Chinese delicacies they wanted tonight. Dina could not make up her mind as which of the many available choices will be pleasing her palate and fulfilling her hunger this afternoon. She looked at Jaime and asked him, "Darling, what are you going to have?". Jaime was just as uncertain as she was. He responded, "I, also am having a difficult time deciding. Why don't we ask Mr. Lee to suggest two or three dishes, that we can share?" Dina smiled, relieved at not having to choose, and responded to his suggestions, confirming her conclusion that it was a great idea. She thought that Mr. Lee always picks delicious dishes which the average, non oriental person, would not know how to order anyway. Jaime told Mr. Lee to surprise them with three house dishes that he recommends. He insisted that one of the dishes had to be his special house fried rice. Jaime also asked for Egg Drop Soup for Dina and Hot and Sour soup for himself.

All of the tables had been occupied by the time the couple finished ordering their meal. The sound waves originating from the many conversations in an assortment of languages bounced against the plastered wall and competed with each other trying fill any absence of sound in the crowded dining room. This medley of voices also provided a shelter for any one wanting to have private conversations at their individual tables.

Jaime sitting across from Dina, at the small table, barely large enough to handle the serving dishes with the ordered three entries, extended his arms and guided his hand to the location where Dina's were resting on the table. Each of his hand took possession of each of her hands and gently squeezed them, communicating his affection and caring. He looked directly into her eyes, wanting to express his most inner feelings without saying a word. Dina, on the other hand, experienced a momentary chill caused by Jaime's intense and penetrating look, focusing his eyes with hers, as if trying to blend their inner soul.. For a moment, their silence was framed by a beehive like bussing sounds and words in different tones, pitches, and languages, generated by Mr. Lee's many other clients. The couple had created a virtual bubble, were the only thing that mattered was the two of them and their voiceless conveyance of what each meant to the other. Dina, as she held his hands, could feel his pulse as his blood rushes through his network of blood vessels, responding to his heart's accelerated pace caused by realization of a dream long restrained. She could likewise feel moisture escaping from her pores on the middle of her palm.

There was much that the couple wanted to share with each

other, and yet neither one could bring themselves to approach the subjects. Perhaps, fearful that the outcome may not be as they wish, and possibly risk loosing what they now had, for the sake of assuring that the future's path is smoothly paved. They recognized that long lasting relationships requires not only sharing their vision for the future, but also unearthing and confronting, if necessary, painful memories, beginning to be laid to rest.

Finally Jaime broke the silence and began to speak "Dina, my darling, these last four weeks have been the most wonderful four weeks that I could remember. The emptiness that prevailed in my life has been filled with nothing but thoughts of you and the wonderfulness of being with you and sharing experiences with you." Before Jaime could express his next thought she responded "Jaime, it is so wonderful to hear you say that, for I feel the same as you do. These last four weeks have refueled my soul. They have motivated me to once again feel alive and to look forward to every morning's birth". Jaime smiled tenderly and continued, "Dina, I do not want us to loose what we have, for it is a wonderful gift. I want to share my life with you for as long as you wish to share yours with me". She responded "My love, nothing will make me happier than to be with you forever!" He continued, "Dina, there is much that we need to talk about as we move forward with our relationship." Before he could share his next thought, the waiter approached the table with the steaming Egg Drop and Hot and Sour soups, which the couple wishfully awaited.

"I am so hungry!" exclaimed Dina "I am, too" he responded. They both picked up their Chinese style soup spoon and quietly began to consume their delicious fare. Their eyes fixed on each other, attempting to continue communicating expressions of love and commitments and the desire to dedicate their life to each other.

Dina commented that her soup was extraordinary and that the

abundance of eggs made it particularly delicious. Jaime also was very pleased with his Hot & Sour Soup and with the delicious mushrooms that had been generously added to his bowl.

Just as Dina and Jaime finished the last drip of the tasty broths, a waiter politely asked them if they had finished. They nodded affirmatively and proceeded to remove the empty soup bowls from the small table. A second waiter was already waiting for the space, occupied by the soup bowls to become available, in order to place a clean dish in front of each of the guests.

The couple resumed their comforting hand holding and visually communicating with each other while waiting for the main course. They were not only filling their stomach cavity with the delicious nutrients, but they were also recharging their being with unexpressed expressions of love.

Mr. Lee accompanied the waiter carrying the three dishes that the young couple will be enjoying. The first dish placed on the table was the famous House Fried Rice. The rice, slightly cream color from the soy sauce, was blended with diced ham, scrambled eggs, chopped onions, bacon bits, peas, chopped scallions, and diced mushrooms. The aroma carried by the escaping steam tantalized the couple's taste buds.

The second dish, Lemon Chicken, was Dina's favorite. Sliced chicken breasts, breaded, then deep fried to a crisp, placed over a bed of lettuce, and generously bathed with a superb slightly tart, lightly sweet and pungent lemon based sauce, and garnished with a thinly slice of fresh orange.

Upon seeing the Lemon chicken, Dina commented to Jaime "I can wait to taste that chicken, it always is my favorite, especially the way they prepare it here".

Mr. Lee placed the third dish next to Jaime, barely able to find adequate space on the crowded table. It was a deep fried Whole Sea Bass, lying gently on a dark sauce, lightly covering the bottom of the dish. The Sea Bass was surrounded by fresh spinach leafs and decorated with thin lemon slices and diced ripe mango.

Mr. Lee picked up a knife and spoon, also sitting on the waiter's serving tray. Using those tools of the trade, he proceeded to expertly debone the Sea Bass, a process and skill which always impressed Jaime. In a matter of a minute or two, Mr. Lee had extracted the entire fishbone from the tail to the head. He placed fishbone on an empty dish, leaving the juicy and delicious white meat for the couple's delight.

Jaime congratulated Mr. Lee for his skillful handling of the spoon and knife combinating to debone the Sea Bass.

As they began their epicurean adventure, the couple requested a pair of Chop Sticks for each of them. The waiter quickly responded with two pairs, each enclosed in red enveloped imprinted with Chinese characters with meanings unknown and of no interest to the couple submerge on the cuisine's pleasure.

Jaime passed the Sea Bass to Dina and his eyes remained fixed on her every move and gesture as she placed a small portion of the moist and inviting fish's white meat on to her plate. He felt contented just watching her delight in savoring the delicious fare after she delicately placed her fish laden fork into her mouth.

The couple's conversation tempo diminished significantly as they focused their attention onto the feast which occupied almost every inch of the small table they sat at. Occasionally Jaime inquired if she wanted more hot tea and or if she needed any dishes to be passed. Her response was always accompanied with a loving smile and a melodic voice, expressing a happiness and fulfillment, which she realized not ever before experiencing it.

All the restaurant's patrons had now been served. Thus, the background noise changed from a beehive like mixture of voices to a melody of muffled sounds from the tapping of utensils and dishware that the diners were using. Voices were clearer to understand, prompting the couple to move their heads closer and lower their volume.

The couple finished their Dinner, commented to each other how delicious it was, and asked which was the preferred dish. They both agreed that the Sea Bass was superb, but the lemon chicken was incomparable.

The waiter removed the Dinner plates and returned with a dish loaded with fresh orange wedges and two fortune cookies. They began enjoying the sweet and juicy orange pieces, simultaneously acknowledging that the oranges served at Chinese restaurants are always very sweet.

Dina looked at Jaime and told him, "Jaime before we started eating you told me there is so much that we need to talk about as we move forward with our relationship'. What did you have in mind?" Jaime smiled, held Dina's hand and told her, "Darling, what I had and have in mind is to tell you how much I love you, to tell you how wonderful these past weeks have been, and to ask you if I could be honored to have you as my wife" Dina squeezed Jaime's hand, fixed her eyes on his, and remained silent and externally composed. Internally, all her body's sensors sounded the alarm, her heart accelerated and her blood rushed at high speed throughout every vessel in her body. Miniature moisture pebbles broke through her velvety forehead skin and a gentle weakness could be felt by her extremities. Dina was momentarily unable to create any sound in response to Jaime's unexpected question.

Jaime feeling insecure by the lack of response and by Dina's appearance of being in another "dimension" said, "Dina" increasing his tone a few octaves, to the point that some of the people at the adjacent tables rapidly turned their heads towards him, trying to satisfy their curiosity. Jaime smile at the curious onlookers, and they lightly embarrassed returned to their previous posture. As Jaime refocused his attention to Dina, her face radiated with happiness, her eyes' brilliance would be the envy of any diamond trader, and her moist and vibrant red lips related the passion and hunger for the same love that he had recently learned to recognize and to cherish. Dina once again squeezed Jaime's captive hands. She pulled them close to her bosoms, fixed her eye sight on his and told him, "Jaime, my darling, your words have made me the happiest girl in the world. Yes!, yes!, and yes!, I do want to be your wife forever" The lovers embraced and kissed passionately as if in the solitude of their alcove, oblivious of their surrounding and of their audience. Their passionate kiss submerged them into that "love dimension" were their mutual souls', physical and emotional feelings are blended into one sense of being. The accompanying restaurant's patron's applause brought the loving couple back to reality.

A mild case of embarrassment overcame them and they decided that it was best to pay for their dinner. They did and graciously exited the restaurant to escape the inquiring eyes and telling smiles from the other diners.

The lovers walked northbound on Mott Street, towards Canal Street, holding hands and looking at the world with a perspective significantly different than what they had experienced earlier. They have committed themselves to each other. They have giving life a different meaning. And they have provided destiny and an opportunity to fulfill their future dreams with much joy.

Coincidentally, they walked past the Transfiguration Church, also located on Mott Street, and he related to her, "Darling, this church was founded in the early eighteen hundreds by a very famous Cuban priest named Padre Varela. He was renown for his self sacrifice and for his dedicated service to the Italian and Irish immigrant communities." Dina was curious and asked Jaime "why would a Cuban priest be serving in lower Manhattan rather than in his own country?" Jaime responded, "He was forced to seek exile in the United States by the Spanish crown because of his outspokenness for individual freedom and liberty." He then added, "Varela continued sharing his passion for Cuba's independence in New York, where he proclaimed Cuba's right to be an independent and free nation."

As they walked past the church, Jaime asked Dina, "Darling, when will you like to get married?" Dina thought momentarily, looked at Jaime with broad smile and said, "My love let's get married tomorrow!" Jaime smiled back and responded "Darling, tomorrow morning we have to pick up Angelina at the port. Did you forget?" She replied, "You are right my love, tomorrow is out of the question. How about Sunday?"

Jaime delayed his response as they maneuvered through the crowded street while approaching the intersection of Canal and Mott streets. He asked Dina, "What about our telling your parents, and your friends before we actually get married?"

Dina looked pensive, yet very sure of herself and of her response to the question, which he posed. She responded, "Darling, I would like for us to find a little church, get married right away and then surprise everyone with the news." She continued, "I do not wish to share that day with anyone else I want you all to my self!"

Because of his love and desire to provide nothing but happiness for her, Jaime was perfectly willing to fulfill her wishes and acknowledge his acceptance of her wedding request saying, "Darling, if that is your desire, it is mine as well"

Jaime asked Dina if she had a particular church in mind. She responded, "Yes, as a matter of fact I do. Last month Diana, my co worker, decided to get married at the last minute, before her boyfriend departed for sea duty. She went to the Little Church Around the Corner, located on East 29th Street. She spoke with the priest and were married that same afternoon after filing the necessary papers."

Jaime then asked Dina, "Did the priest marry them so quickly because her husband had to depart for sea duty?" Dina replied, "According to Diana, this church caters to the "theater crow" and is better known as the Theater Church. The priest of this non denominational church is known to be very accommodating to spontaneous marrying decisions" Jaime continuing to tightly hold Dina's hands while they walked and asked her "Why don't we take the trolley to The Little Church Around the Corner?" Dina kissed Jaime on the cheeks and told him, "I love you", and the couple proceeded to the trolley stop to begin their journey to East 29th Street.

It was six in the morning and Jaime awoke as he usually does every morning, as if sleep had been interrupted by a rooster's crowing. His "internal clock" was more consistent and dependable than any man invented contraction. Jaime turned over towards Dina and admired her angelic facial features, lightly caressed by the soft morning sun rays which invaded the semi-darkness of the bedroom through a partially raised window shade. Not wanting to waken her, Jaime kissed the tip of his right hand index fingers and slowly moved his arms towards Dina's forehead until he could gently touch her and transfer the message of love, which his lips had deposited on the willing fingers. Jaime proceeded to the kitchen to begin preparing breakfast for his soon to be wife.

Jaime could not remember when, before he had felt as fulfilled as he did this beautiful morning. Last night, he once again shared the evening with his lovely Dina. They engaged in another love adventure until their love hungry bodies surrendered to sleep from exhaustion and complete fulfillment.

*

The arrival of his sister, Angelina, had been anticipated for many months and, finally, today he will be able to hug and kiss her. His kisses will not only be for Angelina but will also be for his loving mother and the rest of his family in Cuba.

Angelina's arrival will, as if a piece of Jaime's homeland had been transported on the deck of the SS Santiago, fulfill the vacuum existing in his soul since departing from his homeland paradise.

As Jaime prepared the coffee and fried eggs for breakfast, he began to mentally review the tasks that needed addressing, including sharing his and Dina's spontaneous marriage plans with his sister.

The coffee aroma became the wake up call for Dina. She got up, put on her burgundy colored robe and walked silently towards the kitchen stove were Jaime was preparing the morning meal. She walked quietly, admiring Jaime's robust rear torso, absent of a shirt, and embraced him from the back, placing her velvety cheeks on his shoulder blades. Jaime welcomed the affectionate expression and responded by turning around and embracing his lover with an unbridled passion.

The romantic interlude gave way to the replenishment of energy to be provided by the delicious breakfast which Jaime had prepared. The couple sat down and began consuming the much needed nutrients while reviewing the tasks that required attention during the next couple of days.

Today will be dedicated to Angelina. The couple will go to the Midtown Pier to welcome the ship on its arrival and meet and greet Jaime's attractive sister. They will assist Angelina with custom requirements, if needed, and help her gather her luggage for the trip to Dina's apartment. After Angelina is settled in her room, the committed lovers intent to take her for a walk, and perhaps a trolley ride, if she is not too tired, to begin the city's introduction.

It was ten in the morning when Dina and Jaime arrived at the 42nd Street Pier. The SS Santiago had not docked as yet, but smokestacks could be seen down river. Dina and Jaime rushed to the observation deck to try to see the ship cruising up river to the pier. The river's traffic was very active this morning. Various cargo and cruise ships were navigating up river aided by tug boats and port guide vessels. The SS Santiago, which Jaime quickly recognized by the red, white, and blue lines framing an eagle's painting immediately below the smoke stack, was approximately three blocks away from the 42nd Street pier.

Jaime and Dina, together with approximately one hundred other New Yorkers, looked anxiously as the ship approached. Most began waiving their handkerchiefs while holding hands as their expressions of welcome and as an outlet for their hard to control anticipation of their love one's arrival. The river waters were reasonably calm. An easterly breeze cooled the morning's warm sun rays, and the puffy clouds decorated the clear baby blue skies. It was a glorious morning to be in the city, and the perfect setting to welcome a loved one.

The SS Santiago approached the pier slowly, powered by two tug boats expertly guided by their captains. The ship docked with incredible ease and the crew members quickly picked up the anchoring ropes and dropped them overboard to the waiting land crew to secure the ship to the docks.

The SS Santiago, primarily a cargo ship which transports raw sugar and some tropical products to New York City, also carries a limited number of passengers. This trip apparently was not fully loaded with passengers, if the number of people on the ship's deck provided any evidence.

Jaime searched the ship's deck for his lovely sister and was unable to locate her. He continued looking. Dina also trying to identify Angelina, from her picture, asked Jaime, "Darling have you seeing her yet?" Jaime shook his head and began to respond, when he noticed a very attractive young lady, dressed in a bright red with black trim outfit, and wearing a petite, round, and delicately woven straw hat with a small black bow, and holding a veil like material which covered her exposed hair. That is Angelina, "He exclaimed to Dina. Dina not able to identify the person which Jaime was pointing to, asked anxiously, "Which one darling?" Jaime happily responded, "The girl in the red dress with black trim. Can you see her?. She is wearing a hat with a veil" Once Dina heard Jaime's description, she was easily able to identify Angelina. They both began to happily waive their hands, together with the flowers that Jaime was holding for his sister.

Angelina was also searching the welcoming crowd for her dear brother. Upon hearing her name being called, she raised her eye sight to the pier's observation deck where she spotted her brother and a companion, expressing their welcoming joy by energetically jumping and waiving. Angelina's excitement about seeing her brother, whom she loves dearly, also joined the up and down welcoming ritual, which often takes place when separated love ones make eye contact but are unable to hold each other. Finally, the ship's aft unloading ramp was in place and the passengers began to slowly exit the SS Santiago.

Jaime and Dina quickly walked down the stairs to the customs waiting area. They stood behind a roped area by the exit door where passengers were expected to come out once released by customs. The anticipation and excitement of Angelina's arrival made the waiting minutes appear more like hours. Finally, passengers began to exit into the open waiting area followed by uniformed luggage handlers pushing carts loaded with their luggage.

Half an hour later the loving couple was still waiting behind the rope. Most of the passengers had already exited and the waiting area was becoming desolated.

Jaime was beginning to be concerned that perhaps Angelina was having communication problem with customs.

He turned to Dina, his face expressing the concern that he was experiencing and asked her, "Darling, do you think I should find out what is going on?" Dina responded, "be patient, I am sure everything is fine. Relax she will be out shortly". Moments later,

Dina spotted the bright red dress before Jaime was able to do so. Excitedly, Dina called for Jaime's attention, "Darling, there she is! Your sister is coming. She is beautiful!" Angelina walked graciously out of the customs area, followed by the baggage handler carrying a large, square, leather bound luggage, secured with leather belts almost as thick as the belt which Jaime wore around his waist.

When Angelina spotted her brother, she began to sprint in her high heals to where Jaime and Dina were standing. Simultaneously, Jaime walked under the rope and ran towards his sister. A custom's security guard tried to stop him from entering the cordoned area. Jaime had already reached his sister, kissing, hugging, and moving her in a circular motion, until her feet were airborne. He repeatedly told her how happy he was to see her and how much he missed her.

Jaime finally stopped hugging and kissing her in response to the guard's urging for the brother and sister to keep moving. As they walked to the waiting area, where Dina was anxiously waiting to meet her beautiful sister-in-law-to-be, Jaime, asked Angelina, "Angi", (the affectionate nickname which he uses when addressing her), cuéntame, como esta Mama? (Tell me, how is Mother?)

Jaime and his sister reached Dina, who was waiting somewhat anxious to meet Angelina. Jaime told Dina, "Darling this is my little Angi". The word "darling" surprised Angelina and the surprise was quickly reflected on her facial expression. Jaime, noticing his sister reaction, said, "Angelina, I am sure this will be a surprise to you. I want you to meet Dina, my wife to be, and your soon to be sister in law". Angelina smiled, affectionately hugged Dina, and with a distinctive Cuban accent told her, "Dina, I am so happy that Jaime found some one to share his life with. It is a real pleasure to meet you. I look forward to getting to know you really good, during my stay in New York City".

Dina responded, "Angelina, I am so happy to meet you. I have heard so much about you from Jaime. I welcome you and truly look forward for us to really get to know each other and become good friends." The two of them embraced, as if old friends were meeting once again. Angelina turned to Jaime and with a broad smile said in her broken English "Jaimecito (how he is affectionately called in Cuba), "diablito" (little devil), why did you not write to us, and shared the great news about finding such a wonderful and beautiful love partner?" Jaime smiled, looked at Dina lovingly and gently placed his right arm over her shoulder and responded "Angi, the reason I did not share the news was because we acknowledge loving each other just a few weeks ago. As a matter of fact, I proposed to Dina yesterday and she made me the happiest men in the city when she said "Yes"".

Jaime continued, "It is a long story which we will share with you in the future. The important thing is that we love each other very much and that we will be getting married tomorrow". "Tomorrow!?", exclaimed Angelina having been taken by complete surprise. "Yes tomorrow", repeated Jaime. He added, "And you are going to be our witness, if you have no objections" Angelina smiled, although still a bit flustered by the unexpected news. She once again hugged Dina, kissed her on the cheeks, and told her, "Dina, I am happy for both of you and I am glad that you are going to be part of the family".

The luggage handler coughed lightly, trying to get Angelina's attention. The family gathering was depriving him of the opportunity to help other passengers, and, thus, earn additional tips from them. Jaime recognized the luggage handler's motivation and told the girls, "Ladies let's get moving. We are holding up progress and restricting this fellow from helping other passengers"

Jaime and the girls walked out of the Pier's building onto the sidewalk where he instructed the baggage handler to unload

Angelina's baggage onto the sidewalk. The baggage handler responded without hesitation and, upon placing the luggage on the ground, lifted his hat to Jaime indicating that his mission was accomplished. Jaime extracted a few coins from his pocket and handed them to the grateful baggage handler, who left to serve another arriving traveler.

A taxi driver, upon seeing Jaime and the two girls, brought his cab to the curb next to them and quickly requested their destination. The driver dismounted from the vehicle and with Jaime's assistance, placed the luggage on the top of the taxi since it could not fit anywhere else. He secured the luggage with twine stored in his trunk for similar situations, and proceeded to drive the three passengers to their destination.

The same steps were repeated at Dina's apartment. The taxi driver and Jaime lowered the trunk on to the curb. The two carried the trunk and placed it on the apartment's foyer. Jaime paid the driver including a generous tip, and thanked him very much for his help with the luggage. The driver departed to look for another fare.

The three of them moved the trunk into the house and into Angelina's bedroom. Dina welcomed Angelina to the apartment and told her, attempting to speak a little Spanish "Esta es tu casa (This is your house), and this room is your room. I hope it is comfortable enough for you". Angelina gratefully responded, "Your apartment is beautiful and this room is more than perfect. I am not accustomed to having a room just for myself. At home, I have always shared a bedroom with my older sister"

Dina grabbed Angelina by the hands and showed her the entire apartment, including the kitchen. She told Angelina, "Feel free to help yourself to whatever is in the refrigerator. Remember, you are family and you should always feel that this is your home." Angelina answered, "Thank you, Dina. You are being too good to me". Dina told Angelina, "I am very happy that you came to visit. I want and hope that you have a great time while in New York City." She added, "It is almost twelve thirty. Why don't you take an hour to relax a bit and freshen up. Later, we will begin to introduce the city to you. How does that sound?" Angelina responded, "Perfect!".

At about quarter to two, Dina lightly knocked on Angelina's door and got no response. Suspecting that Angelina may be asleep, she quietly opened the door and confirmed that Jaime's sister was indeed sleeping. She quickly closed the room door just as quiet and returned to the living room where Jaime was reading the introduction to Pearl Buck's Good Earth novel. Dina told Jaime that Angelina was asleep and that they should let her rest at least for another hour. She sat next to Jaime. He placed his right arm over her shoulders and they sat silently, sharing each other's warmth and enjoying the comfort of being together.

Before the hour was over, Angelina walked into the living room and found the loving couple resting comfortably with Dina's head leaning on Jaime's shoulder while retaining his head with hers. They both took and unplanned "cat" nap.

Angelina mischievously said, "I guess I was not the only one that was tired!", awakening the somewhat embarrassed couple from their sweet dreams. Jaime smiled and asked Angelina, "Are you ready to be introduced to the big city!" Angelina responded, "As ready as I will ever be!"

Dina asked Angelina if she was hungry. "Yes, I am starving", said Angelina. Dina turned to Jaime and said, "Why don't we introduce Angelina to a typical New York fare?" Jaime responded, "What do you have in mind, darling?" Dina answered; "Let's take her downtown to Katz's Deli in East Houston Street!". Then she added, "she will have the opportunity of savoring real New York's hot dogs, and the Corned Beef sandwich that you could kill for!". She repeated, "Let's go downtown to Katz". Jaime replied, "That is a great idea". He turned to Angeline and explained that Katz deli is a New York landmark. It started doing business in the year 1888. He added, "During that long period it has been able to gain the reputation that it has deservedly gained for the product quality and unique service that it provides. "Katz it is then" responded Jaime, adding, "Ladies let's get ready to go".

The threesome freshened up, left the apartment, and the loving couple proceeded to introduce Angelina to the city that is always awake. They decided to take a trolley and give Angelina an opportunity to flavor more of the city's reality. They boarded the first and, as it slowly moved over the shinny city's street's rails, Angelina's facial expression communicated her amazement and her inability to absorb and process all the new visual experiences that her eyes were communicating.

After transferring to the South East bound trolley, they finally arrived at East Houston Street, a few blocks East of Katz's deli. They walked west bound, all three admiring their surroundings and the loving couple anticipating the delicious treats that they will soon be sharing with Angelina.

The three arrived at the restaurant, and quickly found that many other people had the same idea as they. The long waiting line to enter the corner deli confirmed the locale's reputation for quality fare has not diminished.

They stood in line and talked about Angelina's trip, which according to her narration, was pleasant and uneventful, including great weather conditions for the most part. She also shared, with a somewhat of a mischievous smile, that there was a young sailor on the ship, with a heavy Italian accent, who appeared to have been going out of his way to be charming and continuously seek her company during the cruise. She added that he was very nice, and laughingly said that she does like bearded fellows.

Finally, the threesome was able to enter the deli and submerge themselves in to the unpretentious facility, which is more than compensated by the aroma and savor of the food, available.

Upon entering the facility, each patron is handed a ticket which represents either the free exit from the facility or the cost of the items consumed. The charges for all items ordered are entered by the counter server, on one or more of the ticket which has to be presented by each of the guests on the way out of the restaurant. Guests who misplaced their tickets are required to pay a restaurant's predetermined sum, before being allowed to exit.

The threesome walked to the counter and waited on the hot dog line to get three of the delicious Kosher hot dogs. They moved to the sandwich line where they ordered a combination platter, consisting of corned beef, pastrami, and brisket of beef, six slices of Jewish Rye Bread, and Cucumber Pickles.

They carried their tray to a not easy to find, empty table. Jaime returned to the serving counter to order a house beer for himself and two Coca Colas for the girls. He returned to the table and they began to share and the anticipated Deli feast.

Although not familiar with the particular Jewish Deli delicacies, Angelina quickly demonstrated that her taste buds welcomed the new flavors and textures by repeating previously served portions.

Once they exited Katz, after finishing their meal and paying at the cashier station, Angelina could not stop complimenting the flavor and tenderness of all three types of meats, which they had ordered and consumed. She added that the Hot Dogs were the best that she ever had, prompting Jaime to comment, "That is understandable since you did not have many hot dogs in Cuba". Angelina retorted, "You know what I meant Jaimecito. Don't be funny"

The soon to be married couple and the New York City newcomer began a westbound leisure walk on East Houston towards Broadway. Angelina was submerged into her new experience; including the buildings' architectures, the clothing styles, the vegetation, the city sounds, and activity tempo. Both Dina and

Jaime enjoyed watching Angelina's reactions and curiosity as she absorbs and savors this new adventure in a strange city, an unimaginable experience for her.

As they approached Broadway, Jaime pointed to the Woolworth Building and shared with Angelina, "That building is owned by the company who owns the Woolworth store in Santiago. It was constructed before the First World War and it was the tallest building in the world until a few years ago, when Chrysler constructed a taller building near Central Station. Angelina looked up to the building's tower and could not help but be amazed by the magnitude of the steel and concrete structure.

Jaime and Dina decided to introduce Angelina to the most beautiful lady in the city. They shared that they are going to visit a tireless lady, whose welcoming message has been a God gift to hundreds of thousands of immigrants who arrive at our nation's shores. A beautiful lady that has maintained, the flame of hope for millions and millions of others and known as the Statue of Liberty. Jaime's sister expressed her excitement when she heard their new destination,. She share that she always dreamed of visiting the "Grandiose Lady in the Bay".

The threesome boarded the southbound trolley once more and enjoyed the early evening's westerly breeze as they crossed Lower Manhattan's streets in their journey to the southern most tip of the island, where the New York Aquarium is located and, nearby, is the popular Statue of Liberty Ferry.

The southern most tip of Manhattan is not only the Aquarium site, but is also full of history. It was an American fort with its batteries pointed SouthWest at the New York Bay. It was for a period of time, known as "Castle Gardens", a popular promenade and beer garden. It became the immigration center during the second half of the 1800's and, more recently, it has been the New York Aquarium's site.

Dina, Jaime and Angelina got off the trolley at the last stop before it began its return trip northbound. They walked leisurely to the island's westerly shoreline until they were able to view the Majestic Lady, lovingly welcoming those yearning for Liberty with the message, "Give me your tired, your poor, your huddled masses yearning to breathe free." Angelina was overwhelmed by the statue's beauty and by the surrounding waterscape provided by an impressive Hudson River Bay. The threesome decided to remain in the area, until it was time to return home, taking in the gorgeous views and submerging themselves in the euphoric enjoyment projected by all the visitors, who, likewise, had taken similar journeys to the historic Southern tip of Manhattan.

*

They returned to Dina's apartment at about nine in the evening. Angelina, although young and generally very energetic, shared with her brother and sister in-law to be, "You both have tired me out, but I loved every minute of it". Jaime teased his sister when he told her with a smile, "Angi, you must be getting old. I never remember hearing words of surrender from you before". Her reply was, "Jaimecito, don't forget that I just arrived from a long trip on the ship!" They both smiled as if confirming that there were no victors in this discussion. The brother and sister appeared to have quickly picked up the one-upmanship game, as if they had never been apart from each other.

Dina asked Angelina if she would like a snack before retiring to bed. Angelina accepted the offer and asked for a cold Coke, if available. Dina showed Angelina were the Coke bottles were stored and lovingly told her, "From now on, you help yourself. This is your home away from home".

After Angelina had been taken care off, Dina turned to Jaime and told him, "Darling, would you like something to eat or drink before returning to your apartment?" This question was not a surprise to Jaime. He and she had agreed that he will not stay over her apartment once Angelina arrived until after they were married. As an older brother and following his homeland tradition, he felt obliged not to encourage his younger sister to behave otherwise.

Angelina finished her refreshment and announced that she was going to bed. She kissed her brother and hugged and kissed Dina while expressing, once again, that it was great pleasure to meet her and that she was trilled to find out she will become a member of the family.

*

After Angelina retired to her room, the lovers embraced and kissed each other with a passion, reminiscent of newsreel scenes, showing sailors saying goodbye, perhaps forever, before departing on their military tour. Recognizing that the romantic temptation was rapidly awakening, the young couple ceased their amorous embrace and Jaime departed to his apartment.

After Jaime's departure, Dina was not quite ready to go to bed as of yet, so she thought. She sat in the living room and began to listen to radio broadcast featuring Guy Lombardo and his orchestra. The soft music, the great meal, and the excitement of the day began to take its toll, and Dina's consciousness was neutralized by the body's need to rest.

Her restful and dreamless short nap was rudely interrupted by the attention demanding telephone bell's ring.

Dina was partially awakened when she managed to pick up the telephone receiver and greeted the caller with a zombielike "Halo..o". The voice on the other end of the telephone immediately said, "This is the long distance operator. I have a call for Mrs. Dina Wagner. Are you Mrs. Wagner?" Dina responded, "Yes operator, this is Mrs. Wagner" Dina was thoroughly confused. The operator following with the usual question, "Will you accept this call?" She wondered who would be calling her long distance then responded, "Who Is calling?" The caller, her close friend, Mary Richard, quickly responded, "Dina it's me, Mary Richards!", followed by Dina telling the operator that she accepts the call. The operator connected the two parties and immediately Mary Richards voice, aided by the modern technological advancements of the period, her friend anxiously responded asking, "Dina, this is Mary Richards, were have you been all day? I have called you three times already and could not get you. Where have you been?, I was getting worried!"

Dina having finally fully awakened by the telephone call and the operator's request and having gained her full consciousness, responded in a firm and motherly like tone, "Mary Richards, I should be the one to ask you that question. I have not heard from you for almost an entire month. Last time we spoke, you were going on a date with Roger. Since then, I have had no idea of your where about."

The sound waves, traveling unencumbered through thousands of miles momentarily ceased and silence overcame the moment. The soundless moment was obvious to both friends. Finally, Mary Richards began to explain, "Dina, forgive me! That night that I went out with Roger, when I asked you to go on a double date, we had such a wonderful time that we wanted to spend every minute of the days together. Roger had to go on a very important business trip to California, and he asked me to go with him". Dina responded, questioning about her responsibility. Mary Richards continued, "Roger turns out to be an associate of my employer. He used his influence to have my employer agree to an early, no pay, vacation. We left for San Francisco the next evening. I am calling you from California right now". "Oh my God!" exclaimed Dina followed by, "You are out of your mind! How can you drop everything and go to California with someone that you hardly know?" Mary Richards' joyful laughter preceded her response, "Love, only love. My dear Dina".

Dina was not surprised with the news shared by her best friend. She knows Mary Richards very well and lack of spontaneity and adventure seeking are not part of her short comings. Dina expressed to her dear friend how pleased she was that her new love adventure was bearing happiness, and that she hoped that it would always remain so. Mary Richards conveyed, "My dearest of friend, this is not a one time adventure. This is the real thing. It is the gateway from searching for an unending love and for fulfillment of long term happiness. We are getting married next spring in New York." Dina excitedly responded, "I am so happy for you. Congratulations. It is great to hear such good news" Mary Richards answered, "Thank you darling".

Dina proceeded to ask her friend when she would be returning home. Mary Richards informed her that she expected to be home in two weeks. Then she inquired, "Why do you ask?" Dina responded, "Because I have a surprise to share with you", she responded, "Tell me now. I cannot wait for two weeks. The curiosity will kill me!" "You have no choice. You have to wait" responded Dina.

The two friends spoke briefly about the beauty and quaintness of the City of San Francisco. She added, the San Fran China Town section of the City reminded her of the good times that the Gang Of Seven shared in lower Manhattan. They then said goodbye, until she returns in two weeks hence, and terminated the call sharing verbal goodbye kisses.

Dina was very pleased to hear the great news about the emerging love between Mary Richards and Roger. She was pleased not only because of the joyfulness that her closed friend appears to be experiencing, but also, and perhaps, selfishly, because of her own action. Mary Richards' secretly running away with Roger without sharing it with her, before hand, may ensure that their friendship not be permanently damaged when she finally tells her friend about her marriage, without first sharing that secret with Mary Richards.

Dina turned off the living room lamps and quietly walked to Angelina's room before going to sleep, to make sure that she was fine and to find out if she needed anything. She partially opened the door to the room and confirmed that Angelina was deep asleep. Dina retired to her empty and lonely bed to begin dreaming about the recent love adventures that she has shared with Jaime, adventures that she was yearning for.

Jaime was up earlier than usual. The clock alarm's, fulfilling its task to break the early morning silence at half past five, was not necessary today. Jaime was already dressed in his Sunday suit and was ready and anxious to depart to Dina's apartment.

Before leaving, Jaime checked that he had gathered the needed documents for the wedding. He had a copy of his birth certificate, his passport, and his residence card already tucked in his suit pocket. He checked to make sure that he had an adequate amount of cash and, last but most important, he confirmed that he had the keys to Dina's apartment. Once satisfied that he had not forgotten anything, Jaime left the apartment and began his walk to Dina's place.

The walk through the quiet streets, bathed by the soft and brilliant morning sun rays, and refreshed by the virgin Northern breeze, invigorated him. That feeling reinforced his self perceived good fortune of being alive in perhaps one of the greatest cities in the world, and about to marry the most wonderful women that God had created. He could not help but to repeat to himself, "What a glorious day this is!"

Jaime's brisk walk got him to Dina's in record time. The street was desolate, other than the occasional squirrels chasing one another as they climbed the three trunks and branches, with the pursuing canine envious of their agility. Jaime arrived at

Dina's apartment and carefully and quietly unlocked the door and entered the apartment. There was complete silence, a confirmation that the ladies in the house were fast asleep, as he had anticipated.

Jaime entered Dina's bedroom and verified that she was indeed asleep. He resisted his desire to kiss her, so as not to disturb her peaceful rest. He removed his suit jacket and tie and proceeded to the kitchen to prepare breakfast for the two ladies that he loves dearly.

This morning's breakfast is to be unforgettable, for all three of them will be celebrating not only Angelina's arrival, but more important, they will be celebrating a love's journey's beginning. A journey of two lives from two very different origins, which crossed each other's path, and will merge forever into one promising and unending sharing of happiness, brotherhood, and mutual loyalty, until death breaks that bond.

Last night, before departing to his apartment, Jaime had added spices and lemon juice to three small Strip steaks, which will be the main course for this morning's extra special breakfast. After taking the steaks out of the refrigerator, Jaime began to peal three medium size potatoes. Once pealed, the potatoes were cleaned and cut various times until achieving the desired French fries size. Jaime placed the steak on the hot frying pan, then added oil to another deep pot for the French fries. He then turned on the gas under the percolator, already filled with grounded coffee and water.

Jaime's game plan was to awaken the sleeping beauties as the aroma from the percolating coffee and the frying steak permeated throughout the apartment. Thus enticing the ladies gastronomical sensors to awaken them from their deep sleep.

Shortly after the coffee began percolating, Jaime heard water running and the toilet being flushed. He smiled and complimented himself for having succeeded in awakening at least one of the ladies with the power of his cuisine. The question which he asked himself was, who will it be?. Shortly after hearing the water running, Jaime looked back at the table and found that the two loves in his life had quietly entered the kitchen and sat silently and anxiously awaiting their breakfast treat, both looking more beautiful than ever.

Jaime placed the small fried Strip steak on each of the three plates. He then served the French fries in equal portions, placing them adjacent to the steak. The only missing component for this morning's meal was the fried egg to be placed on top of the steak. The pan and the hot oil were ready for the three eggs to be placed on the frying pan and fried. Jaime broke the eggs, dropped them into the hot oil, and began the "easy over" frying process The eggs were perfectly fried and placed on top of the steak, in no time at all.

Jaime placed the breakfast plate in front of each of the ladies, and in front of the chair next to Dina where he will be seating. He served the coffee, removed the sliced bread from the oven and placed it on the table as well. He sat down, smiled, and told his ladies, "Von appétit1". The three devoured their breakfast. The girls congratulated Jaime for his excellent cuisine, and suggested that he is welcomed to perform an encore any time that he desires. Jaime smiled and told the girls, "Ladies it is my pleasure to please you with a hearty meal. Besides, today is a memorable day and I wanted to make sure that you both have adequate nourishment to deal with the excitement and emotions of the day."

Jaime continued, "This is the game plan. We need to be at the Little Church Around the Corner, located on East 29th Street by ten o'clock. That is the time when the nondenominational mass will begin. At the end of the mass, we will meet the pastor at the rectory and take care of the bureaucratic requirements. By the way, Angelina, we need a witness for our marriage. As I mentioned before, Dina and I will like you to be the witness, if this is ok with you. Angelina did not hesitate. She quickly responded, "Off course, I will be honored to witness you and Dina's commitment to a lifetime of happiness."

Jaime suggested to the girls that it was such a beautiful morning that perhaps they could walk to the church and enjoy the gorgeous day. Both Dina and Angelina agreed to walk rather than to take a taxi. Dina got up and said, "Well, if we are going to walk, it is best that we get moving getting ourselves beautiful for the wedding", Angelina responded, "Good idea, let's get ready!" Jaime smiled and told the two ladies, "You are both already beautiful so it should not take you both very long". The two girls laughed lightly and walked to their rooms to get ready.

Jaime followed Dina into their room to be and closed the door behind them. They looked at each other and Jaime asked her, "Dina darling, what is wrong? I know you better than you think. You smile and laugh, but you can not hide from me the fact that something is bothering you. Are you having second thoughts about our getting married? Do you need more time? Would you rather have a formal wedding?"

As Dina looked at Jaime, the overflowing droplets of crystal clear tears began to gently escape from their natural reservoir, slowly traveling down each of her cheeks. Jaime took out his handkerchief and gently captured the escaping evidence of sadness before they could reach her inviting lips. He kissed her lips gently, and waited for her response.

Dina looked at Jaime and locked her eye sight on his. She then told him, "Jaime darling it is nothing of the sort. It is just that I have to remove the rings that Vincent gave me. They are the last linkage between our lives. Part of me feels that doing so is a betrayal of the love that we shared. That is the reason for my sadness and my tears". Jaime embraced Dina. He held her close to him momentarily, without saying a single word. Dina began to sob quietly, burying her face on his chest and thus avoiding looking at him, while he comforted her.

Jaime held her chin gently and moved her face upward until both sets of tearful eyes were once again communicating with each other.

He kissed her forehead and said, "Darling, no one more than Vincent knows that you loved him with all your soul. No one more than Vincent knows your loyalty and dedication to him and your loyalty to your marriage bow. I am sure that no one, more than him, would want your life to be nothing but full of happiness"

*

Jaime slowly raised and held her left hand with his. He gently placed his thumb and index finger over the ring and said, "With this ring you and Vincent promised to love each other until death does you part. You both fulfilled that promise. You have, and will have for evermore, a special place in your soul for that beautiful love. Not unlike you, I have a special place in my heart for my friendship and brotherhood with Vincent." Jaime began to slowly remove the ring from Dina's finger while both of their eyes followed its movement. Jaime added, "This ring represents your love and fidelity to Vincent and it shall be safeguarded in a special place, just as you are safeguarding that unforgettable love in a very special part of your heart." Once the ring was removed, Jaime placed it on her left palm and gently closed her hand, symbolizing the closure of a short lasting, but always to be remembered, an unconditional love between Dina and Vincent.

Dina walked to her dresser, located a small black jewelry box, carefully placed the ring inside and closed it. She stored the black jewelry box in the dresser's lower left hand drawer. She returned to Jaime. She embraced him, and rewarded him with a love longing kiss, signaling the true beginning of her new life with him. They both smiled, their expressions conveying true happiness, having found a resolution to a burden that was "weighing" their relationship and mellowing the happiness to be had. Once again, they hugged and kissed, as if reconfirming their love and unbridled dedication to each other.

Jaime affectionately tapped Dina's lower back and lovingly told her that she better put a move on or they will be late for their wedding. Dina, whose eyes were once again brilliant and projecting nothing but happiness, smiled and told him, "Not in your life. There is no way that I will be late for my wedding with such a handsome and wonderful man!".

Dina began to walk away towards her closet to get the dress that she will be wearing for the wedding. She turned around and with a grin she told Jaime, "You better leave the room so that we do not get distracted, as I try to get beautiful for you". Jaime, without a second of hesitation, replied, "Darling there is no way that you can be more beautiful than what you already are". Jaime left the bedroom and walked to the living room where he turned on the radio and let his mind just wonder endlessly without a particular destination as he enjoyed the soothing piano music.

Angelina entered the living room, bringing Jaime back to the reality of the moment. She asked, "Jaimecito, how do I look?" She then turned around as if modeling for her brother. Her dress was forest green with white trimmed collard, pockets and sleeves. The dress was tight enough to divulge her young and beautiful figure. Yet not enough to convey excessive promotion of her beautiful physical attributes. Jaime smiled and told his sister, "Angi you look gorgeous. If you were not my sister, I would take you on date" They both laughed heartily.

Dina returned to the living room and asked the brother and sister, "What made both of you laugh with such gusto?" Angelina replied, "Jaime said that if I was not his sister, he would take me out on a date" Dina smiled and told Jaime, "What nerve have you, thinking of asking a beautiful young lady to go out with you on our wedding day?". The threesome looked at each other and heartedly laughed.

Jaime looked at Dina. She wore a straight white linen dress which reached her mid calf. The dress softly contoured her attractive figure. White embroidered flowers framed the collarless oval neckline and delicate pockets. A vertical row of small but shinny Ivory buttons ran below the collar down to the belt line. Each of the pockets was also decorated with identical ivory buttons. An ivory color belt with a matching Ivory buckle, emphasized her youthful waist line. The beautiful dress, the joyful smile, and the bright red lipstick contrasting with Dina's pearl white and perfectly shaped teeth, filled Jaime with desire and pride,

 having the fortune to be able to share the rest of his life with her.

Jaime looked at Dina's eyes and told her, "My love, you look radiant". Dina smiled, having received the confirmation which she was seeking. She responded, "Thank you, darling."

The soon to be married couple and Angelina departed from the apartment and began their leisurely walk to The Little Church Around the Corner. They crossed streets and avenues enjoying the gorgeous morning and blending with the many New Yorkers, just as elegantly dressed, in their journey to their place of worship.

The wedding party of three arrived at the Little Church, just in time for the beginning of the mass. They sat on a pew near the rear entrance and submerged themselves in the religious service.

At the end of the mass, all three proceeded to the rectory and joined two other couples, who likewise, were going to exchange their vows, this unforgettable morning.

The pastor gathered the three couples, the marriage witnesses and instructed them about the procedure which was about to take place. They will all go to front of the altar where the pastor will perform the religious marriage ceremony. The couples will exchange vows. Afterwards, each couple will meet separately with the pastor to complete the state's administrative legal requirements.

The pastor shared with all there present, including the marriage candidates, that he will perform a combined ceremony for all three couples. At the appropriate time each couple will individually state their marriage vow, as per his predetermined order. Dina and Jaime will be the first couple to state their marriage vows.

The wedding parties exited the rectory, preceded to the front of the altar, and waited for the pastor's arrival. The simple, but memorable ceremony began with the pastor quoting bible passages and sprinkling marriage wisdom to the newlyweds to be.

The long awaited moment, when the pastor will ask the couples, "Do you take this woman for your wedded wife, and do you take this man for your wedded husband" arrived, both Dina's and Jaime's expression reflected a mixture of pensiveness, nervousness and excitement.

Sharing a loving smile, and each reaching for the other's hand, Jaime assertively responded, "I do!". Dina, radiating her beauty, excitedly also responded likewise, "I do!"